Praise for

Crystal Clear Persuasion

"Once again Ann Jeffries takes us into a mesmerizing tale of the human experience, enchanting us with family, faith, and friends. The winner, in the midst of all of this, is the reader!"

—Bella Fayre, Author *Sisters of the Scorned*

"Ann Jeffries' latest novel Crystal Clear Persuasion, in the Family Reunion—Wisdom Of The Ancestors Series, doesn't disappoint its readers. While reading, you will travel along with the family and their friends through their trials, turmoil, and true love. The dynamic characters will be brought to life that you will love, while disliking others intensely; as Ms. Jeffries excels at painting each character and scene into reality."

—Connie Scruton, Columnist, *Everyday Women*.

Ann Jeffries offers a romantic and suspenseful tale. Not only are her fictional characters beautiful and successful, they endeavor to right some of the world's wrongs. I definitely want to live in the world she creates."

—Rebecca Bridges, Author, *Blue Ridge Mountain Escape*.

Crystal Clear Persuasion

Another Family Reunion Novel In The Wisdom of the Ancestors Series

Book Two of the Chi-Town Girls Trilogy

Ann Jeffries

Published and Distributed By
New View Literature
820 67th Avenue N, #7603
Myrtle Beach, South Carolina 29572
annjeffries@newviewliterature.com
www.newviewliterature.com

Jenetha Hollis, Editor
Quill Editorial Service

Jessica Tilles, TWA Solutions
Cover and Interior Design

ISBN: 978-0-9915003-2-1 Print
ISBN: 978-1-941603-66-6 eBook
Library of Congress Control Number: 2014947430

First printing August 2018

Acknowledgements

I bow in humble gratitude to:

The Creator

My Ancestors

Jenetha Hollis, Editor
Quill Editorial Services

Jessica Tilles, TWA Solution
Interior and Cover Art

The Carolina Forest Authors' Club

My precious and faithful family, friends, and fans

The journey continues and the struggle for literary perfection
shall never end.

I remain faithfully yours,

Ann Jeffries

Other Ann Jeffries Titles
In The Family Reunion—Wisdom Of The Ancestors Series

In print and e-book formats:
Southern Exposures
Another Point Of View
Northern Exposure
Uncommon Choices
An Unguarded Moment
Moments To Remember
The Better Part of Valor
Walking On Uneven Ground
Ask Me No Questions—I'll Tell You No Lies
Touch Me In The Morning
All Goodbyes Aren't Gone
A Different Frame of Mind
Judicial Indiscretion
Crystal Clear Persuasion

In audio-book format:
Another Point of View
An Unguarded Moment
Moments to Remember
Walking on Uneven Ground
Touch Me in the Morning

In Production:
Southern Exposures
Northern Exposures
Uncommon Choices
The Better Part of Valor

I am no one just peaceful girl
Who trusts every caring hand
And believes love breathes in every heart
But now I am a prisoner and in band

I am no one just a little girl
By Shima Nesari Haghighi Fard

Prologue

The gunfire was sporadic, but persistent with loud and deafening staccato sounds. The air was hot and heavy with the smell of blood and cordite that burned the nostrils. Sick to their stomachs with fear and scared beyond terror, twenty young girls huddled tightly together in the small, dark, dank smelly cellar with no way to know whether they would live or die from moment to moment. They had been there in that space for hours, though it seemed like much longer, awaiting their fate.

Their parents, African royalty all, sent them to the English-speaking school in the fervent hope they would be safe and learn to lead a better life through the benefit of education and exposure to a world outside of their villages. The girls were expected to one-day rule their people. That was not going to happen if the militant Jihad terrorists got their hands on the girls who were between five and twelve years of age. The Boko Haram respected no one's status in life and would force the older girls into motherhood as child brides for the soldiers, hostages for ransom, and the younger ones would likely be sold into the sex trade. Every girl at the school knew and understood what she was in for if found. So, they remained still and quiet packed in like babes in the womb in the underground earthen tomb while a war raged above their heads.

Little did they know at this moment a tightly-knit group was there to search for and destroy the terrorists. The nighttime helo jump was successful. Moving like ghosts through the thick forests, night vision goggles made them appear otherworldly, but they handily dispatched the last of the insurgents as the mission dictated. Now they were on a recon mission to tag and bag each Jihadist for posterity. Photos, fingerprints, and DNA samples were quickly and efficiently collected to add to a database of criminals when one of the group discovered the hidden trapdoor in the floorboards in a kitchen storeroom.

Guns at the ready with lasers sites engaged, the trap door was opened, and twenty pairs of frightened young eyes looked up gasping in fear.

"Well, hell," said the leader in a decidedly female voice with a midwestern, American accent into a face mic. "Delta, we have a problem. How do you read?"

"Reading you five-by-five, Explorer One. SitRep."

"Helen of Troy found twenty little people, all female. Suspected missing royalty. They weren't kidnapped as originally reported."

"Breathing?"

"Affirmative."

"Execute: Gravedigger. Extraction. Secure for transport. Extra helos dispatched. Head 'em up and move 'em out, Explorer One. Let's see how quickly you can make it to the landing zone (LZ). Your time is running out. Watch your six. You've got insurgents crawling all over the region. Other teams are going combat ready and wheels up to replace you."

"Copy that, Delta. Mission complete. Asses on the move. Thirty clicks from the LZ. This is the Explorer One. Over and out."

As the girls were helped out of the space not much bigger than a Napa Valley wine barrel, one of the Ninja-clad, squad members would step up and the child was secured by harness piggy-back style to the human carrier. When the last child was on board, the Jihadists who were not already buried were dumped into the hole and the trapdoor secured, the squad triple-timed it through the thick woods without leaving so much as a leaf or blade of grass out of place. Some of the squad members, recon-turned-rescuers took point while others spread out to cover both sides and the rear.

Not knowing their fate, but somehow trusting, the girls clung tightly to their personal carriers not uttering a sound. The night was pitch black with no stars or moon to see their way, but somehow they were moving swiftly and soundlessly through the dense forest.

They were suddenly stilled by the sound of trucks up ahead coming toward them through the woods in a space no wider than a goat path. Their carriers melted like mist into the foliage and the girls instinctively knew they had to hold their collective breaths and remain still.

What the girls couldn't see, but the night-vision glasses revealed, was another group of about twenty to thirty militant Jihadists standing on the back of two transport trucks with guns scanning the thick woods while the trucks slowly tried to navigate the narrow path. The girls also couldn't see the fluorescent hand signals only visible through night-vision goggles. Or hear the voice commands that passed among their carriers or the other Ninjas who had scrambled like silent monkeys up into the trees.

Yet, suddenly what looked like fireflies centered on each terrorist bloomed blood red, the trucks stopped moving as did the Jihadist who all seemed to collectively and, without a sound, simultaneously melt into the floorboards of the trucks. Each driver and his companion in the windowless front seats slouched down like melting goo. The headlights continued to glow in the dark and the engines ran, but that was the only sound that could be heard.

Quickly, another tag-and-bag operation took place, but with no time to bury the dead, they were hoisted up into the tall trees and tied to thick branches where they could not be seen from below. Then the ninjas were again off on a dead run.

Still in the dark, just before daybreak, the ninjas spread out in a circle around a clearing facing the woods. They had not uttered a word, but MREs, meals ready to eat, and bottles of water were silently passed over their shoulders to each girl. The carriers never took their eyes off the woods and collected each scrap of debris after the girls had their fill. Remaining as still and quiet as a petrified tree trunk, the girls were still tethered securely in harnesses to their carriers.

A huff of air signaled something and the ninjas went on heightened alert. Then without otherwise hearing a sound, huge, black, bat-winged aircraft were suddenly filling the clearing. The ninjas, with their charges intact, sprinted backward toward the crafts and were shortly airborne at treetop level and whisked across the land at dizzying speeds that made the lushly green landscape blur below them. Land gave way to light-brown, sandy shores, a deep blue ocean, and what appeared to be specks on the vast watery horizon. The crafts bulleted toward what soon became a super, nuclear-powered, aircraft carrier surrounded by an armada of other battleships.

They landed on the deck of the huge aircraft carrier long enough to transfer the girls into the waiting hands of soldiers wearing the American flag and medical badges on their uniforms. The crafts were refueled and then another crew of pilots, both male and female, took the bat-winged aircraft off again carrying a different group of Ninjas. They flew toward the place they had all just left as the sun came up over the Mediterranean and the far horizon.

Chapter 1

"*Ooh, baby!*" Wilbur Hardy bit out through clenched teeth as he sank repeatedly into his wife's womanly core. Sweat trickled down the sides of his face coming together at his chin. "You feel so *damn* good, baby! So tight! So wet! Ahhh!" he moaned. Then his voice became inaudible grunts, groans, sounds of sucking air through his teeth as he climbed higher into his ecstasy.

With one hand, Cheryl Lawrence-Hardy's long, slender, well-manicured fingernails rhythmically stroked her husband's moisture-laden back while trying to psyche herself up into feeling a little of the passion she was giving to him. With the other hand, she pushed against the leather padded headboard to keep her head from being bounced against it from the force of her husband's hard, strong, almost spastic thrusts. Little did he know, or perhaps even care, she was not with him on his rush to climax.

Cheryl was a 21st-century woman, highly educated, financially independent, and acutely intellectual. Yet she believed it was a wife's duty to please her husband, even if she was not being pleasured in return. Cheryl lifted and then rotated her toned hips causing Wilbur to swear he was *"the man."*

Nothing could have been further from the truth. She had never thought much of women who faked an orgasm, but, over the past six months, she had raised the practice to an art form.

Cheryl's marriage to Wilbur was a year old. They should still have been ensconced in the throws of honeymoon bliss, but Wilbur's refusal even to consider starting a family had left Cheryl feeling alone and lonely—and very much unloved, even in the heat of his passion. She envied her friends, particularly Kristen Bryant Marshall and Vivian Alexander Montgomery. They both had the kind of husbands, Thomas Ashton Marshall and Charles Patrick Montgomery, and families people read about in romance novels. Her marriage to Wilbur wasn't anywhere near that idyllic. Maybe Kristen's and Vivian's marriages were more stable because they were both judges on the Federal Appeals Court.

Even her friend since childhood, Tina Justice, although single, had much more satisfying relationships than what Cheryl felt she had experienced with Wilbur. Men wanted Tina to be the mother of their children, but Tina was nowhere near ready to make the commitment to home and hearth the way Cheryl was. Although she admitted, only to herself, she had not truly been *in love* with Wilbur when she married him, she had hoped she would find some semblance of love and comfort with him. As he hiked her legs up around his waist and gripped her bottom, pumping her harder and harder like a fired-up piston to satisfy his needs, she knew this intimacy would end in another joining toward unproductive sex.

She moved her body to coax him toward reaching his peak, but the pattern and graduating colors of blues, greens, and grays on the coffered ceiling held more interest for her than her own climax. Where Wilbur's body was bathed in sweat, Cheryl's body was cool and unaffected. Where his body was bunched into hardness, hers was relaxed and languid. She felt not the first bit of amour or even a tingle of want or need. Thank goodness for KY Jelly. *She loved this man, didn't she? If so, why couldn't she push aside her own need to be filled with the fruit of his loins? Wasn't it enough they appeared to be a financially comfortable, upwardly mobile, loving couple?* She was enjoying a very prosperous Washington, DC law practice at one of the best-respected, strategically diversified, and most prestigious law firms in the country, Alexander, Carter, Chandler, Charles, Lightfoot, and Towson, PA. The firm had been headed by her undergrad classmate, Vivian Alexander, now Vivian Alexander Montgomery, who would soon ascend to the US Supreme Court of America.

Wilbur, twelve years Cheryl's senior, was a tenured professor at the University of Maryland. They had a beautiful home in Havenhurst Estates; a private, gated, seventy-two-hole, golf club community and Equestrian Park in a rural area of Maryland, equal distance between Washington, DC, Baltimore and Annapolis, Maryland. Yet, it was one of the wealthiest communities in the nation. They had good friends around them and a very active social life. So, what, if most of her friends were starting families? What difference should that make? She was not one to keep up with the Joneses. Yet, the fact she felt incomplete without a young family to raise, children to love and care for, did bother her tremendously. Each time she broached the subject with Wilbur, their discussion turned into an argument. To stem the downward spiral of their marriage, Wilbur suggested that, if she was feeling maternal, she should buy a dog.

A dog!

Really? He was serious.

Tears banked in Cheryl's eyes comingling with the salty sweat that dripped from Wilbur's face into her eyes. She wanted children, not a dog. The fact Wilbur would not even consider the matter of her bearing his children, not even one child, emotionally tore at her both day and night. She had reached nearly all of her professional goals, but her personal life was falling apart. At thirty-one, her biological clock was ticking loud and clear. The passage of time was not her friend.

"*Ooh, baby!*" Wilbur lustfully crooned near her left ear, his sweat plastering her hair to her temple just before he released his life-giving fluid into an ever-present condom. "You should come home early more often." He kissed her cheek, feeling the stream of her tears. When he lifted his head to look into her eyes, she turned her head away. "Damn it! Why do you always have to ruin everything?" he accused and abruptly uncoupled, rolled off her, and settled heavily beside her breathing hard. He didn't even touch her; just lay there seething.

Quickly, Cheryl, not usually given to tears, brushed the tears from her cheeks, turned her back toward him, and curled up on her side. What could she say? She said it all at least once a day for six months. They reached an impasse.

Wilbur rolled off the bed, snatching his robe as he stomped to their ensuite bathroom. Over his shoulder he flung, "You better get yourself together! I'm sick and tired of this baby shit!"

The slamming door punctuated his petulant point. Simultaneously the telephone rang, but Cheryl did not bother to answer it. Clara Brown, the housekeeper, would take a message. Cheryl was in no mood to talk to anyone.

A few seconds later, the intercom on the bedroom telephone rang. "Yes, Clara?"

"Sorry to disturb you, Cheryl, but it's Peter Brock on the telephone."

Few people would have caused Cheryl to take their call in her present mood; Peter was one of them. Drying her eyes with a tissue, taking deep, calming breaths to regain control of her emotions as best she could, she thanked Clara, and, then depressed the blinking light on the cordless telephone console.

"Hi, Peter," she said while simultaneously snatching another tissue from a box on her nightstand.

"Hey, kid. How about doing a favor for a friend?" he jovially asked.

"Sure, what is it?" she sniffed in a deep, tremulous breath.

"I need…Cheryl, is something wrong? Did I call at a bad time?" he asked with concern lacing his voice.

Peter Brock was one of her oldest and dearest friends from Chicago; they were as close as siblings. Their parents, along with Kristen's and Tina's, were the best of friends and neighbors long before she and Peter were gleams in their daddies' eyes. The Brock, Lawrence, Bryant, and Justice families were still close and lived on the same street in the same neighborhood within spitting distance of one another.

She and Peter were now both junior partners at the same law firm. At one point in her life, Cheryl thought herself in love with him. He, however, was not in love with her or even aware of her feelings for him.

Rather, he was in love with one of their best friends, Kristen Catherine "KC" Bryant. Peter almost got KC to the altar when, out of the blue, the dashing and dauntingly handsome Thomas Ashton Marshall, III, a Rick Fox look-alike, stepped into the picture and claimed Kristen, who closely resembled former Miss America Vanessa Williams, as his wife. Peter was heartbroken, and, clearly on the rebound, married Denise Lombard, a woman he dated while in undergrad. A cougar in training.

Peter and Denise now lived next door in the same private Havenhurst community with Cheryl and Wilbur, continuing the close, supportive relationship that began between them as children. Denise didn't want to live in the rural county. She much preferred the glitz and glitter of city life They were neighbors then as now, but for the life of her, Cheryl admitted to herself she could not seem to warm up to Peter's wife, Denise. The feeling was apparently mutual as Wilbur had an aversion to Peter. Nevertheless, in an effort to change that dynamic, they socialized as a foursome. That was at least something they could agree on. They enjoyed traveling to interesting places around the globe. Since Denise and Peter did not have children, it was easy for them to go out to the theater or clubs and dinner together often. She and Peter were still good friends and, at times like this, she needed a friend. Still, even this heartache, her need to be a mother, she could not share with Peter.

"What's up, Pete?" she asked pulling herself together.

"Well," he hesitated. "Maybe it's not such . . . ."

"Come on, Pete. What's on your mind?" she coaxed.

"I tried to reach you before you left work today. Your assistant said you left early."

"Last minute details for tomorrow night. I had to meet with the caterers, Greenfield Brothers, to go over the final decoration plan, so I came home early. Why were you trying to reach me?"

"I was going to ask you for a ride to work tomorrow morning. Denise's car is in the shop and she wants to use mine instead of a rental. If it's an inconvenience, I can rent a car for tomorrow. I know you're very busy with all the planning for the reception and dinner party for your new clients."

"It's not a problem, Peter, if you don't mind leaving work early tomorrow. Cocktails are at 6:00 o'clock, but I want to get home early enough to meet with Isaac Greenfield to make sure everything is set. Jackson Chase is one of my most important new clients to date and the largest land developer in Mitchell County. I want everything to go well. Capri McAllister Kennedy and I both share him as a client. She does his lobbying work and I handle his corporate requirements. This is an important event for both of us. He's partnering with some heavy hitters who will transform Mitchell County into the most livable county in the state."

"It will go well, Cheryl. The entire firm's founding members and the senior partners are very impressed with you. It seems that everyone is planning to be at your house tomorrow night. I don't mind leaving work early. In fact, I could use a few extra hours of downtime myself. It's been a hellified week."

"Does that mean the McCoy Hotels case is going well?"

"So far, so good. Factions of the remaining Delaware family claim the government colluded to illegally separate the Delaware Hotel Group from the extensive holdings on behalf of Justin McCoy and McCoy Hotels. Their argument has no merit, but I'm glad I don't have to be in court again until next week."

"I owe you a favor anyway for letting me use two of your paralegals last week."

"Anytime, Cheryl, you know that. Thanks again for the ride. I'll see you in the morning."

"Bye, Peter," she said and then hung up. She did not notice Wilbur's return to their bedroom.

"Who was on the telephone?"

As if he didn't already know, she thought. She believed he listened in on her conversation via the extension in the ensuite. Nevertheless, she played it off. After all, unlike Wilbur, she had nothing to hide.

"Just Peter," she said gathering a robe from their walk-around closet and slipping it on.

"Humph, what did he want?" his tone nasty as he followed her inside their double closet.

"He needs a ride to and from the office tomorrow. Denise's car is in the shop."

"Probably not all he wants," he mumbled derisively.

Cheryl heard the comment on her way to the bathroom and stopped in her tracks. She pivoted to face Wilbur. "What does that mean?" she asked, her brows furrowed, arms folded akimbo.

"You know what it means," he said, morosely, not looking at her while he rummaged in his underwear drawers.

Instantaneous, heated ire rose in her. He could not even look her in the face she noticed. "Of all the patently absurd things you've come up with, you've finally reached the bottom. Peter Brock and I have known each other since we climbed out of our cribs. Not in all of those years has anything at all passed between us except deep and abiding friendship. I do not understand why you don't like him, but I am sure it has nothing at all to do with me! Moreover, I'm not the one whose fidelity is in question!"

With that said, it was her turn to slam the bathroom door. Almost as quickly as the door closed, Wilbur opened it and stalked in. Cheryl spun to face him, her hands planted in tight fists in the pocket of her robe

"Are you back to that again!" he bellowed, flailing his arms in the air. "Just because some young, foolish co-ed calls you up claiming to be my lover, you take her word over mine!"

Cheryl's chin came up a notch higher as she stood her ground. "One co-ed, maybe, but in the last year, more than four women have called this house—."

Wilbur threw up his arms in exasperation or an academy award attempt. Which one, Cheryl wasn't sure. What was worse, she was beginning not to care.

"Here we go again!"

"Not again, Wilbur, still!" Cheryl shot back, and then she tried to tamp down her pique. She briskly combed her fingers through her shoulder-length hair. "Look, Wilbur," she breathed with near exhaustion, aggravation, and wanting to avoid the acrimony. "I am trying to get past this. I'm trying to love you and be a good wife to you, but you've got to meet me half way."

Hands on his narrow hips, he studied her. "You want me to get you pregnant, I suppose? Is that it, Cheryl? It's all about what you want; not what I want. You want a baby. Lately, that's all you talk about. Is that what it will take for you to stop nagging me about some stupid college kid's crush?"

Cheryl sat down on the side of the large whirlpool tub, buried her face in her hands, and restlessly rubbed her face. Then resting her elbows on her thighs, hands clasped together, she looked up at her husband. Wilbur was still as handsome now, a light brown-skin George Clooney version, as he was when she first met him. She was in her sophomore year at Maryland U when she took his class on Ethics preparing herself for law school. That was when she was still so excited he chose her to be his lady. Despite his advanced age, she thought him the most sophisticated man she ever met and he was interested in her. After her class ended, they dated steadily for over a month before they made love for the first time. He was so romantic all other men she had known seemed to pale by comparison to him. She was on cloud nine. Half the women on campus thought he was God's gift to womankind. It was six months later when she learned he was sharing his "gifts" with many women in the standard metropolitan population of the Washington, DC, Virginia, and Maryland areas. Devastated by his betrayal, his behavior, and embarrassed by her naiveté, she transferred to Spelman College with her friends, Kristen Bryant and Tina Justice, for her junior and senior year.

It was not until years later after she graduated from law school, passed the bar exam, and was clerking for her friend, Judge Kristen

Catherine Bryant, she literally bumped into Wilbur at one of the most popular nightspots, H2O, in Washington, D.C. At the time, Peter Brock and another one of their childhood friends, Constantina 'Tina' Justice, were also working for Kristen. Fighting her feelings for Peter, Cheryl once again surrendered to Wilbur's considerable charms. After a short, whirlwind courtship, she and Wilbur were married in a small, civil ceremony on Maryland U's campus. The first six months of their marriage were blissfully happy.

After a year on the bench, Kristen Bryant stepped down and took a leave of absence. She, her husband, Thomas Ashton Marshall, III, and their young son, Thomas IV moved to an island paradise, Plaza de Masquerada, in the Pacific Archipelago. Kristen started a professional dance troupe that began touring the world, performing before sold-out audiences. Thomas continued managing his international law practice with offices in Portland, Oregon, and Washington, DC.

Tina Justice went back to their hometown of Chicago to start a television production company, Sweet Justice, and began a new career as a talk show host.

Peter and she stayed in Washington and signed on with Alexander, Carter, et.al, as junior partners. All prospered from their career changes.

She was concentrating on her career and Wilbur was supportive. She often had to work late and sometimes on weekends, but Wilbur agreed she should do whatever she had to do to be successful and professionally content. She had loved him for what she thought was his self-sacrifice and unyielding support…that is until the telephone started ringing. At her office and at home, young female college students took perverse pleasure in telling her, often in graphic detail, what intimacies they shared with Wilbur. One young woman was so bold as to try to come to their home. When the gate guard asked whether to admit the young woman, Cheryl could no longer deny Wilbur's claims of innocence and fidelity did not have merit.

Yet, wanting her marriage to work, she tried just that much harder to make Wilbur happy; hoping against hope it would all work out in the end. However, the harder she tried, the worse things got. Then Wilbur's unyielding refusal to start a family tore the frail fabric of their marriage nearly to shreds. Her energy level was nearly depleted. They had to *work* together if they were going to *stay* together.

"Wilbur, after the dinner party for my client tomorrow night, why don't we go to the beach house for a long weekend? I can change a few appointments around and you don't have any lectures to prepare for until later in the week. We haven't spent a lot of time alone together at the beach house this summer. Maybe we could talk," her voice calm, even, expectant.

Some of the hostility seemed to have stilled in him as well. "We'll go to the beach house, Cheryl, but let me make myself perfectly clear; I do not want to have children!"

Wilbur walked out of the bathroom closing the door behind him. Cheryl's emotions plummeted. She wrapped her arms around her waist, her empty womb, and resting her head on her knees, she released her pain in silent tears.

Chapter 2

Peter Brock replaced his cordless telephone in its cradle and sat back in his deep, wine-colored executive chair. His thoughts were still on his long-time and close friend, Cheryl Lawrence-Hardy. A hand clasping his square chin with his index finger, he unconsciously brushed his mustache brought on by a perpetual five-o-clock shadow, brows furrowed. For months, he noticed some of the sparkle was missing that usually resided in Cheryl's beautiful, hazel-colored eyes. Generally, his friend had buoyancy in her voice and demeanor that lifted his spirits just being in her company. Her infectious laughter was genuine and deep, but the woman he just spoke with had none of those characteristics. In fact, she sounded as if she was crying; something he had never known her to do. She was a strong, independent woman who never seemed to need coddling. A hell of a good lawyer, she held her own and bested many inside the law firm as well as in the courtroom or across a negotiating table. Although she busted the glass ceiling vigorously and energetically, she knew how and when to turn it off, too. She could party with the best of them and dance up a storm.

Absently, Peter wondered whether things were going well for her at home. He had to admit to himself, he did not like her husband, Wilbur, but for Cheryl's sake and for the sake of their friendship, he tried to, at least, get along with the man. Wilbur was what women would call a "pretty" man; smooth, light-brown complexion and wavy hair, tall muscular build, and an air of confidence that bordered on arrogance. Wilbur enjoyed the attention his looks brought his way.

He and Wilbur had nothing in common and it was difficult for Peter to have pleasant conversations with the man. Even more perplexing was Peter's inability to understand Cheryl's attraction to Wilbur. In fact, it came as a big surprise to every one of their close friends and families when Cheryl announced she planned to marry Wilbur. Not that Cheryl was not most men's fantasy woman, because she was, but she was grounded. Although a heart-stopper, she paid little, if any, attention to the many compliments she usually received from men. Peter had known her long enough to know she was clueless about the effect she had on the opposite sex. When he thought of Cheryl, the terms tall, leggy, and luscious came to mind, as well as aggressive, impressive, and intelligent.

After Cheryl and Wilbur married, Peter continued to date Denise. He invited them on outings and they got to know each other better. Peter's cabin in the mountains was one of the things Cheryl enjoyed and it took him nearly a year to complete it doing a lot of the work himself as an outlet for his idle time. Wilbur and Denise found "roughing it" in a four bedroom, three and a half bath, thirty-five hundred square foot chalet on a lake in the Western Maryland Mountains near Camp David, uninviting. As children, Peter and Cheryl relished going camping; a throwback from their youth in Chicago when their parents sent them to camp each summer in Wisconsin. They, Kristen, and her brothers, George and Clarence, and Tina with her six brothers were sent to live among the Justice's paternal grandmother's people, the Sokaogon Chippewa and Oneida. Recently, Tina built a chalet and wild-horse ranch on her family's land and the friends still enjoyed spending a few weeks together there when they could manage it. Given Wilbur's and Denise's distaste for living in the wild, Peter knew Cheryl enjoyed helping Tina and him to design, build, and decorate their cabins as much as she could.

Peter thought of other times when he and Denise went on vacations with Cheryl and Wilbur. Scuba diving in Martinique, white-water rafting in the Grand Gorge, skiing in Aspen and St. Moritz, even horseback riding in the Grand Canyon or on Tina's wild horse ranch in Wisconsin. Wilbur and Denise did not enjoy the demanding physical exertion it took to do those things three or four times a year, but Cheryl seemed to be in her element just as he was. Wilbur's and Denise's idea of a vacation included two weeks of gambling in Monte Carlo, shopping in Paris, France, Rodeo Drive in Hollywood, California, or shows and dinners in New York City, Las Vegas or Venezuela. When Cheryl suggested an African sojourn, Wilbur and Denise suggested she had lost her mind, but Peter, excited by the prospect of visiting African nations, supported the idea. They were planning to begin their African holiday the day after the University broke for Christmas and New Year so it wouldn't interfere with Wilbur's class schedule.

The telephone rang, taking Peter's thoughts from his seemingly troubled friend.

"Yes, Meka?"

"Your mother is on line two, Mr. Brock."

A smile curled his lips as he picked up the phone. "Happy birthday, Mom." He smiled.

"Ooh, baby boy, you really out did your self!" Cassia Brock said and giggled with glee.

"Then you like it?" he asked.

"Petey, it's so beautiful, I couldn't believe it! And the flowers, you must have bought out every florist in Chicago!" She giggled again.

It made Peter's heart nearly burst with love and pride that he could make his mother smile. She had so little to smile about recently. His father and mother had been married for forty years, but recently his father was becoming the personification of the rolling stone. How his mother put up with his father's adulterous behavior was clearly one of the wonders of the world, but she loved that man and vehemently defended him. His father was still a handsome man who looked a lot like Denzel Washington and, as owner of a chain of laundry and dry cleaning establishments throughout Illinois, very wealthy in his own right. Peter knew his father had a mistress he kept in high style, but his mother acted as if it was not true. She was Mrs. Peter Linwood Brock, Senior, and she defied anyone who did not appreciate what that meant to her. True, his father rarely spent the night away from Cassia, even though they slept in different bedrooms. Nevertheless, that was their life. Peter hated to see what it did to his mother, so he lavished her with gifts and flowers for any and every occasion. The diamond pendant he sent to her cost a mint, but Cassia Brock was worth every cent and more.

"No, Mom, not *every* florist. Just those on this side of the Rockies," he teased.

"Petey," she said almost wistfully, "you make me so happy, but you spend entirely too much on me. Last Mother's Day you sent me and my friends for a spa week at that exclusive place in Palm Springs, California, just because I said I had never been to California."

"It doesn't compare to all those times you were there for me, Mom. It always made me feel good to know, no matter what I did, you were in my corner. No one could ask for a better friend or a better mother."

Peter heard her sniffle and knew the tears were probably flowing down her beautiful face. He gave her time to gather herself. "So, what's my birthday girl going to do to celebrate?"

"Well, your Aunt May, Cheryl's mother, Tina's mother and Grandmother Anna Lettie, my new neighbor, Stella, and I are going to a theatre play. Then we have reservations for a late dinner at Bouchard Justice's restaurant. Tina gave me box-seat, theatre tickets for all of us. Oh, and Clarence Bryant and his new wife, Governor Sheila Marshall, are in town. We haven't had much time to welcome her to our group. So, I'll call her and see whether she wants to join us."

The muscle in Peter's jaw tightened. "Where's Dad, Mom?" he asked tightly.

"Oh, honey, you know how busy your father is."

Not too busy to be with that floozy, Peter knew. Still, of course, he kept silent knowing to express himself would break his mother's heart. He would deal with his father in another way. For now, his mother seemed content and that made him harness his anger at his father.

"You have a good time. Maybe Denise and I will fly up to Chicago in a week or two and take you out to paint the town red."

Cassia laughed. "I've still got my dancing shoes, Petey, but I know Denise ..." she hesitated. "Well. It would just make me so happy if you two could manage to give us, your father and me, a grandbaby or two to spoil."

Peter's heart constricted. He wanted more than anything to have a son or a daughter. He had hoped by now Denise would be ready to start a family, but she wanted to hold off until she could build her clinical psychology practice. He spent a lot of time, money, and energy to help her over the year of their marriage, but, unlike his skyrocketing legal career, Denise's clinical psychology practice was faltering. As a result, he did not press her about getting pregnant, but now he was a man on a mission. He planned a romantic getaway for just the two of them at their cabin in the mountains. He was excited by the prospect that, in less than a year, he would finally be a father.

"I'm working on it, Mom."

"You take care of yourself, Petey. Say hello to Denise and hug Cheryl for me. Tell Cheryl I said thank you for the beautiful Waterford crystal vase. I'll call her next week."

"I will, Mom. I love you."

"I love you more, baby. Bye now."

Peter sat for a moment before he picked up the telephone again and dialed his father's office. When his father's executive assistant said his father was unavailable, Peter demanded she forward the call to him. She did so and a sultry female voice answered the phone.

"Mr. Brock, please."

"Who should I say is calling?" the woman asked seductively.

"His son," he said tersely.

"Oh, we haven't met yet, but I'm—."

"Look, is my father there or not!" Peter cut her off, his hand tightening on the phone. The woman sounded young enough to be his father's daughter, instead of his lover. He did not want to know this woman or anything about her. Infidelity in a marriage was his father's thing, not Peter's. He was faithful to Denise and would never dishonor her by having an illicit affair. His marriage was important to him and so was his family, the family he wanted to have; the grandchildren he and his mother wanted so dearly. Whatever it took, he would make that dream a reality.

Peter's father cleared his throat, bringing Peter back to the situation at hand.

"Son? Is something wrong?" his father asked.

"I'd say so. Do you know what today is?" he asked tersely. Silence stretched into moments. "Well, do you, Dad?"

"Yes, Petey, I know what today is," he answered quietly. "Did your mother call you? Is that why—."

"Mother has too much class to call me and ask me to do something like this for her. She's a lady which is more than I can say about that whore—."

"Peter!" his father's sharp reproach reached through the miles between Chicago and Washington. "That's totally uncalled for! Ginger is—."

"I don't give a damn what or who she is! What I care about is the fact today is my mother's, your wife's, sixtieth birthday, and she's spending it without her husband!"

Again, silence. Then the elder Brock spoke. "I love my wife. You do not have to remind me what today is or of my obligations. I've been married to Cassia for forty years."

"Then act like it, Dad. Goodbye."

Peter hung up and rocked back in his chair. How could his father claim he loved his mother and then lay up with some high-priced whore? Peter shook his head and closed his eyes for a moment. His father was a good man and, in spite of his behavior, he loved him. What he could not reconcile was his father's conduct. Strangely, Peter believed his father when he said he loved Cassia but saying it was not enough. With Denise, he tried to show her the depths of his feelings. No matter what the circumstances, it was a man's duty to love, respect, honor, and cherish the woman he married.

He hadn't been head over heels in love with Denise when they were first married and, the truth be told, he hadn't reached the depths of feelings he believed he should have at this point in their lives together. At the time Denise entered his life again, he was reeling from the lost opportunity to love and marry his long-time friend and would-be fiancée, Kristen Catherine Bryant. All he wanted was to love someone and have his love returned in equal measure. Kristen could not and would not offer him what he needed he understood on an intellectual level, but Denise had. Shortly after Kristine married Thomas Marshall, he married Denice and vowed he would make it work between them. Of course, he was building a career over the year of his marriage to Denise and she had been working to build her practice. Their private life was comfortable, if not truly satisfying or complete. He thought it was his fault for not giving her all she needed in their marriage, giving himself totally over to being in love and attentive, but he made every effort to see to her financial security and hoped by doing so, their love would someday grow and blossom into something to hold on to.

Well, it had not happened yet, but with renewed determination, he would make a family for them to focus their love on and then on each other.

"Mr. Brock?" MeKa asked over the intercom. "Do you have a few minutes for Zack Cooper?"

Peter pushed the intercom button. "Sure, send him in," he said sitting forward at his desk.

Moments later Zachary Cooper, another junior partner in the law firm, came in.

"How's it goin', my man?" Zack grinned.

Peter shook his head and grinned as he continued jotting notes on one of his cases. "You got it, my man."

"Not yet, but I'm working on it."

Peter's head came up and studied Zack. "All right, man, there's only one reason for you to have that shit-eating grin on your face. When does Tina get into town?"

"Tina? Man, if I can't have the best, then I'll take the rest."

Peter narrowed his eyes. "What are you talking about?"

"That phine, phine, super phine, Cheryl. Who else, man?"

"Cheryl? You mean, as in Cheryl Lawrence-Hardy?" he asked, instantly not liking the way this conversation was going.

Zack, a tall, well-built, and handsome man, had only been with the law firm for a matter of months, a little over half the year. In that time, Zack dated every available woman at the firm . . . and a few who were not so available. He was a playa and everyone knew it. The fact he was also an excellent trial attorney was no surprise to anyone. Zack had charisma which made women swoon and a masculinity which made men want to identify with him. He had an impressive winning record in court and not many other attorneys wanted to tangle with him in the trenches. However, Zack faced Cheryl in court and across the conference table on several occasions and lost each time. Yet, Cheryl was so impressed by his legal skills she recommended to the partners he be hired by the law firm. The senior partners agreed and were also impressed with Zack and his work, if not his philandering.

Cheryl introduced Zack to their friend Tina, Constantina Justice. Tina, since leaving Washington, after clerking for Kristen, was a high-profile, hot commodity television personality, and more than time enough for Zack. She led him on a merry chase and he was having difficulty keeping up with her.

"Yeah, Earth to Brock. What's wrong with you, man? The chick is *phine!*"

"She's also very married, my man," Peter said, liking even less Zack's reference to Cheryl as a "chick."

"There must be something wrong with you old, married types. Your hormones must go into remission or something. Man, the woman is A, number one prime!"

"Chicken, beef, man, you must have a food fetish or something," Peter said trying to laugh it off and lighten the sour mood he was quickly slipping into. The memory of the conversation he just had with his father about fidelity wasn't helping things. "I presume you had a reason for stopping in to see me."

Zack hiked a hip on the edge of Peter's desk and then conspiratorially leaned forward. "Look, I hear the powers that be, the founding partners, are looking to move some people up to senior partner. Two of the senior partners are considering retirement."

"So, what does that have to do with me?"

"Man, are you lunchin' or something? You, my man, are on the short list. You and Cheryl. I sure as hell don't want to get next to you, but Cheryl . . ."

Peter came to his feet in one swift, smooth motion and leaned across his desk toward Zack who quickly hopped off the desk and backed up a few steps. "Look, *my man*, if you want to make some orthodontist rich, you just keep talking about Cheryl Lawrence as if she's on your dinner menu!" he hissed lowly through gritted teeth.

Zack quickly put his hands up in surrender. "Hey, man, I'm sorry. I didn't mean it like it sounded. I know you and Cheryl are tight, but I wouldn't disrespect the lady. Yeah, I wish she wasn't hooked up with that tool, Wilbur, but, hey, a man can dream, can't he? I'm only lusting after her in my heart."

"In your dreams. You bring that bull in here again and I'm going to be your worse nightmare!"

"Sorry, man," Zack said back peddling out of the office. "Just thought I'd give you a heads up."

As soon as Zack left, MeKa knocked and entered Peter's office.

"What did the walking groin want?" she asked facetiously.

Peter smiled at his very astute executive assistant as she handed the legal briefs she finished typing to him.

"Something about potential openings for senior partners," he offhandedly remarked giving her the edited version of the conversation he had with Zack as he stuffed the legal briefs in his already cluttered briefcase.

"Oh, that," she said. "Yeah, the managing founding partner's executive assistant told me all about it on Monday. Seems you and Cheryl Lawrence-Hardy are on the A-list. You've been in court all this week with the McCoy case or I would have told you about it. Doesn't surprise me, though. Both of you work real hard. When you win this case and Cheryl signs up her new clients, you're both in the executive dining room. I think I'll like having a corner office just like the other senior partners' executive assistants. Of course, that big raise won't be anything to sneeze at either!"

Peter smiled again. The grapevine in the law firm was alive and well. He'd have to make a note to mention this news to Cheryl in the morning.

"Don't call the interior decorators yet, MeKa," he teased. "Anything else?"

"Your wife called to remind you to pick her up at her office. She wanted to know what time you were scheduled to leave today and made me swear I'd give you the message." MeKa wrinkled her nose and muttered. "Like I'm too dumb to ring a bell."

Peter heard the remark but didn't respond to it. He knew Denise sometimes appeared to be condescending and, all too often, short-tempered with his staff. Talking to Denise about her behavior toward his team proved fruitless. She didn't consider them worth her time or attention. His people tolerated her but clearly didn't like her in the least.

"Peter, if that's all, I've got a dental appointment. I'll see you in the morning."

"Thanks, MeKa, I'm leaving now, too."

"Oh, well, you're leaving earlier than I told your wife. She's going to blame me for that too, so drive slowly."

He laughed, but he knew MeKa was right about Denise's attitude.

Less than an hour later, Peter parked in front of Denise's office in a large business park he owned, not far from their home. Checking his watch, he noted he was indeed early. He got out of his Porsche and walked into the reception area. Betty Jones, Denise's secretary, looked up with a big smile.

"Hi, Mr. Brock."

"Hello, Betty. Is Denise with a client?"

"Yes, she is, but I'll tell her you're here." She picked up the telephone and relayed the message.

Shortly, Denise opened her office door carrying her purse and briefcase. Peter rose from his seat and walked toward her reaching for her briefcase and moving to kiss her on the cheek.

"Hi, babe. Betty said you were still with a client. Are you ready to go?" he asked.

She moved away from him. "Please, Peter. Not in front of the help."

He immediately noted the chill in Denise's tone. "Yeah, wanting to kiss my wife in her reception area, what could I possibly have been thinking?" he muttered.

Betty looked back toward Denise's office, a quizzical expression on her face. "Mrs. Brock, isn't there still someone in your office?"

"Goodnight, Ms. Jones. Please lock up before you leave," Denise said curtly to Betty's confused expression.

"Goodnight," Betty said lowering her eyes, but Peter noted the anger before Betty looked away.

Peter seated Denise in his car and then slid in behind the wheel. "Now, Mrs. Brock, may I have a kiss?" he asked turning the ignition.

"Peter, I don't want to smudge my make up or mess up my hair. We only have thirty minutes before we're due at the Mitchells for cocktails.

"Cocktails? What are you talking about, Denise?"

"State Senator Julius and Mrs. Norah Barkley Mitchell from Mitchell County. You know them, don't you? The family represents the old guard in Maryland business and politics. Tonight they're hosting the . . . didn't that ditsy secretary of yours put this on your calendar?" She huffed in annoyance. "Really, Peter, you should fire that woman. She's totally incompetent."

Peter rolled his eyes to the ceiling of his car. "Honey, it's been a tough week. I've been in court every day. Couldn't we skip this thing tonight? We'll be at Wilbur and Cheryl's party tomorrow evening, remember? I'm really beat and I'd like to spend a quiet evening at home, just the two of us." He put his arm around her and squeezed her gently close to his body. Kissing her ear, he whispered. "We could hop in the Jacuzzi, snuggle, and soak for a while. Then make love and have a late supper with . . ."

Denise looked at him as if he had grown two heads and backed out of his embrace. "That's always your way, Peter, isn't it?" she sharply questioned. "Whenever it comes to *my* professional commitments, you're too busy or you want to skip it, but let me not show up at one of those boring founders or law partners' confabs *you're* always going to, and you hit the ceiling! Of course, if Cheryl crooks her little finger, you're always there at her beck and call."

It wasn't true, but rather than start an argument, Peter surrendered. The Jacuzzi would have to wait.

Later that night, after they returned from the cocktail party, Peter lay in bed, his fingers laced behind his head waiting for Denise to come out of their bathroom. He had champagne in an ice bucket beside the bed, scented candles lighting the room, and soft music playing. He already showered, shaved, and was relaxing listening to the music while waiting for his wife.

Because of his heavy caseload, it had been weeks since they spent any quality time together and tonight would mark a change in the distance that seemed to separate them for far too long.

Peter watched intently as Denise came into their bedroom wearing a lacy, canary-yellow teddy, a matching, flowing, sleeveless silk robe, and stiletto slippers. Her long, shapely legs and svelte body looked like she ought to be a runway model. She was not classically beautiful, like his friends, Tina, Kristen or Cheryl, but she knew how to accentuate her positive features. Her New Orleans mulatto heritage was strong in her dusky skin tone, dark eyes, and chemically-treated, dyed, long, dark-auburn hair. Her mouth was wide, her lips thin, a narrow nose that turned up at the end, and sunken cheeks. She had small breasts, a narrow waist, and nearly non-existent hips. Luscious didn't come to mind when he thought of his wife, as it did when he thought of Cheryl. Rather Denise seemed more dry and detached; perhaps more stately and very distant.

"Peter, would you transfer ten thousand dollars to my account tomorrow?" she asked brushing her hair while she sat in front of her dressing table. The question asked as if she were requesting he pick up a loaf of bread from the grocery store on his way home from work.

Peter narrowed his eyes. "Ten thousand? I just transferred that much to your account last month. What is all this money for, Denise?"

"I have expenses, Peter, darling. You know that. It takes time to build a good clinical psychology practice. Things will turn around. That's why tonight was such an important networking opportunity. One of the major health maintenance organizations in the area is offering to add my name to the list of psychologists they'll refer their patients to. I've also been asked to give a speech at a conference next week in Chicago. Everyone who's anyone in the field of psychology and psychiatry will be there."

"That's wonderful, honey. I'm very proud of you," he said sincerely. He probably should have asked for a more detailed accounting for why she needed the money but chose not to raise questions at this particular time. It wasn't as if the funds were an issue for him, because they weren't. Rather, he was trying to set the mood for a romantic night.

"Then you'll transfer the money?"

"Yes, first thing in the morning," he said slipping off of the bed and approaching her. "Maybe I'll be able to go to Chicago with you. I talked with my mother today and told her we would come for a belated birthday visit."

Peter kissed her on her right shoulder, slipped a diamond studded necklace around her neck He kissed her left shoulder as she swung her hair to the right and continued to brush it.

"That's nice, Peter." She smiled looking at the bobble and then continued brushing her hair. "You needn't change your schedule to accompany me. I won't have time to socialize while I'm in Chicago. I'll call Cassia and give her our regrets."

Peter wanted to discuss the trip more, but he didn't want to argue. He would deal with the question of whether they were going to Chicago together after he knew what his court schedule next week would be. For the moment he had something else on his mind. "How about some champagne to celebrate?" he asked when she seemed unaffected by his attention. "I have something I want to talk with you about."

"Really, Peter, isn't it a bit late. You said you were tired earlier. It's nearly midnight. Frankly, darling, I'm very tired now, too. It's been an exhausting day. I'd like to just go to sleep."

"Honey, we really need to talk." Then rushing on, he said, "I've been thinking it's time for us to start a family and . . ."

Abruptly, Denise tossed her hairbrush on the vanity and glared at Peter in her mirror. Her face contorted into a sneer. "What is it? Is there something in the water at that damn law firm of yours? Cheryl has been nagging poor Wilbur for months about having a baby and now here you are pushing that same foolishness at me! I've told you, Peter. I don't want to have a baby!"

Peter was taken aback by her vehemence. He stood behind her, crossed his arms, and his eyes narrowed. "Are you saying you don't want to have a baby now . . . or ever? Also, what's this about *poor* Wilbur?' I didn't think you and Cheryl were close enough to discuss or confide intimacies with you about her and Wilbur."

Like a chameleon, Denise seemed to change before his eyes. Her demeanor softened. She stood and put her arms around his neck, nuzzling his throat with her nose and kissing his bare chest.

"Darling, let's not talk about them." She stroked his head. "Let's just concentrate on us."

He set her an arm's length away from him, searching her eyes. "You didn't answer my question, Denise. Are we going to plan to have a baby or not?"

"Of course, we are, darling," she said stroking his chest, "Just not right away." She turned away from him, grabbed a bottle of perfumed lotion and began applying it to her arms. "My career is just taking off. In a few years, five at most, everything will be perfect. We can plan to have a family . . ."

Peter turned her to face him. "*Five years?*" Peter thundered. "Denise, I'm thirty-four years old now. You're thirty-nine. I don't want to wait that long to start a family."

Denise snatched her hands away from him and pursed her lips. "You would have to remind me that I'm older than you, wouldn't you?" Her chin lifted defiantly. She dropped her robe to the floor and put her hands on her hips. "Does this body look like I'm a day over nineteen?" she asked rhetorically. "No, it doesn't and I'm not going to ruin my body by carrying some little crumb snatcher—"

"So," he said as his insight improved. "Your reluctance to have a baby now has nothing to do with reaching your career goals, does it? It's all about what pregnancy will do to your vanity!" Peter closed his eyes briefly in frustration. Tamping down his anger, he pulled Denise's stiffened body into his arms against his hardened length. "Look, honey," he said calmly and quietly, caressing her gently. "If you're worried about whether I'll love you, I promise I will. I want to feel our child growing inside you. I'll kiss every stretch mark, we'll do the Lamaze classes together, and, after our baby is born, I'll become your personal trainer to help you get back into shape. I'll sit up with our baby every night if I have to. I'll even become Mr. Mom so you can go back to work, if you want." He kissed her lips gently. "I promise, honey. This will be a wonderful and exciting experience for both of us."

His sexual need was great, but he didn't miss the stiffness in her demeanor. Slowly, languidly, he kissed her mouth until she opened to him. He moved them to the bed, relieved her of her teddy, and made slow, drugging love to her before he buried himself unshielded inside her. He prayed this was the beginning of a new life for them. A life filled with the love a baby could help cement.

A future.

Chapter 3

Cheryl rolled her head to the left and peered at the small, square, gold, antique clock on the nightstand. It was five-thirty in the morning. Dawn was just beginning to crease the darkness of the bedroom. Her head rolled to the right and she noticed Wilbur was so far away from her in their king-sized bed as he could qualify. It was as if he was as sleeping in a different zip code. Inwardly she sighed.

Wilbur left the house yesterday after their argument. When he returned, they went to different parts of the house like two prize fighters going to neutral corners of a ring. She ate dinner alone and went to bed early. Most of the night she thought of and dismissed every possible argument she could use to persuade Wilbur that starting a family was the right thing for them to do. Each counter-argument he might use made her less certain she could be persuasive.

It was late when he came to bed, but, as usual, no matter what the hour, he wanted to have sex. He woke her from a sound sleep several times during the night. The man was insatiable but never failed to wear a condom.

Tired of the uncertainty and needing to concentrate on the dinner party, Cheryl rolled out of bed, looped her hair into a top-knot ponytail, and dressed for her morning run.

Outside the moist thickness of the August air immediately clung to her body. She bent and stretched for ten minutes to limber her muscles. Shortly she took off at an easy pace and joined other early morning runners on the golf-cart paths that meandered through the seventy-two-hole, championship golf course that comprised a substantial part of the large, private community. Custom-built, mansion-sized homes of all types and descriptions were each nestled on at least seven-acre, well-landscaped parcels. Rolling lawns professionally designed and maintained added to the carefully planned community. A private security force protected the residents from intruders. Wealthy families paid dearly for the peace, security, amenities, and tranquility Havenhurst Estates provided.

Cheryl's usual run took her past the tennis courts, the country club with its five-star restaurant and upscale nightclub, and the marina at the man-made lakes that flowed throughout the neighborhood. Passing runners, she barely noticed a few county executives, a state court judge, and four members of the Washington Redskins. She spotted her friend, astronaut Dr. Tate Kennedy and his wife Capri McAllister, an attorney and lobbyist with her own DC law firm, Kitt, Kenmore, and McAllister. Many of the people she passed would be in attendance at her dinner party that night. For now, they all ran in silence with their concentration on the movement of their bodies through the morning air.

Up ahead of her, Cheryl noticed the rhythmic movement of a pair of white running shorts with navy blue piping along the edges. She'd know that firm butt, those long, strong, muscular legs, maple-syrup skin tone, and Adonis body anywhere. It was Peter Brock and his pace was as strong as it had been when they were young children. They both ran track for their private prep school, Ridgefield Academy in Chicago, and he and she also ran in college. He added bulk to his tall frame and he wore it well. Given his pace this morning, Cheryl knew she would never catch him. Since she did not confirm what time he would be ready to leave for work, she took an alternate route that would cut a mile from her run and put her ahead of him.

Her plan worked. Cheryl ran in place waiting for Peter's long legs to close the distance toward her. Without a word spoken between them, they fell into an easy stride together for the last mile back toward their respective homes. Silently they ran along the golf-cart track that passed the ducks and geese paddling in the still lake waters. The water spouts were on and the array of dancing waters made the lake that much more tranquil. The sun darted out creating a rainbow effect from between large oak trees and the pine trees perfumed the cloying air. Sweat glistened on their bodies and trickled down to saturate their clothing. On they ran in perfect symmetry coming first to Peter and Denise's English tutor styled home. There they walked in figure eights to cool down and steady their breaths.

Peter didn't want to notice how Cheryl's T-shirt clung to her full, rounded breasts as they heaved up and down or how her running shorts contoured her heart-shaped bottom. Nor did he want to notice how a few stray hairs escaped her long ponytail and blew against her cheek and her full lips. Her legs were long, strong, sturdy, and shapely. Not a skinny woman, but without question, a woman. It had to be Zack's conversation the previous day that had him scoping his best friend's physique, for probably the first time, he really looked at his friend, his buddy, his ace, Cheryl. Immediately he saw what other men probably saw, a woman so beautiful she could make time stand still.

Because their parents were the best of friends, he had known her for all of his life and hers. As children, they spent so much time at each other's homes they were more like sister and brother than just friends.

Peter did a mental head shake to take his mind away from the direction his thoughts were heading. It must have been the wakeful night he had after he and Denise made love… well, actually, after *he* made love *to* Denise. She, on the other hand, did all the taking and giving little, if anything, in return. After she reached her climax, she rolled from beneath him before he could reach for his own satisfaction. The entire affair left him painfully aware something was seriously wrong with their marriage. He had gotten out of bed and gone to his library. For a few hours, he just sat in the darkness trying to reconcile his concerns. Later, he worked on the briefs his assistant finished. Dawn found him asleep curled up on one of the sofas in their library. Before the sky brightened, he was out of the house and running to expend his pent-up energy and attempt to clear his mind. Now he was having a *hard* time, literally and figuratively, keeping his eyes off Cheryl's body.

"Peter? Did you hear me? What was Cassia doing to celebrate her birthday?"

Peter dragged his thoughts away from Cheryl's sexuality and climbed out of his fog. "Uh, she and your mother, Tina's mother and grandmother, KC's stepmother, her friend, Stella, and my Aunt May were going out together. Something about box-seat tickets for a theatrical play Tina gave her and her friends. Then they're going for a late dinner at Bouchard's restaurant for her birthday." His mouth was dry and he knew it had nothing to do with the run he had just finished. "Mom loved the crystal vase you sent to her and said to give you a hug from her. I'm a little too gamey for that right now." Peter wasn't about to touch Cheryl in his present heightened sexual frame of mind, not even to deliver a purely platonic hug from his mother.

"Mmm," Cheryl smiled around the tone. "I thought she might like the vase. She's a beautiful person inside and out, much like that Waterford crystal. Tina thought she and your dad might like to hear the singing sensation, Loretta, perform live. She's touring the country with her Broadway hit show *Jelly's Last Jam*."

"You've always had a soft spot for my mom."

Cheryl's smile broadened. "It's because she baked the best double chocolate brownies I've ever tasted. My mother couldn't tell you whether she had any cooking utensils in the house."

Peter laughed. "Yes, but Helen Kendall-Lawrence won prizes for investigative reporting. She didn't need to know how to bake."

"She's still winning awards. She and Dad love each other to distraction, and me too, but your house always smelled like home. Like the time Cassia helped me bake all those cookies for my Girl Scout retreat. Or when I had to host a high tea for one of my cotillion events. My mom and dad were always jetting around the world for some late-breaking news story. They were there for me with the big events, but the little things that made my childhood so special all revolve around sitting in the kitchen of your home with you and your parents."

Peter tilted his head and smiled at Cheryl. "You failed to mention I was the one who ended up having to clean up the kitchen after you and my mother made your sweet treats."

"I helped," she defended, "at least I did when I was tall enough to reach the sink," she said giving him a mischievous grin. "I was the one who had to go get your smelly underwear and socks out of your room and wash your clothes," she averred.

"It was your excuse for snooping into my business," he feigned anger.

"Well, nobody told you to keep those X-rated magazines between your mattresses," she countered.

"They weren't between my mattresses, Cheryl Annalisa Lawrence, and you know it. They were in the crawl space above my closet."

"Mmm, you're right. So were your petrified socks. I just followed the scent," she teased. "Still, you got me back when you insisted on going with me when I went on my first date with a boy. Poor Melvin Gates will probably never get over how you made him sit two seats away from me in the movie theater. I was crushed."

Peter laughed. "That's what I wanted to do to *poor* Melvin when I found out what the brother had in mind for you later that night."

"Yeah, I know." Cheryl sighed. "Tina told me you and her brothers heard in the boys' locker room Melvin was out to *make his bones* that night with me." She absently shrugged.

Peter noticed the distant look in her eyes. "I'm still around if you need someone to talk with, kid."

Cheryl smiled. "Last one ready for work is a rotten egg," she challenged and then dashed away.

Peter watched her until she rounded the bend of the road out of sight, shook his head and trotted into his garage. Whatever was bothering her, she wasn't ready to discuss it yet, but he'd be there for her. After all, she was still his friend. In fact, Cheryl was probably his closest friend. Maybe she might offer insight from a married, professional woman's perspective about having children and maintaining a career. Perhaps they could make time for coffee sometime soon to discuss it. At this point, he could use all the advice he could get. What better place to seek counsel than from someone whose counsel he respected?

Later that morning, Cheryl slammed out of her house into her garage. She tossed her briefcase and purse into the back seat of her BMW convertible, hopped in the front seat, and stabbed the ignition button. The engine roared to life and she peeled rubber driving out of her long driveway.

To say she was pissed was a gross understatement. Wilbur had acted like a barbarian when she refused to submit to his sexual needs after she was dressed and ready to leave for work. He tried to force himself on her in the kitchen. He bent her over the kitchen table and tried to rip off her thong. The palm of her hand still hurt from slapping his face. What was worse was he seemed to enjoy the rough treatment. She had never seen him so aroused. The only thing that stopped him from taking her there in the kitchen was her threat that, if he touched her, she would leave him and file for divorce. She still didn't know or understand why she made the threat. After all, it was only the day before when she pleaded with him to start a family. No matter where the thought of divorce originated, what frightened her more was she meant it. She was seriously considering a divorce from Wilbur.

Cheryl was still steaming when Peter swung out of his front door and covered the distance to her car in a matter of seconds. She wondered what had set *him* off. The scowl on his handsome face bode no discussion. In any event, it matched her mood. As soon as he was buckled in, Cheryl drove away. At the guard post, Cheryl and other motorists had to wait for little children to board a school bus. She watched the proud parents as they waved goodbye and blew kisses to their youngsters. The children smiled happily returning the gesture and waved to their parents. It was such a tender scene to see a father hug his son or a mother kiss her daughter that Cheryl was almost reduced to tears. She wanted so much to be among the parents hugging her own little ones. The painful thought she might never be a parent wrenched her gut.

Peter was transfixed with watching one of his neighborhood friends, Calvin Pollard, a pilot with Adventurer Executive Airlines, holding his son in his arms and waving the baby's hand at his daughter, who was only six or seven years old, as she boarded the school bus. Calvin took his children with him wherever he went; working in his yard or to the hardware store or even to sports events. Calvin's wife, a professional woman, owned commercial income properties and ran her own, large real estate company. Calvin recently shared, at a backyard barbeque, that he and his wife, Laura, carefully planned their family and enjoyed parenting. Peter envied few people, but the sight of Calvin with his baby in his arms pulled hard at Peter's heart.

Calvin noticed him and Cheryl waiting for the school bus to pull away. Peter waved and Calvin gave them a big smile waving, too. Looking at the happy father and son, some of Peter's anger dissipated. He asked Denise again this morning about plans for a romantic getaway to their cabin. She said she was too busy preparing for her trip to Chicago and in the same breath reminding him to transfer the money to her personal account and to leave his car keys where she could find them. He hoped last night's lovemaking would have put her in a more romantic mood, but this morning when he tried to kiss her, she acted as if he didn't exist. When she buried her face in a fashion magazine during breakfast, he knew talking about starting a family would have been an exercise in futility.

Cheryl's right turn on two wheels as she headed down the ramp onto Route 50 East into Washington, DC, brought him back from his thoughts. It was clear to him something happened to change Cheryl's sunny mood between the time she left him to dress for work and the time she pulled in front of his house to pick him up. The set of her jaw told him it was not the time to ask. Her focus was on the building traffic as she skillfully wove around slower moving cars. The early morning sun reflected off of her dark sunshades. Her straight, shoulder-length, chestnut-brown hair whipped by the wind in the open convertible danced around her high cheekbones. Small pearl and gold earrings hung on her lobes. Her navy-blue fitted business suit rose thigh high as she shifted gears. Her shapely legs were in navy, open-toed pumps that gave a peek at her red, polished toenails. A white, silk, shell blouse molded to her high, firm, ample breasts by the wind, outlined a lacy white bra. The scent she wore was fresh, clean, and vibrant, much like the wearer herself.

Peter felt no qualms about leaning back in the rich, comfortable leather seat and closing his eyes. It was either that or salivate over his best friend who happened to be another man's wife. Peter took the lesser of the two evils. Cheryl was driving fast, but very carefully and skillfully. Besides, closing his eyes might help him focus his new awareness of her away from the aroused state he found himself in just from sitting beside her. He had seen Cheryl in various states of dress or undress as the case may be. From wearing a bikini that covered less than dental floss to bundled from head to toe in her ski wear. He had appreciated how well she looked, but he didn't recall being aroused to half-mast on any occasion. Now, he was and, as he squirmed uncomfortably in the contoured seat, he was *hard*-pressed to deny his thoughts about Cheryl.

He respected Cheryl and knew he would never approach her on any level other than friendship. He also knew his less than satisfying sex life with Denise was on his mind. He never claimed to be a fantastic lover, but he thought he was, at least, adequate. He enjoyed being romantic, taking his time with foreplay, cuddling and caressing. Nothing they agreed on in the bedroom was out of bounds. However, that was where they were at the opposite ends of their marriage. Denise's patience with his approach was sometimes limited, at best. She wanted their intimate moments to be hard and fast, much like a military maneuver. No tenderness. No long lingering kisses. He loved touching and being touched, caressed, fondled, nuzzled, and stroked, but his wife rarely, if ever, offered any of the pleasures he craved. He talked with her about what pleased her and what pleased him. He didn't believe his expectations in the bedroom were outside the norm, but she seemed not to have an interest in pleasing him.

It seemed somewhere along the way, rather than coming closer together they were moving further away in different directions. Denise preferred to be out and about every night. As a result, he often felt like a trophy husband; someone to escort her or chauffeur her around. He didn't mind going out to have a good time, but she seemed to find ways to get on the A list of every society shindig happening in a three-state area. However, when he had a particularly busy court schedule, he preferred more quiet evenings unwinding at home.

Peter admitted to himself that he was not the most exciting guy. Although he enjoyed meeting people, he did have his limits. He could hold his own as a conversationalist. They lived in a community where the country club had a nightly entertainment schedule, first-class bar, and comfortable comradery with like-minded people to socialize with. He was a sports enthusiast. Playing a round of golf a couple times a month wasn't quite as exciting to him as a game of basketball or racquetball, but he kept his body in shape with a daily five-mile run and working out every other day in his in-home gym.

Occasionally, he preferred inviting a few close friends to join them at home for beer and pizza or screening a popular movie with hot buttered popcorn in the sanctity of their in-home theater. He liked to throw a few steaks on the grill, toss a salad together and dine alfresco with his wife by candlelight and a good bottle of wine. Denise didn't want quiet evenings or small gatherings at home.

Maybe what they needed was to see a therapist, he concluded. Perhaps they weren't communicating with each other in the right way. In a way that would bring them closer together, because, if the last twenty-four hours was any indication, they had to make some positive moves, and soon, before their marriage was really in trouble.

Clearly, sitting next to Cheryl and having carnal thoughts—wondering about how she responded to a man in bed—was taking him in the wrong direction.

".... and there is a seventy-percent chance of rain tonight. Showers should move in late in the evening and be followed by an even hotter day tomorrow. Temperatures are expected to reach the high nineties in the last gasp of summer," the meteorologist on the radio was saying when Cheryl snapped her attention away from Peter's nearly prone body.

For some strange reason she didn't even want to explore, the sight of Peter's erection sent warm thrills down her spine. She was glad she was driving and had to keep her mind and eyes on the road and the traffic because, when she reached to change the radio station, her breath had caught in her throat. Peter hadn't said two words to her while they were riding along. That was okay. They didn't have to carry on an inane conversation. He seemed to be lost in his own thoughts. She guessed he was having some erotic thoughts about Denise from the way his body seemed to be reacting.

When he reclined his seat and stretched out his long legs, she absently noticed his well-tailored, gun medal-gray business suit, crisp, muted-pink thin pinstriped shirt with white collar and cuffs, and silk gray and white tie that perfectly matched his ensemble. His suit jacket lay on the back seat with a handkerchief that matched his Hermès tie sticking out of the breast pocket. She always thought of him as an impeccable dresser. He didn't dress to impress, but he knew style and he wore it well. She noticed his fraternity ring on the third finger of his right hand and his silver wedding band on the third finger of his left hand. Other than his Piaget watch and rings, he wore no other jewelry.

Still, his hands! His hands were massive, long fingers, and masculine. She always had a fetish about a man's hands and the sight of Peter's hands was driving her crazy. His nails were clean, round cut, and well-manicured. She wondered how they would feel stroking her…never mind.

Funny how until now she hadn't noticed how long, strong, and expressive his hands seemed to be. His skin tone was the color of strong tea. His usually dark-brown hair was a shade or two darker despite frequent exposure to the summer sun, but thick and naturally wavy. Judging from the way his hair curled over the neck of his shirt collar, he needed a haircut, but the longer length added to his overall sex appeal. He had a strong, impressively, handsome face. Not a pretty face. Rather, Peter looked like a proud African warrior. He and the singer, Brian McKnight, could have passed for siblings: Intelligent, almost omnipresent, eyes, a broad nose, devilish mustache over kissable lips. His strong, square jaw was hairless so far today, slightly cleft at his chin, and his corded neck and noticeable Adam's apple proclaimed his athletic prowess as did his broad, straight shoulders, wide chest, firm, flat abdomen, and nicely proportioned hips and butt.

Why she was thinking of him in terms of his maleness, virility, and awesome attributes today was a surprise and a bit disconcerting. She would never seduce or allow a married man anywhere near her. She respected herself and other women, including Denise. Although, at one point in her younger life, she fancied herself in love or in lust with Peter Brock. Of course, that was just a schoolgirl crush and well over with before Wilbur…wasn't it? She put her youthful yearnings for Peter away when she accepted Wilbur's offer of marriage. Now, for some odd, inexplicable reason, she was aroused just sitting next to Peter on the drive to their office. Although she would never act on her thoughts, she believed Denise Lombard-Brock to be a very lucky woman to have a man like Peter to love her. Other women tried unsuccessfully to turn his head, but Peter was committed to his marriage.

He had a warm, loving personality, but professionally, he was any opposing counsel's worst nightmare. He always kept a cool head, even in the heat of a legal battle. His greatest gift was his ability to lull his opponent into a false sense of security with his meticulous legal arguments, and then, blast them out of the water without raising his deep, melodious voice. He was often called upon as a speaker or lecturer at bar association meetings or dinners. He mentored law students at Howard and Georgetown and some from Maryland University's law school in Baltimore. His efforts helped the firm find and hire law school students who displayed great potential. His energy and knowledge of the law seemed boundless and he was eager to help his associates at the law firm where they worked.

Yes, her friend, Peter Brock, was a rare and truly wonderful individual. She both loved him and respected him for the surrogate brother he was to her all of her life and for the man he was today.

That didn't keep her from admiring Peter, the man, with thoughts of how she would feel with that tall sip of pleasure wrapped around her body. She groaned at the thought.

"Did you say something?" Peter asked turning his head to look at Cheryl. She looked so beautiful in the early morning light.

Cheryl took a deep breath. There should be a law that prohibited Peter from looking so damn good. She would have to write a letter to her congressional representatives to have a bill introduced in Congress to ban Peter from being such a heart-stopper. "No, not really. I was listening to the weather report. There's a high possibility of a storm later tonight. I'm going to have to have the Greenfield Brothers put up one of their larger tents over the entire patio. With over two hundred guests expected tonight, I'm going to need the extra elbow room in case it rains." She couldn't see his eyes through his dark, designer shades, but she had a strange sense he was studying her for some reason. She thought he'd guessed her earlier foul mood was directly related to Wilbur, but she would neither confirm nor deny his suspicion.

She did need a sounding board though, but she didn't want it to be Peter. Their friend, Constantina Justice, was flying into town to do her syndicated television talk show, ***Sweet Justice***, from the US Supreme Court. If all went well, another friend of theirs, Vivian Alexander Montgomery, would become the youngest American woman of primarily African descent to sit on the high court. The President nominated Vivian and confirmation hearings before the United States Senate were scheduled for after the Congressional summer hiatus. Vivian granted their friend, Tina, an exclusive interview. After the interview Tina, Vivian, and she had planned a decadent lunch at a high-priced day spa in the city and were also planning to spend the better part of the early afternoon pampering themselves into oblivion.

"What are you wearing?" Peter asked before he could harness his thoughts.

Cheryl thought the question odd. "I haven't decided yet."

Peter laughed. "No, I mean the scent you're wearing now. Not what you're going to wear tonight."

"Oh," Cheryl said while she thought. "Frankly, I don't remember." She was so angry with Wilbur, and in such a rush to leave the house, she didn't consider which perfume she wore.

"Whatever it is, it's nice. If you remember the name, let me know. I'd like to buy a bottle of it for Denise," Peter said covering his *faux pas*. The scent was softly alluring. He doubted Denise would wear it. On Cheryl the fragrance had his senses wired.

"Nothing," Cheryl said.

"Nothing?" Peter asked.

It had just dawned on Cheryl she hadn't put on perfume that morning. She had showered using a moisturizing, cleansing body wash, but nothing else. "I mean, I'm not wearing perfume."

"Oh," was all Peter could manage to say around the lump in his throat.

Cheryl's body flushed with heat so intense she thought she might be pre-menopausal. For the rest of the ride to work, neither Peter nor Cheryl said a word, but they were keenly aware of each other.

Chapter 4

"Oh, that feels too good," Constantina Justice, known to her friends as Tina crooned.

"You can say that again," Vivian Alexander-Montgomery purred.

"This feels so good it has to be either sinful or illegal," Cheryl added with a deep sigh.

"I'll plead guilty as long as I can keep feeling this good," Tina said. "If your hands feel this good on my body, the rest of you would be mind-numbing."

A deep male chuckle pierced the air.

Vivian and Cheryl lifted their heads from their massage tables and looked at each other while shaking their heads. Vivian said to Tina, "Uh, all that money for your legal education and you're laying yourself bare, no pun intended, to be charged with making an illicit proposition in front of witnesses. Officers of the court no less."

"Foreplay," Tina quipped. "I'll marry the man."

Another deep male chuckle. "I don't think my husband would go for it. He never learned to share."

"Now you want to add bigamy to your list of crimes. Really, Tina, you've got to get out more," Cheryl said and laughed.

"Or finally put one of your many male admirers out of his misery and get married," Vivian suggested.

"I'm not that brave," Tina deadpanned.

The room erupted in laughter as the three, male masseuses continued to work on their clients.

"Speaking of the brave, how is Peter, Cheryl?"

"He's fine, but why do you call him brave?"

"He's married to a challenge, isn't he?" Tina asked.

"WOW, I walked right into that one," Cheryl joked.

"Denise?" Vivian asked. "Why would you call her a challenge? It's not like you to be derogatory, Tina."

"The woman calls my office every few days. She wants to be the expert clinical psychologist on my show."

"What's wrong with that?" Vivian asked. "It just means she's an aggressive businesswoman. You should understand that trait, Tina. You're definitely not the shy, retiring type yourself."

"Aggressive I like. Denise would also have to be competent, which she's not. I'd do almost anything for Peter's sake or even to give a sister a break, but according to other experts in the industry, Denise's talents are nil-to-non-existent. According to my own researchers and contacts, if it wasn't for Peter's resources, Ms. Denise would be looking for a new line of work."

"That's not nice, Tina," Cheryl said seriously.

"*Nice?* Nobody ever accused me of being *nice*, Cheryl. That's your logo. I call 'em as I see 'em. I hate to see a good friend, like Peter, get taken for a ride. Denise is a user just like Wilbur. You and Peter would have been much better for each other than ..." Tina cut off her thought. "Sorry, Cheryl, I shouldn't go there."

Vivian frowned at Tina and then turned her head toward Cheryl. "You okay, kid?"

Cheryl turned her head toward the wall. "Yeah, I'm fine." Yet, she wasn't fine. The thought Denise was using Peter crossed her mind, too. She didn't like it, but she wouldn't interfere in Peter's life. The reference to Wilbur as a user did sting. She knew Tina and Wilbur didn't get along, but Tina's straight-forward, no-nonsense approach was one of the things that glued their friendship together since they were children. Tina never pulled her punches. If you didn't want honesty in a friend, Tina wasn't your type of pal. Tina, Peter, Cheryl, and Kristen grew up together in a very tightly-knit neighborhood in Chicago. If anyone else made a statement about Wilbur being a user, Cheryl would have taken offense, but coming from Tina, the statement ran too true to be denied.

Nearly three hours later, Cheryl, Tina, and Vivian left the spa feeling on top of the world. They were pampered from head to toe; full-body scrubs until their skins felt refreshed and renewed, fed a scrumptious lunch including champagne, soaked in a whirlpool tub, massaged, given facials, mani-pedi, bikini wax, hair coifed, and makeup expertly applied. It was well worth the high dollar amount each woman spent. They hugged goodbye and headed in different directions. Cheryl strolled along the fashionable Connecticut Avenue corridor window shopping the *haute courante* displays. Moving without looking, Cheryl literally bumped into Peter as he left a high-end male barber salon.

For a moment they just stared at each other.

"You look . . . amazing," Peter said when he could have said much more. Everything he was thinking would have sounded like a come on, and, wisely, stifled his thoughts.

Cheryl struggled to find the words to speak. Peter was breathtaking. His hair was freshly washed and cut, his perpetual five-o'clock hairs trimmed and his nails manicured. He wore a healthy male glow that enhanced his virility. Obviously, he had a facial too. He had a natural panache that was hard for most men to achieve, yet he wore it extremely well. Swallowing hard, she smiled. "Thank you. You don't look half bad yourself."

Peter felt he would blush at any moment. It was a good thing his complexion would keep his secret. He dug his hands in his pockets. "Where are you headed?" he asked

"Back to the office," she said nodding in the direction of their office building just a few blocks away on Sixteenth Street, not far north of The White House.

They fell into an easy stroll together finding it hard to talk. Each one was feeling something akin to a strong attraction to the other, but not wanting to sully their long-term friendship with inappropriate comments, so they merely talked about the office. Peter relayed the office gossip about potential senior partnerships.

"You don't sound interested in moving up to senior partner, Cheryl. Why?" Peter asked.

"If I'm selected, it would mean I'll have to put in more hours in the office than I do now."

Peter laughed. "That's the idea, Cheryl. Billable hours are the reason we're here. It pays the bills."

"I'm not saying I'm not ambitious, because I am, but I'd like to have more control over my hours."

"You sound like me. I'd like to move into private practice. Develop my own clientele. Take on cases that are not only interesting but also challenging."

"I know exactly what you mean. I've been thinking along the same lines. If Wilbur and I start a family, I'd like to be able to work from home when I want to. At least more than I do now. Spending time being a mother, like Cassia, would be ideal."

Peter didn't understand why the thought of Cheryl having Wilbur's child bothered him. He chalked it up to the fact he didn't like Wilbur. Cheryl, he thought, deserved a better man than her husband; a man who seemed too self-centered to be a good father. He made no comment for fear he would say what was on his mind and offend her. Cheryl loved Wilbur and he didn't want to say anything that might upset her or their easy friendship.

"I agree. When Denise and I start a family, I want to have more time to be at home, too."

Cheryl involuntarily winced at the thought. Denise, a mother? Now, there was a scary thought! Frankly, Cheryl didn't think Denise had a maternal bone in her body. Of course, she would never tell Peter that. After all, Denise was his wife and he loved her. If Peter and Denise were planning to start a family, she would give them all the moral support she could muster. She still held the slim hope Wilbur would, at some point, consent to have a family. Then they could raise their children together the way she and Peter had been raised as if they were siblings. She clung to that hope with tenacity as she and Peter returned to their offices.

Chapter 5

Later that evening, Peter straightened his tie while looking at himself in his closet mirror, considered it, and then removed it. He didn't feel like wearing a tie tonight. It was entirely too confining. Mrs. Moore, the housekeeper, picked up his clothes from the cleaners. His favorite ban-collar shirt hung in a plastic bag on his closet rack. Quickly, he changed his shirt, took off his socks and donned a pair of more casual shoes. Then he checked his watch again. It was six fifteen and they were already late for the start of the party. Cheryl and Wilbur lived next door so they didn't really have that far to go.

"Denise, are you ready?" he called for the third time as he went downstairs. He didn't want to make an issue of her tardiness considering he had completely forgotten to transfer the money she requested into her business account. He would make time the next day to take care of that task. For now, he just wanted to get going.

A short time later, Denise, dressed in a short, silver, strapless body dress, shimmering silver hose and slippers, slowly descended the steps clipping a diamond stud earring in her right earlobe. Peter looked up and smiled at her. "You look lovely, honey," he said holding out a hand to her. Then he took both of her hands in his and kissed her knuckles, mindful of the fact Denise didn't like to be kissed or fondled when her hair and makeup were completed.

"Thank you, darling," she crooned, then appraising his attire, she said, "but why aren't you wearing a tie and socks? Really, Peter, you should be more careful of your appearance in public. Your attire is rather Bohemian. You should have a professional, personal shopper select your wardrobe as I do," she complained.

Behind her back, Peter rolled his eyes to the ceiling as he turned to open the front door. Denise rarely liked his choice in clothes or anything else. He had long ago decided to please himself, and not anyone else. He was comfortable with what he was wearing, particularly since it was going to be a long, hot evening. Rather, he was still looking forward to convincing Denise to make the getaway trip to their cabin in the mountains. He'd been able to clear his schedule for the next week. Alone in the isolated area without outside distractions and then on Denise's business trip to Chicago, he hoped he could convince her of how important having children was to him.

Cheryl and Wilbur stood in the wide vestibule by the glass and wrought iron, double-door entranceway of their home forming a receiving line of two and greeting their guests as they arrived under the *porte-cochère* where parking attendants swiftly moved cars to the parking area. A jazz combo played festive music in the expansive, open-concept living area; bartenders served drinks in the library and on the rear terrace overlooking the manicured lawn, pool, gardens, and lake. Greenfield wait staff carried champagne in fine crystal and served hot and cold hors-d'oeuvres from silver trays lined with fresh, leafy aromatic spices. Three gaily-festooned buffets were set up in the dining hall and three on the screened, glassed-in and open-air patios. Twenty-two round tables of twelve were dressed with fall-colored cloths, roses, and scented candles on the lower patio at each end of the three-tiered lighted waterfall that emptied into the large pool lagoon. Crystal goblets, bone china, and silverware sparkled under the huge tent with its hanging lanterns. Beyond the patio, additional tables surrounded the swimming part of the lagoon and lawn chairs were strategically placed throughout the garden down toward the lake. The large, round gazebo was also lit, as well as the dock at the edge of the lakefront where Cheryl kept a pair of kayaks, jet skis, and a small skipjack. Music filtered through the speaker system covering all of the entertainment areas in the house and on the terraces, in the garden and yard.

Many of Cheryl's closest friends and neighbors came, including Roderick and JaiHonnah Hawkins Baylor, and Tate and Capri McAllister Kennedy, and Tate's brother and sister-in-law, singing sensation Matt and Audra Kirkland Kennedy. There were also members of her staff in attendance, other junior partners in the law firm, and all of the founding members; Charles and Vivian Alexander Montgomery, Alan and Melissa Charles Lightfoot, David and Gloria Towson Carter, William Chandler; and the senior partners and their spouses or plus ones. Wilbur's colleagues, professors, and their spouses from the university were also in attendance making a nice mix of people from different walks of life. Cheryl was very surprised to see Thomas and Kristen Bryant Marshall arrive. Although the invitation was extended, she hadn't really expected them to leave their island paradise in the Pacific Ocean just to come to her cocktail and dinner party. Nevertheless, she was thrilled to see her old friends. She and Kristen kissed each other on the cheek and shared a long, warm hug.

"What are you doing here?" Cheryl excitedly asked Kristen Catherine, KC to her friends.

Kristen smiled warmly at her friend. "My year-long hiatus is over. Since Vivian may be moving to the Supreme Court, I've accepted her seat on the DC Circuit Court of Appeals—again," she said, laughing.

"That's wonderful, KC, but I thought you were going to give up the law and continue to manage your dance company."

"I would if I could, but I have to stay put again." She grinned.

Confusion on Cheryl's face changed to insight. "You're pregnant?" Cheryl asked very excitedly. KC nodded and smiled broadly. "That's wonderful," Cheryl smiled warmly and hugged her friend again. She was truly happy for Kristen and Ashton. They already had a wonderful little boy, Tommy, Thomas Ashton Marshall, IV, but Cheryl's heart broke with the knowledge she may never feel the wonder of a life growing inside her. Her mood would have slipped into despair, if her thoughts were not interrupted. Only Peter's greeting broke through Cheryl's melancholy. Cheryl looked up at him and immediately her heart skipped a few beats. Her body flushed, heated to her core. Her skin became sensitized and her nipples hardened. He looked fantastic in his cream-colored, ban collar chambray shirt, matching cream-colored slacks and a navy- blue sports jacket. When her breath returned to her body, she remembered Peter had once been very much in love with Kristen. She excused herself and immediately moved to greet Peter and Denise. "So glad you could come, Denise. You look wonderful."

"It must be old home week," another voice interrupted the group.

Everyone turned to see Constantina Justice enter escorted by Zachery Cooper. Tina didn't just enter a room; her arrival was a kind of event unto itself. She swept in like Jackson through Vicksburg, capturing everyone's gaze and admiration. Her beauty was legendary. A light smattering of applause from other guests accompanied her arrival. Some even approached for her autograph or to take a picture with her. When she satisfied her fans' requests, she turned her charm first on their friend Peter.

"Mumph, Peter, if you get any more handsome and sexy, I'm going to have to adopt you," Tina teased kissing Peter on the mouth. Everyone chuckled. "And you Ashton," she said hugging him, "how does it feel to be every woman's heartthrob? Never mind, don't answer that. There are so many media moguls here, your response would end up as the lead story on CNN or MSNBC tomorrow." Then turning to Wilbur, she simply acknowledged his presence. To Denise, Tina extended her hand. "So nice to see you again, Denise. I hope you've been taking care of my good friend, Peter," her smile laced with larceny.

"But, of course," Denise smiled hauntingly. "Peter and I are wildly happy, aren't we, darling?"

Peter stood beside Denise in the circle of his oldest and dearest friends, but his eyes strayed more than they should have to Cheryl. She was, in a word—incomparable—in a thigh length, black, lacy, wrap dress that bared one shoulder. Sheer, black hose with black lace tops and single-strap, four-inch, plat-formed, high heels completed the alluring package. Her hair was piled on top of her head with wisps of hair dangling around her beautiful face. Even among the throng of beautiful women, Cheryl stood out to him. Her clear, clean, crisp smile, even pearl-white teeth, full delectable mouth, wide-set, shinning, golden-olive eyes and perfectly shaped nose were a ringing endorsement of her Afro-Cuban heritage. The diamond studs that sparked in her earlobes and the teardrop diamond suspended around her neck didn't match the sparkle in her eyes. Yet, he noticed her smile, though genuine, didn't reach her eyes either.

"Peter!" Denise hissed lowly.

Denise's tug on his arm brought him back to the conversation. "Yes, honey?" he asked feeling the embarrassment of having not heard a word she had said. "What were you saying?"

"I just told Tina you and I are wildly happy. Wouldn't you agree?"

That was really putting him on the spot. All eyes were on him. He caught Tina's devilish grin. He knew she had set him up. Of the three women he had grown up with, Tina, Cheryl, and KC, Tina was the trickster in the group. He had her number this time.

"Well, Tina, what do you think?" he asked around a devilish grin of his own.

"I think you're too slick for pay TV," Tina said grinning back. "Which reminds me, when are you going to put that all too handsome face of yours on my television show? My Q rating would go through the roof."

"Ah, but, Tina, you know Denise is the television star in the Brock household. We'll be in Chicago next week. Denise has business in town. You two should make time to talk about her regular or recurring appearances on your show," he grinned a 'gotcha'. "Tonight too soon for you, my friend?"

It was rare to see the incomparable Constantina Justice, maven of her own law and consumer court television show, nonplussed, but Cheryl knew Peter had done it again. She gave him an attaboy wink and then noticed something in the way he looked at her. She smiled, but her brows beetled and she was hard-pressed to look away. Fortunately, her client, the guest of honor, Jackson Chase, a property developer, bank owner, with partners in his New York Stock Exchange office, Gregory Alexander, Margo Chandler, Jason and China McAllister Goins, Peter and Joyce Montgomery Callaway, Jeremy Lightfoot, Adam Atterly, and Troy Jackson, all Wall Streeters, came into the foyer and she and Wilbur pulled away from their group of friends to continue greeting their new arrivals.

Peter watched Cheryl walk away with Wilbur to great newly arriving guests, and then turned his attention to the rest of the crowd. "How have you been, Ashton?" he asked addressing Kristen's husband.

Ashton gave him a hardy handshake. "I keep thinking it couldn't be better, but it always is." He smiled at his wife as she slipped her arm around his waist.

"You look radiant, KC," Peter said. "How's little Tommy?" he asked.

"Thank you, Peter. Tommy is wonderful." She giggled. "Ash and I could bore you to tears with the pictures and stories about our son."

It was always good to see Kristen and to know she was so happy. Ashton was the right man for her, Peter admitted to himself. He still loved Kristen, as the sister she was to him his whole life; another strong woman who he respected, trusted, and admired. Ashton was a lucky man to have found a woman like her and Peter never regretted being the catalyst that put them together. He knew he had finally put his feelings for Kristen in their proper perspective.

During their conversation, Peter held his wife's hand and constantly brought her into the conversation. At one point, Ashton mentioned he and Kristen were expecting their second child. Peter let go of Denise's hand to embrace Kristen and to shake Ashton's hand again. When he looked around, Denise was nowhere in sight.

As Peter moved from area to area, outside on the wide, deep terrace, the lower patio, or on the lawn talking with other guests, occasionally he saw Denise on her usual networking bent. None too discretely, she was handing out her business cards as she worked the rooms. For some odd reason, he chose not to approach her. Instead, he continued to mix and mingle with the crowd.

Often during the evening, he spotted Cheryl and Wilbur as they introduced her client to other guests. Wilbur was charming to the wives or companions of Cheryl's clients and seemed very attentive to Cheryl. Peter noticed when Wilbur's hand slid down Cheryl's bare back and squeezed her perfect bottom. However, he also noticed Wilbur perform the same maneuver on the wife of one of their neighbors. The woman in question returned the intimate caress. Wilbur was slick with his behavior. Kissing Cheryl on the neck while simultaneously feeling up a woman at his back. The crowd was densely packed, so if he wasn't specifically looking for the little indiscretions, they would have gone unnoticed. Yet, Peter noticed. It wrenched his gut Wilbur didn't appreciate what he had in Cheryl or respect her in the sanctity of their own home. In Peter's view, Cheryl was far more beautiful, more sexually appealing than most of the women in attendance. Not only was she wonderful to look at, she was also beautiful on the inside; smart, kind, loving, compassionate, amiable, considerate, generous, and gentle. Not for the first time, he wondered why thoughts of Cheryl and Wilbur together annoyed him. Taking a deep, steadying breath he turned his attention away from Cheryl and Wilbur. The sight of her continued to harden his phallus to painful proportions. He recognized the emotion. Lust. In his view, lusting in his heart for Cheryl was as despicable as what he had witnessed in Wilbur's behavior. He walked away to distance himself from his thoughts of Cheryl and continued to mingle with the crowd.

It must be the heat, Cheryl thought as she walked out to the patio to catch a breath of fresh air. She had been on her feet for hours, circumnavigating each area and assuring her client and other guests were enjoying themselves. It was the shank of the evening. The combo was playing dance music, and she danced with more men than she cared to count. Everyone seemed in a very festive mood. The law firm's founding members and senior partners were thrilled and told her the gathering was an unqualified success. Her client was eager to retain her as his sole legal counsel for corporate matters related to land acquisition and development and even promised her many more business contacts through the bank he owned in Mitchell County and the business dealings he had than she had thought possible. Her assistant even had to whip out a calendar to schedule appointments over the next month. Two of the Washington Redskins wanted her to handle their contracts with sportswear companies. A local movie producer wanted her to handle his contracts with the talent for his next movie. A regional food chain owner thought it was time to review his contracts with farmers. Even a few county school board members asked whether she'd sit on a citizens' panel that handled the review of the county's school budget. She passed a pocketful of business cards she received to her assistant. The list of contacts seemed endless, but what had her attention most of the evening was on one Peter Linwood Brock, Junior, Esquire.

Cheryl chastised herself, time and time again, during the evening because her thoughts about Peter were inappropriate at best and carnal at worst. Her musings were far from chaste or pure. Rather they bordered on prurient interest, having no socially redeeming qualities what-so-ever. He caught her furtively looking at him a few times and she had flushed with embarrassment, shrugged non-committedly, and looked away. Peter was her friend, not a man to be gawked at like some matinee idol boy toy. Just because he looked indescribably delicious was no excuse either. He was a happily married man, a neighbor, and one of her closest friends. From her home, she could see his house, for chrissake! More importantly, she was a married woman! She was faithful to her marriage, although she strongly suspected Wilbur was often unfaithful to her. She would never entertain the idea of being disloyal to him, not even for a chance to be with Peter. Her marriage was sacred to her, even in its weakened condition. She believed in her wedding vows and would never do anything to dishonor them, Wilbur or herself.

Cheryl was by no means a fool, however. She would never convict Wilbur of infidelity on gossip, innuendo, speculation or hearsay alone. Any evidence of Wilbur's disrespect for the sanctity of their marriage would have to be irrefutable. She prayed that would never happen, but if it did, she would have no option but to leave him and dissolve the very vows she held most sacred. She was a realist. No marriage was perfect and too many of her friends and acquaintances, both male and female, stayed in a bad marriage for all the wrong reasons.

"Cheryl? Are you all right, Cheryl?"

The voice and the concern she heard in that voice brought her back to reality.

"Yes, Isaac, I'm fine. What is it? Is there a problem?" she asked Isaac Greenfield of Greenfield Brothers' caterers. Isaac and his brother, Wesley, were both friends as well as the best caterers in the metro area. Both brothers and their wives were also in attendance as guests

"We're low on everything, beer, wine, and alcohol. I asked Wilbur nearly an hour ago if he would unlock your wine cellar so we could replenish the bar."

"Why didn't he just give you the key, Isaac?" Cheryl asked annoyed.

Isaac shrugged. "He didn't say. He said he would take care of it himself and not to bother you about it. Then he seemed to disappear. I, and my people, have looked for him everywhere, but I can't find him. I apologize, Cheryl, but we really need to restock. Everything is stored in your wine cellar and—."

She stood on tiptoes while looking around trying to spot Wilbur, but he could be anywhere. She did spot Peter just as he turned in her direction. "That's all right, Isaac," she said giving up on her visual search for her husband. There were just too many people to spot him. "I understand and appreciate you for bringing this to my attention. I have a key in the kitchen. I'll get it and—."

"Problem?" Peter asked, suddenly standing beside Cheryl.

"No, uh, not really," she said craning her neck and trying to spot Wilbur in the burgeoning crowd. "Wilbur hasn't unlocked the wine cellar or brought up more beer, wine, and liquor from the wine cellar. He must have gotten sidetracked and we're running low at the bars."

"Look, why don't I give you a hand?" Peter offered. He too was a friend of the Greenfield brothers and a fan of their catering service. Their food was top-of-the-line and their party planning a complete package.

"What about Denise? Won't she miss you?"

Peter laughed. "Denise was working the crowd the last time I saw her more than an hour ago. Come on. This shouldn't take long. We can use the dumbwaiter to get the things Isaac needs upstairs," he said taking her elbow, following Isaac, and guiding her through the massive crowd. "Great party, Cheryl. Everyone I've talked with said you're quite a hostess."

"Thanks, Peter. This was a very important event and I think it's gone very well."

People spoke to her and Peter as they descended the wide staircase to the lower level of her home. The recreation room and game room were just as crowded as the upstairs and yard. People were shooting pool, playing ping pong, chess, backgammon, and air hockey among other games. It took a few moments to weave through the group of well-wishers, but she and Peter stopped short when they saw people crowded around the door to the wine room. The people were listening intently to something and then laughing and giggling. Cheryl, Isaac, and Peter approached the crowd.

"What's going on?" Cheryl asked, confusion bunching her brows.

"Just listen for a moment," one of her co-workers said, stifling a giggle.

Faintly at first, Cheryl and Peter could hear over the music the all-too-familiar sounds of two people having sex.

"It's been going on for nearly an hour," another offered. "Somebody's getting some mighty good love," a tall, slender man snickered.

"Look, everyone," Peter said ushering the people away from the door with Isaac's help. "Why don't we leave them alone? We wouldn't want to embarrass anyone."

As the crowd reluctantly dispersed, Isaac closed the door that led to that part of the basement, the restroom, and side door exit. Cheryl was glad Peter and Isaac were with her and had taken charge. Frankly, she didn't want to have to deal with the situation at all and certainly not alone. However, she had to get the bars restocked and the only way to do that was to interrupt the ardent lovers. She couldn't imagine who had gotten into her wine cellar, but she was certainly going to give whoever they were a piece of her mind.

"Maybe Isaac and I should do this alone, Cheryl," Peter offered. "It's probably a couple who have had a little too much to drink. I can take them out this side door so no one will see them."

"Thanks, Peter, and you, too, Isaac, but I resent anyone using my home as a motel, drunk or sober," she insisted while inserting the key in the lock. She turned the knob and reached for the light switch.

The lovers lay buck-naked on a wine-tasting table in the center of the room. They were so engrossed in their heated passion they didn't immediately notice the light was on. When the lovers looked up, time stood still. Peter and Cheryl spoke simultaneously.

"Wilbur!"

"Denise!"

Chapter 6

Twenty months later . . .

Cheryl remembered the night of her party as if it were yesterday. The heavens opened up and rivers of tears flowed along the streets and highways. Actually, twenty months had already passed since her marriage ended. Now it all came back to her as she sat across a conference room table looking at Wilbur's pleading expression as they prepared to sign the terms and conditions of the final divorce decree.

The night of the party, Wilbur and Denise looked like animals caught in the glare of oncoming traffic. The scene would have been comical if she and Peter hadn't been wearing similar stricken expressions. When the shock wore off, Peter went after Wilbur with a vengeance. Fortunately, Isaac was there to intercede. Then Peter snatched Denise from her repose on the wine room table, shoved her clothes at her, and took her butt naked out of the side door through the pouring rain to their home.

The entire time Cheryl's gaze was riveted on Wilbur as he quickly dressed, all the time pleading and begging with her not to jump to any hasty conclusions. Claiming he loved her and this wasn't what it seemed to be. However, her mind had shut down, closed up, and turned off. She was numb. All she could do was stare at Wilbur, not hearing a word he said.

Thankfully, as the rains came that night, the party quickly ended. The valet service delivered cars two abreast under her porte-cochère to load up her guests. She stood silently beside Wilbur saying their farewells to their guests. It was three o'clock in the morning when she tore off her clothes, pulled a duffel bag from her closet and began to pack a few clothes and toiletry items. Wilbur pleaded, begged, groveled, and then turned angry when she ignored him. She moved like a robot on an appointed mission until Wilbur suggested it was she who had failed in their marriage; that her career was more important than he was to her. All pretenses, that what she witnessed between Wilbur and Denise was a one-time event, were gone. Wilbur had the audacity to claim their marriage needed some spice. They should practice spouse swapping with other couples in the neighborhood of the private compound. He had all but admitted he and Denise were enjoying the practice with other people for nearly a year. She never in her life hit anyone with malice and forethought, but when he accused her of having an affair with Peter, Cheryl hauled off and punched him in the nose so hard it bled.

When she slammed out of the house, the rain was falling like Niagara Falls, but she didn't care. Three hours in the spa and a new coifed hairdo vanished in a matter of moments. She barely missed hitting Peter's car as he hurriedly backed out of his driveway. She didn't realize he followed her until she pulled up under the portico at her beachfront home. She immediately went to the deck railing overlooking the dark, expansive ocean, and screamed her anger at the raging storm. Then, as if all the air seeped out of her, she sank to the wet, wooden, deck floor hugging her legs as tight to her body as possible. Peter wordlessly came to her. Sitting behind her on the deck, mindless of the pouring rain and their clothes, he pulled her between his legs and into his arms, her back to his chest. Resting his head on the nape of her neck, he spoke not a word. He simply held her, rocking her in his comforting embrace as the rain, like healing waters, beat down on them both.

Sometime during the rest of the night or in the early morning, Peter tucked her into bed and talked with her parents about their flight information. After her parents arrived later that day, Peter left. Her parents stayed with her while she went through the heartbreaking tasks of separating her life from Wilbur's. When her parents saw she was back in some semblance of control over her life, they left and returned to Chicago. Cheryl cleared her schedule enough to stay two more weeks at her beach home. The weeks that she spent alone helped her to heal her heart and her soul. On the last weekend of her stay at the beach, Labor Day, her friends, Kristen, Vivian, and Tina, came to be with her. They laughed together and cried together. When they all left the beach to return home, she felt stronger for the renewed bond they shared. She was prepared to move on with her life.

At her instruction, before she returned from the beach, her attorneys notified Wilbur to move out of their home. He didn't know where she was but thought she would come back to him, so initially, he refused to leave. However, his name was not on the deed to the property, therefore, he wasn't entitled to demand any benefits from it. When her attorneys served him with the signed petition for divorce, he had no choice but to leave, so he left, taking most of their furniture and many of their priceless art with him. He cleaned out their joint checking and savings accounts, but she anticipated he would. He couldn't access the accounts she maintained in her maiden name alone. Sacrificing their joint accounts was a small price to pay to have him out of her life.

In the months following her decision to divorce Wilbur, Cheryl buried herself in her work. She spent the holidays with her family in Chicago and her friends. She and Tina spent a mid-winter vacation at Kristen and Ashton's home on an island, Plaza de Masquerada, in the Pacific. When Cheryl returned from the island, she started working with young women in the county school system. Teenage girls who, because of their challenging home environments were identified by the county child protective service officials as "at risk" of dropping out, doing drugs, or getting pregnant. The work was mentally, emotionally, and sometimes physically demanding, but as her group of twelve young girls began to show improvements in their self-esteem, behavior, and work ethic, she redoubled her efforts and immersed herself in them to continue her own healing process.

Although they were friends, neighbors, and now senior partners at the law firm of Alexander, Carter, Chandler, *et al.*, Cheryl rarely saw Peter. They only talked about business during senior partners' meetings and never about their estranged spouses. She knew, through friends and co-workers, Peter moved out of his house until Denise left. He stayed at their friend Vivian's Watergate condo, which was within walking distance of the office. Many nights she saw the lights on in his office long after everyone else left for the day. Then again, she only saw him working late because she was putting in extra hours too. During the holidays, his parents came to be with him in Maryland. They helped him put back in place the things Denise either took or destroyed when she left. From all accounts, Peter was handling the situation and she was pleased he was also on the mend.

As the months rolled by, Wilbur vigorously fought the divorce proceedings; his attorney delaying the proceedings with frivolous motions. However, she authorized her attorneys to hire Slade Richardson's Investigation and Securities' firm to document Wilbur's behavior during their marriage. Wilbur sent flowers almost weekly and cards or letters daily proclaiming his undying love, begging and pleading for forgiveness, and for a reconciliation of their marriage. He even offered to start a family, if she would not divorce him. She was appalled once she received Richardson's final report. When she refused to even consider reconciliation, the divorce turned as ugly as Wilbur could make it. He demanded she pay alimony, sell their home and split the profits, permit him to share in her retirement account, and other valuable assets. Still, when her attorneys trotted Isaac Greenfield, Richardson's investigators, and one witness after another up on the stand to testify to Wilbur's infidelities, his attorneys advised him to drop all claims and count himself lucky she was willing to settle for a modest one-time payment.

That was why they were now sitting across the table from each other. She refused to see him over the last twenty months and felt nothing for him now, not pain or pity.

"Ms. Lawrence, if you will sign these documents where I've indicated, this will conclude the proceedings."

"She's still Mrs. Hardy!" Wilbur angrily shot back.

Cheryl didn't even raise her head as she signed the documents. "Not anymore I'm not. The court granted permission for me to resume using only my maiden name," her voice was even, strong, and matter of fact. "It's over, Wilbur. I wish you nothing but the best for the rest of your life," she said and she meant it.

"Mr. Hardy, if you'll sign here . . . ."

"It's not over, Cheryl! Not by a long shot. You make four or five times as much as I do and you're giving me a mere pittance of what I deserve! No man will ever love you the way I have! No man!" he shouted angrily.

"Thank the Creator and my ancestors for looking out for me," she deadpanned. Then rising from her chair, she shook hands with each of her attorneys and walked out of the conference room. Her steps were a great deal lighter. She felt a weight was lifted from her shoulders. She could even smile as she walked out of the building and headed to her home to meet her students. *Free at last!*

Chapter 7

"Hey, Ms. Cheryl, what dat?" Lena, age fourteen of Eurasian descent, and the smallest of the group, asked pointing out toward the lake.

Cheryl looked up and smiled sardonically. "Lena, do you want to ask the question again so I can give you an answer?"

Lena rolled her eyes and blew a hard, exasperated breath. "Ms. Cheryl, what are *those* things in the water?"

"Very good, Lena. Those are ducks and geese. There are a lot of them because they are gathering to fly south for the winter."

"I ain't never seen no geese and ducks before," Cookie, a fifteen-year-old girl of Afro-American descent said peering at the creatures from a good distance away. "Do dey bite?"

"Naw, but theys good eatin'. My grandma she used to shoot em down in the old country and cook em when we didn't have no food." Shenesca offered, her German accent whispered through her urban indoctrination. Then turning to Cheryl, she asked, "You shoot them, Ms. Cheryl?"

Cheryl shook her head. Most of the time her twelve rainbow coalition girls remembered how to speak properly, but they weren't paying attention today. They were on her back lawn raking leaves. Their school counselor, Darrin Johnson, a tall, handsome man of thirty-eight was also with them. He brought the girls to Cheryl's house in a school van and always accompanied Cheryl and the girls on outings.

He looked at Cheryl and gave her a lopsided grin. "It's still an improvement over this time last year," he said knowing her frustration with the girls' lapses in speech.

"What you be talkin' bout, Mr. Darrin?" Soledad, a fourteen-year-old Latina, asked.

"Oh, no you don't, young ladies. We have a lot of leaves to rake. If you're going to eat tonight and have that fashion show we planned, you'd better get busy."

The girls groaned knowing Cheryl had caught on to their ploy to get out of work.

Darrin winked at her. "You're swift, Cheryl."

She returned the wink with a smile. "Sometimes."

The girls worked until all the leaves were raked into several piles around the lawn, but before they could get them bagged, a leaf fight broke out. The girls were laughing and giggling as they threw leaves at each other and at Cheryl and Darrin, too. Both adults joined in the fun and frivolity that lasted nearly an hour.

Peter got out of his car, leaving his coat and briefcase inside, then walked to the end of his front yard to his mailbox to get his mail. As he walked back toward his garage, he could hear laughter and a lot of hoops and hollers that seemed to be coming from the back of the property. Curious, he went inside to deposit his coat, briefcase, and mail before he went out on his rear terrace. Leaving his property, he walked through the thinning fall foliage toward Cheryl's house. The noise grew louder as he approached. When he was in sight of Cheryl's lawn, he saw a bunch of teenage girls sprinting around the yard tossing handfuls of dried leaves at each other or trying to stuff them into each others' clothes. It was a hilarious sight. Then he noticed Cheryl, and a man he didn't recognize, frolicking like the teenagers. She was obviously having a lot of fun. She giggled, laughed, shouted, hooped and hollered with glee as she dashed away to avoid being pummeled by leaves. It did his heart good to see Cheryl so happy again, the way they were when they were children. They had many a leaf, water balloon, and snowball fights in their youth. Even at thirty-three, Cheryl's youthful and sometimes devilish expressions belied her age.

Standing at the edge of Cheryl's property, Peter continued to watch and laugh at the girls' antics. When Cheryl tripped and plopped down on her backside in a pile of leaves, the girls rushed her, piling on more leaves until she was almost completely buried. The man with them valiantly tried, in vain, to rescue Cheryl and ended up being a victim as well. Cheryl and the man finally got to their feet and the girls scattered in every direction. Two or three of the girls ran right at him and then tried to hide behind him and the tree he leaned against. Quickly, it became a game of hide-and-seek as Cheryl and the man searched among the garden, trees, and bushes for the girls laughing all the time.

When Cheryl spotted Peter leaning against an oak tree, arms folded across his chest, and legs crossed at the ankles, his powerful masculinity caused her heart to skip a beat or two. The older he got, he was more handsome, more virile, more sexy, and sensual. He was grinning at her as if he had a guilty secret, then she noticed two heads pop out and then back behind him. She and Darrin found most of the girls, all but three, and Cheryl had a feeling she knew exactly where they were hiding. She whispered to Darrin, and then they split up going in different directions. As soon as the girls spotted them sneaking through the trees behind them, the race was on.

Peter laughed until his sides ached. He hadn't had so much fun in far too long. Yet, looking at Cheryl's lawn he remembered that night. The night Cheryl's party turned his life upside down. He literally pulled Denise from beneath Wilbur and dragged her through these same trees to their home. He realized now he removed her from Cheryl's sight, not so much for his own wellbeing and state of mind. Rather, Cheryl was the reason he even touched Denise. He couldn't have just walked away and left the emotional mess for Cheryl to carry alone. He could not do that to her. So, he took Denise out of Cheryl's sight.

Moments later he and Denise were inside their house. While he packed, Denise berated him, screaming at him that he was less than a man. She swore at him shouting she was in love with Wilbur and had been his lover from the moment she met him. He stood and momentarily listened to her, watched the venom dripping from her lips, the anger contorting her features. She went on about how she and Wilbur Hardy met secretly in her office, in Wilbur's office on campus at Maryland U, and even in his bed and in Cheryl's. She named dates and times when they all went on vacation together. While he and Cheryl went scuba diving, Wilbur and Denise were making love. When he and Cheryl were skiing in Aspen, she and Wilbur laughed behind their backs. Denise was proud of the love she felt for Wilbur and believed he loved her as well. He apparently told Denise the only reason he was with Cheryl was because of the money she and her family had. Denise admitted that was why she married, too, because Peter's family was wealthy and he made a lot of money as a lawyer.

Denise physically attacked him for ruining her life. To add insult to injury, she confessed with glee she had surgery shortly before they were married to ensure she would never have children. She became so vile, contemptuous, and violent he stormed out of the house to avoid her physical and verbal attacks. He felt the sickening disgust and revulsion as soon as he got into his car to leave. Then he saw Cheryl driving fast and erratically in the pouring rain, and all thoughts of his own pain diminished. He followed her; afraid every minute she would hurt herself. When he realized where she was heading, he knew she needed to be surrounded by love. He called her parents from the road, who thankfully were both in the country. Her father was in Chicago and her mother in New York filming an exposé. They called him to let him know they were on their way. When they arrived at Cheryl's beach house the next day, he explained what had happened. They begged him to stay. Cheryl's mother had tears of pain in her eyes for him. Though he loved Cheryl's parents nearly as much as he loved his own, he couldn't stay and have them pity him for his stupidity. Besides, Cheryl needed them to help her through her own traumatic experience. So, he left knowing Cheryl would not be alone and drove to his cabin in the mountains.

He was emotionally and physically spent when he reached his mountain retreat. He slept fitfully off and on for two solid days. Every time he closed his eyes, Denise's loathsome and hateful words cut him to his core. Denigrating his manhood, laughing at the love he foolishly tried to share with her, tearing at the fabric of his being. When his parents showed up unexpectantly, he was in terrible shape. Slowly, but surely, they surrounded him with their love, kindness, and patience.

He reached a new level of understanding when his father tearfully confessed he was impotent. In his embarrassment, his father contrived to make it appear he was having an affair and keeping a mistress to force his wife to leave him. His father didn't want his mother to suffer years of a sexless marriage because of his inability to make physical love to her. The telephone call Peter made on his mother's birthday broke his father's heart. He went home and admitted to Cassia why he behaved so scandalously. Cassia knew all along and, not wanting to add to her husband's pain, suffering, and humiliation, had kept quiet about what she knew. She never doubted her husband's love and devotion for one moment and still loved him unconditionally.

For months after leaving Denise, Peter worked harder than ever before. He moved into Vivian's Watergate condo for eleven months until Denise moved out of their house. Once Peter cut off all forms of financial support, Denise went to his parents for help. Peter's attorneys already cautioned his parents not to intervene on her behalf. Although he continued to pay all household expenses, Peter cut off all other contact with Denise, except through his attorneys.

When they appeared in court, Peter remembered every word she said on that fateful night. Cheryl and Isaac Greenfield testified to what they witnessed and Wilbur admitted his role in his long-term, adulterous affair with Denise. From the witness stand, when Wilbur declared he still loved Cheryl and desperately wanted reconciliation with her, Denise bolted from her seat and attacked him, drawing blood as she clawed his face before anyone could restrain her. She claimed Wilbur admitted he only married Cheryl because she came from wealthy parents and had a higher-earning capacity than anyone else he dated. Somehow, Denice contrived to blame Peter for Wilbur's change of heart, claiming Peter had paid Wilbur to lie. Then she claimed Peter was not only mentally, but also physically abusive to her. That claim died almost as quickly as she raised it. His attorneys couldn't have been more brutal if they were cross-examining a witness at a murder trial. They cut her lies to shreds. Along with the discovery of her secret Cayman Island bank account, which she failed to disclose during the pre-trial, discovery period, came the knowledge she failed to complete all of the necessary training to be a certified clinical psychologist. She illegally hung out her shingle without a license. Her reputation in shreds, eminent prosecution for misrepresentation in the works, and the threat of an Internal Revenue Service investigation, all contrived to convince Denise to take a divorce settlement far less than what she envisioned. She quickly signed the divorce decree and moved to Hollywood, California, to pursue an acting career.

Although alone, and too often lonely, Peter almost completely withdrew from social affairs. Women propositioned him, but he didn't date or otherwise seek out their company except on strictly business occasions. He was happiest when Denise moved out and he was able to move back into his home in Havenhurst Estates. The peace and tranquility of his lake-front home were the things he enjoyed. His friends and neighbors continued to visit him and ask him out to special events, but otherwise, they seemed to understand his need to be left alone without taking offense. He thought himself in love with two women, first Kristen and then Denise. He lost them both. He regretted losing Kristen, but not Denise.

Now, fifteen months since that fateful night, standing and watching Cheryl so happy and full of life, something in him was revived. Instantly he knew he had been to hell and back and that he was still alive. Denise had not killed the love in him. He would live to love again and, maybe the next time, he would be loved in return.

Had it always been there, that special feeling that now enlivened him as he watched Cheryl? Had he stifled what she meant to him to hold on to his marriage to Denise? To hold on to his friendship with Cheryl? To deny his love for Cheryl? Whatever the reason, his feelings for Cheryl were now as crystal clear and bright as the setting October sun.

Yet, what of her feelings? Was she too hurt by Wilbur's betrayal to ever trust a man again? Was it too soon for her to consider dating and especially how would she feel about going out with him on a real date? Not as a sister and brother might do or as colleagues, but as two single people with the world before them and the time to explore it. He didn't know the answers or even know all of the questions. He would have to take it slowly and feel her out, but he was ready, willing, and able to find out what her feelings were…and now was the perfect time to start.

"Ms. Cheryl, who is *that*?" one of the girls asked with youthful interest.
"He is such a hunk!" another proclaimed.
"Looks like a walking dream, like Bryan McKnight!" one added.
"Yeah, a wet dream!" another said, and giggled.
Cheryl didn't have to guess who inspired all of their interest. She only had to look at all of their faces and notice their collective mouths hanging open to know Peter was walking toward them. They were swooning audibly. She would have swooned too had she been alone. She could have drastically improved on the girls' not-so-chaste or innocent remarks.

Darrin grabbed her around her waist and hauled her to her feet as Peter's long powerful and impressive strides covered the distance until he stood before her. She could feel the heat gathering to flush her body. A light sheen of moisture covered her face, not from the exertion of romping in the fall leaves, but from the indescribable feeling that stole her breath and quickened her pulse.

"Hello, Cheryl," his voice rumbled like distant thunder.

"Hi, Peter," she managed to squeak out around a strange lump that settled in her throat. "You're home early."

"I planned to do what you're doing. Raking leaves, I mean," he said feeling foolish, but not taking his eyes from her bright, wide ones. "I didn't have the benefit of assistance from such a charming group of young ladies to help me."

"Oh, uh, yes uh, well uh," she stumbled. "This is the Lawrence Twelve Crew," she said by way of introduction. "My crew is the best leaf rakers in this county, aren't you, ladies?"

Not a sound was forthcoming. All of the girls' mouths still hung open and all eyes were trained on Peter.

"*H e l l o*," Cheryl said with emphasis, to get the girls' attention. "Ladies, this is Mr. Peter Brock, my neighbor and also one of the finest attorneys in the country."

"You got that right, Ms. Cheryl. He sure is phine!" one of the teens spoke up and made Peter chuckle.

"Ms. Cheryl, now I know I want to be a lawyer!" one of the other girls offered with emphasis.

All of the girls giggled, but when Peter smiled, they all lapsed into exaggerated, audible swoons.

Cheryl laughed at their antics and introduced each one to Peter. Each girl was on her best behavior around him. Not a dangling participle in the group. Even their diction and elocution improved dramatically. She would have thought they were being presented at a cotillion which sparked an idea. They were perfect angels causing Cheryl and Darrin to exchange speculative looks in amazement, and then simultaneously shrugged their shoulders in a "Go figure" motion.

"All right, ladies, let's get these leaves into bags and then make dinner."

"Mr. Brock, would you stay and help us, please?" one of the girls begged. Quickly all of the others chimed in pleading with him to stay.

Peter chucked, and then said, "Give me a moment to change my clothes and I'd be honored to assist you."

Three girls immediately offered to help him change his clothes. When Cheryl elevated one eyebrow at the trio, the girls immediately amended their offer.

With reluctance, the girls let him leave. When he returned dressed in well-worn sweats and tennis shoes, every one of the girls wanted to help Peter fill the bags with leaves. The task was completed in record time. After the girls helped Peter and Darrin stack the bagged leaves at the curb for pick up, they joined Cheryl in the house. She had started the water boiling in a huge pot for spaghetti, and the sauce was simmering in another pot. She put the girls, Darrin, and Peter to work. The table set, garlic bread buttered, and popped in the oven, the salad tossed, punch made and glasses filled with ice, and in an hour they all sat down to dinner.

The conversation around the dinner table was lively and enchanting. The girls barraged Peter with questions. He fielded each one, even the most unorthodox ones as if he were reading it off a cue card. He was magnificent with the twelve girls and made them laugh and giggle. Once dinner was over, Peter and Darrin led the cleanup crew. An hour later, the girls foraged in Cheryl's expansive, walk-around closets for clothes to wear for an impromptu fashion show. The girls delighted in modeling the clothes for Cheryl, Darrin, and Peter for over two hours. The music the girls chose for the fashion show was by no means demure. They strutted their stuff wearing some of Cheryl's most expensive *haute couture* designer pieces, shoes, and jewelry. The evening was even captured on video and scads of snapshots were taken on camera phones. The most dramatic pictures ended up on several social media sites.

All too soon, to the girls' way of thinking, the evening drew to a close. Cheryl and Peter walked the girls to the van and made sure each one was safely buckled up. Peter observed the big hug and kiss Darrin Johnson gave Cheryl. He witnessed the scene with a mild sense of jealousy. He hadn't known whether Cheryl was dating again, but, if she was, he wasn't going to let the opportunity pass to ask her out. She introduced Darrin Johnson as a vice principal and one of the counselors from the county schools. He knew, from talking with Darrin, that Cheryl started volunteering to work with the girls after the beginning of last year. He also noticed the unmistakable admiration in Darrin's eyes, when he talked about the contribution Cheryl made and the difference she was making in the lives of the girls. According to Darrin, she was one of the most popular volunteers and he thoroughly enjoyed working with her. As they waved goodnight, Peter was determined to find out how Cheryl felt about Darrin.

When Peter didn't seem eager to leave, Cheryl invited him to stay for coffee.

"Frankly, Cheryl, after that crew of yours, I could use something stronger than coffee."

"You're right." Cheryl laughed as she went to a liquor cabinet concealed in an étagère.

Peter studied the library. He hadn't been in Cheryl's house since the night they found Denise and Wilbur together. Everything in the house was completely redecorated. The new, gray, lavender and white motif was warm, sophisticated, and inviting. Peter settled into a comfortable spot on one of the sofas and watched Cheryl pour Amaretto into two crystal snifters. Even in her jeans and an old, bright-orange sweater with her hair in a comb clasp ponytail, she looked youthful and alluring. Leaf flakes were still in her hair. She looked like a wood nymph as she approached and handed his drink to him.

Cheryl wasn't sure why Peter seemed to be studying her all afternoon and evening. She found him looking at her as if they had just met for the first time. It was a strange feeling, but not at all uncomfortable. In fact, she kind of liked the way he was looking at her, especially now while she was fixing drinks. A warm, cozy feeling spread through her. Peter seemed relaxed and untroubled, except for his watchfulness whenever Darrin was near her. Thinking of Darrin, he surprised her, too, with his affectionate embrace and even surprised her more when he kissed her on the cheek barely missing her mouth.

"I had fun this afternoon, Cheryl. Your girls are really quite a handful."

"Tell me something I don't already know." She gave him an exhausted smile, plopped on the sofa, laid her head back against the cushion, toed off her moccasins, and put her feet up on a hassock, crossed at the ankles. She wiggled her painted toes. "They have enough energy to power the city into the next millennium." Then sobering a bit, she turned her head toward Peter and said, "Thank you for helping out. You were a big hit with them."

Peter's attention was on Cheryl's sexy feet. He never realized he had a foot fetish, but suddenly he wanted to suck her perfectly formed toes. Clearing his constricted throat, he said, "I'm glad I could help." Drawing his attention away from her bare feet took supreme effort. Then he took a slow, meandering look up her body to her face. She looked totally edible all over. "I'd like to do that again, if it's all right with you."

Cheryl blinked. "Sure. It's all right with me," she said in a voice she barely recognized as her own. Peter's gaze made her feel like she was hot fudge; his favorite flavor and he just licked the spoon clean. She felt delicious. She cleared her voice before she spoke. "You'll have to register with the county as a volunteer, though. There's a minor clearance process you'll have to undergo, including a security check through the local and state police departments, but that shouldn't be a problem. The county schools desperately need volunteers."

"I'll look into it on Monday. How did you end up with your crew and Darrin Johnson?"

"The school system pairs a volunteer with a professional counselor. They try to place one man with one woman and the teens are selected for the group. I did some necessary training about how to work with young people, met the families, talked to the girls' teachers, and, based on my research, I try to come up with interesting things for us to do. You know, projects that are both educational and fun. We get together sometimes two or three times a week. Some days we just have fun, like today, or Darrin and I tutor them with their studies. We go to local museums or art shows, boat shows, anything that exposes them to something new or novel. I took them to the beach house a couple of times this summer and we camped out in tents on the sand. We're going to the County's Oktoberfest and the Maryland Renaissance Festival.

"Each girl has to set a goal for herself and work to achieve it. They monitor their own progress so they can feel a sense of accomplishment." Smiling, she tilted her head to the side. "I'm proud to say, we worked over the summer in school and between last school year and so far this school year, each one of the Lawrence Twelve Crew has brought her grade point average up at least one full point in most of their primary studies."

Peter grinned at her obvious pride in the girls' accomplishments. "With you on the case, how could they not improve? You're obviously a positive role model for them."

"Thanks, Peter, but what Darrin and I are trying to accomplish is to help them improve their self-esteem. Each of my girls comes from home environments that are challenging at best. I've had to take on a few of their cases just to ensure they are safe in their own homes. I try to help them learn how to handle themselves in any situation. Essentially, how to think. We're not trying to teach them *what* to think, but how to go through the thought process to reach decisions that are solid and based on sound judgment."

"It's working?"

"Yes, Darrin thinks so. He's been working with young people his entire professional career. He believes, even if we help one young person to make the right life decisions, to stay in school and away from drugs and alcohol, not permit herself to get pregnant before she's emotionally and financially ready, and to look toward setting some early career goals and objectives, we will have accomplished a lot."

Peter hadn't missed the number of times Darrin's name came up in Cheryl's conversation. Curiosity was getting the better of him. "I imagine it's hard on Darrin's family that he gives so many off-work hours to the kids."

"Oh, Darrin's not married and he loves his work. He has two brothers who also work with young adults; Trevor is a cop and David is a businessman."

"You seem to know his family fairly well."

Cheryl narrowed her brows and took a quick sip of her drink. Something was definitely different about the conversation she and Peter were having. She wondered why, but before she had time to ponder it, the phone rang. Taking a quick look at her watch, she noticed it was getting late. Excusing herself, she rose from the sofa to pick up the extension on her desk.

"Hello."

"Hi, Cheryl, it's me, Darrin. I know it's late, but I have two reasons for calling."

"Hi, Darrin, what is it? Is everything all right?"

"Everything is fine. First I wanted to tell you the girls were all delivered to their homes safe and sound."

"That's good to know, but I was sure you'd take good care of them." She laughed. "What was the other reason for your call?"

"I wanted to ask you out. On a date. I mean, out to dinner and a movie or something."

Cheryl was surprised, to say the least. She thought Darrin was a wonderful person, but she hadn't considered dating him.

"Cheryl, are you still there?"

"Uh, yes, Darrin, I'm still here, but—."

"Look, Cheryl, I know you've just come out of a pretty bad relationship and it might be too soon for you to considering seeing someone—."

"It's not that, Darrin, I mean—."

"Oh, then maybe I'm right about Peter Brock. You two have some history together."

Cheryl laughed at the thought. "No, not in the way you think, Darrin. We're just friends."

"Uh, Cheryl, the way he looked at you tonight when he thought you didn't notice, I'd say he may want more than just friendship. So, I want to make sure you know he's not the only one interested in you."

Now Cheryl was truly perplexed. She quickly glimpsed Peter relaxing on the sofa before turning her back to Peter and returning to her conversation with Darrin.

"I'll think about it, Darrin. Is that okay with you?"

"It beats the hell out of a no any day."

"Thanks. I'll talk with you next week."

"Good. Goodnight, Cheryl."

"Goodnight," she said and then hung up.

Peter gleaned, from what little he'd overheard from Cheryl's side of the conversation, it was Darrin Johnson on the telephone. The bewilderment on Cheryl's face bolstered his belief Darrin's late-night call was a surprise to Cheryl.

"Problem?" he asked.

Cheryl, still baffled, said, "Uh, no. No problem. That was just Darrin on the phone. He wanted me to know the girls got home safely," she said leaving out the question he posed about going out on a date. That little bomb had to settle in her mind before she could discuss it. More perplexing was Darrin's observations about Peter. What was that all about? she wondered.

"Just Darrin." That bolstered Peter's comfort level even more. Cheryl still had confusion written all over her face. He had seen that expression

many times when Cheryl was pondering an issue she had difficulty solving. His experience with examining and cross-examining witnesses in the courtroom convinced him there was far more to the conversation between Darrin and Cheryl than her edited version. His instincts told him Darrin said something which confused her, but he wouldn't press the issue. Not now, at least.

Downing the last of his drink, Peter rose from his seat. "It's getting late. I should be going." His gaze washed over her from head to toe, especially her still bare toes. *She has a hell of a great curvaceous body* he thought and his body was beginning to flame with desire. If he didn't get out of there soon, he'd display his needs in plain view.

When Cheryl sat down she noticed Peter's movements more than she heard his words. As if coming out of a dream, she looked up at Peter. Was it possible Peter *was* interested in her? She and Peter hadn't said much to each other over the recent past. Darrin had to be mistaken. That's all there was to it. Immediately she dismissed the thought.

Rising from her seat seconds after sitting, she took Peter's glass and placed it on the wet bar. Then she dug her hands in her pockets and preceded Peter to the front door. She didn't realize Peter was so close to her until she turned to face him. Her eyes were level with his mouth. His very kissable mouth which slowly curved into a lopsided grin. His usual five-o'clock shadow was just beginning to make its appearance on his square jaw. Before she could get her hands out of her pockets, Peter reached up and plucked a few remaining pieces of leaves from her hair. He smelled good, like the fresh, fall air. For a moment she almost closed her eyes and inhaled.

"A memento for your memoirs," he said holding the leaf chips between his fingers.

"Mmm," she intoned, unable for a moment to speak. "I'll rush right out and buy a memoir book at first light." She smiled.

"I have a better idea," he said lifting her chin to his eyes.

Cheryl swallowed hard and wondered why she tingled at his touch.

"What? You think I ought to write a novel about today?" she asked trying desperately not to look at those devilishly kissable lips.

"No," he said, grinning. "Run with me in the morning."

"Uh, in the morning?" she asked worrying her bottom lip.

"Yes, Cheryl, that period of time between night and afternoon," he teased, but her teeth biting her sweet lips had him transfixed.

"Uh, no can do." She smiled impishly. "I have a date."

Eyebrows bunched, Peter took a step back, arms folded across his chest, and asked, "A date? That's pretty early for a date, isn't it?"

"The two men I'm seeing tomorrow are early risers," she said and smiled girlishly.

"*Two* men?"

"Two very handsome men," she said and smiled broadly, but she couldn't keep the giggle in her throat. Peter looked totally perplexed. "I'm babysitting for the Marshall boys, Tommy and Eddie. Ashton and Kristen have some errands to run, so I begged them to let me keep the boys. They will be here early in the morning."

Relief flooded Peter. For a moment there she really had him going. She looked so excited he merely shook his head and smiled.

"I see. Well, in that case, you'll just have to go to dinner with me tomorrow night. Of course, your dates are invited to attend," he grinned.

"I couldn't get that lucky."

"Excuse me?"

Her smile broadened. "I only get to hold on to them until early afternoon. The boys have other engagements in the evening. They're going to a birthday party for one of Chuck and Vivian's children."

"Sorry to hear that. Then you'll just have to settle for me at dinner. I won't even ask you to cut up my food for me," he teased.

"I'm good at it, you know. I can cut up a dinner into itsy-bitsy, teeny-weeny pieces and . . . ." she used her fingers to demonstrate the size.

Peter's laugh was hardy and heartfelt. He held up his hands to stop the litany. "If you insist. See you about eight."

Before the smile disappeared from her face, Peter pulled her into his arms for a quick embrace and those very kissable lips were on her forehead. Why her knees felt like jelly, she didn't know, but before her mind fully registered the answer, Peter was walking out of the door. His hands dug in his pocket, and a blast of chilly air replaced the spot where he had been. She stood for a moment and watched him leave. She could have sworn she heard him whistling. She shook her head to clear it and started to walk away from the door. She had gone three steps before she stopped dead in her tracks.

"Did I do, what I think I just did?" she asked the empty house. "Did I just agree to go out on a date with Peter?" She stood in one spot searching her memory of the conversation they just had. "Naw," she said shaking her head at the thought. "Really, Cheryl, old girl, you have to stop reading so many romance novels." She set the security system, turned out the lights, and headed for her shower.

As Cheryl stood in her shower alcove washing her hair and soaping her body with a sponge and fragrant shower gel, the conversation with Peter replayed in her mind. He asked her out to dinner and she hadn't said no. She was so excited about having Tommy and Eddie she completely missed the part about going out with Peter. Peter was too good of an attorney. He slipped that one right past her, but the thought was not unappealing. It was a very long time since she went out to dinner with a man purely for pleasure, instead of for business. Of course, Peter wasn't just *any* man. He was, after all, a friend, a surrogate brother she had known for more than thirty years. What could be more natural than having dinner with an old friend? They were, of course, law partners, too. In their office, the partners often went to lunch or dinner together. Sometimes they even had breakfast meetings that weren't always strictly business related. It was usually just to talk about cases or business in a relaxed atmosphere. It wasn't purely social. Maybe that's why Peter suggested it. Maybe he had a case he wanted to discuss with her. That had to be it. He wanted to discuss a case . . . right?

The thoughts tumbled in her head as she continued to soap her body. Then she stopped and looked at her plumped nipples and registered the tingling sensation flowing through her. Heat pooled in her womanly core. She couldn't be aroused from the thought of going out to dinner with Peter . . . could she? What were that hug and kiss about? It wasn't as if he hadn't hugged her before or even kissed her. It was a brotherly hug and kiss . . . wasn't it? This didn't feel like that at all . . . did it?

Chapter 8

Peter turned over in his oversized bed and buried his face in his pillow. This was definitely one of the longest nights in history. All night he thought about Cheryl. His phallus was still at half-mast. Lying on his stomach, he stretched his long, six-foot, four-inch frame until his muscular body burned and he gritted his teeth. Nearly two years of celibacy was getting the better of him. The thought of someday having Cheryl snuggled in his bed next to him was working on his psyche. That's where he envisioned her all night long. It wasn't only about sex, though. He didn't bed women just to work off a hard. He had more self-control than that. He had to feel something for them, something more than the physical release he could achieve.

Before he married Denise, he dated all types of women, not all of them stunningly beautiful, emotionally secure, physically appealing, intellectually stimulating or charmingly aggressive. Some of the women may have had a few of the attributes, but Cheryl Annalisa Lawrence encompassed all of those characteristics and many more. No, what he wanted from Cheryl went far beyond the surface of an affair for their mutual, physical satisfaction. He wanted what he never had from Denise or from any woman he had known . . . he wanted to be loved, wanted, and even needed.

Raising his head slightly, he looked at the clock on his dresser. It was still early, but he needed to expend his energy or he'd never get through the day as a sane man. Tossing back his navy-blue, thousand-thread-count sheets and comforter, he got to his feet and walked bare-bodied into his closet. He was so painfully aroused he could barely get his phallus into the jock strap. Finally, he was dressed in a Stanford Law warm up, running shoes, and a towel around his neck.

Outside the October air was brisk. It was going to be a beautiful day. Not a cloud was in the predawn sky as the first fingers of the sun began to illuminate the brilliant autumn colors. Peter stretched in his usual warm-up positions, raising alternating knees to his chest and behind his back, bending from the waist, and stretching his arms as far over his head and behind his back as possible. The deep breathing expanded his lungs and he started off running with an easy gait toward the golf course cart path. As he ran, he cleared his mind and centered his thoughts on his inner peace. His spirit was alive and now healed. His life was back on track and he was the wiser for the tumultuous experience he endured, but endured he did. Only one regret still grabbed at his heart. He still wanted to be a father. To have at least one son or daughter was his goal; someone to be close to and share with. That wasn't going to happen now, not without a wife.

He considered adoption. There were many children who needed a home and someone to love and care about them. At last count, his friends, Chuck and Vivian Alexander Montgomery, adopted twenty-one children of their twenty-six and were wonderful parents. They adopted children who were abandoned and health challenged. Vivian's husband, Chuck, adored her. She had one son from her previous marriage and together with her second husband, they had four biological children. They didn't show any signs of slowing down. She was independently wealthy and a sitting Supreme Court Justice. Chuck was also independently wealthy and a medical doctor who, with other doctors, founded Physician's Hospital. He also had a full-time, private practice he conducted within eyeshot of his and Vivian's working ranch. If they could handle twenty-plus children with their very busy and demanding schedules, surely Peter felt he could raise one or two children on his own. His life wasn't that complicated. Even without a wife, he thought he could be a good father and friend to children who needed a home. He certainly had the home for raising a family; six bedrooms and four floors with seven acres of land surrounding it. It was a mansion by any definition, but it would be a wonderful place to raise a family.

Then there were his friends, Wesley and Rosalyn Greenfield, who took in three orphaned children years ago and raised them as their own along with the two children born after they married. Five children might be a few too many for him as a bachelor, but two, maybe three children he believed he could do successfully.

As Peter continued his run, he decided he would talk with Chuck and Vivian, and Wesley and Rosalyn to get more information about their experiences with adoption. The future was now and he was ready for it to begin.

Cheryl was so excited she was grinning from ear to ear. She had Tommy and Eddie all to herself for hours. She fed them lunch and put them to bed for a nap. Still, she couldn't leave the bedroom. So, she sat in a rocking chair and watched the boys sleeping. She marveled at how much they looked like their father, Ashton. Both Tommy, almost three, and Eddie, a toddler, had thick, curly, black hair, dark eyes and eyebrows, like their father, but a lighter skin color, a cross between their parents, one of her BFFs, Kristen Catherine. The boys were perfect angels whenever they were with her. Well-adjusted, they didn't cry or fret when Ashton and Kristen Catherine left to run errands. In fact, the boys smiled and waved goodbye. Cheryl played with them all morning, romping around on the floor, coloring pictures, building blocks, and playing video games. Of course, Eddie was a little young to use the controller, so he just crawled up into her lap and helped her play. Tommy was a whiz at the games and very bright for his age. When Eddie crawled into Tommy's lap, Tommy didn't miss a beat but cuddled his little brother close to him. It was such a wonderful scene Cheryl forgot she was playing and just sat watching the two brothers together and taking pictures.

Now sitting in the rocking chair between the two beds, she stroked the thick, black curls on Eddie's head. He was sleeping on his back and apparently having a wonderful dream, his little angelic face smiling. What she wouldn't give to have at least two children just like these boys . . . or girls, for that matter. That was what was missing from her life. She had everything else a human being could want. She was professionally successful, financially secure, and emotionally stable. All of the elements were there to have a family, but there was one vitally important missing link that would close the circle of her life; she didn't have a family of her own.

As an only child, she could only live vicariously through the children of her friends. That wasn't nearly enough for her. She wanted more. She had only one life to live and she didn't want to live it without knowing the love that a family provided.

She thought of going to a sperm bank. Inquiries were made with a few of the more reputable ones recommended by her college friend and gynecologist, Dr. Savannah Logan-Flack. A good candidate, they told her because she was healthy and fit and would likely have no trouble conceiving, carrying, and delivering a healthy baby. She laughed when they told her she could select from any number of characteristics. It seemed so detached, so clinical. Yet, without many other options to choose from, artificial insemination seemed a reasonable alternative.

It wasn't a decision she came to lightly. She considered the impact a single-parent household would have on her baby. Her preference would have been a two-parent household like hers had been. Both of her parents, even with their high-powered, busy schedules, shaped her growth and development. She wondered whether it was selfish to think only of her own needs, but she was confident she could surround her child with so much love and support, a missing parent wouldn't have an adverse impact on her child's development. She could use the same semen to have more than one child from the same gene pool. One day she might even meet a man who could share her life and love her child or children as she would. Someone, like Darrin Johnson, who loved children and would make a wonderful father or someone like . . ."

Her thought hung in mid-air when she heard her front door chime. Peeking at her watch, she hoped it wasn't Ashton and Kristen returning early from their errands. She wasn't expecting anyone else and the gate guard would have announced an unexpected guest. It had to be a neighbor, she surmised as she reached for the telephone and pushed the intercom button.

"Yes?" she said quietly, not wanting to disturb the children.

"Cheryl, it's me, Peter. Do you have any more leaf bags? I ran out and—."

"Yes, Peter, come on in," she said pushing a sequence of buttons on the telephone to release the lock on the front door. "I'm upstairs in the third bedroom on the right."

Shortly, Peter came into the bedroom and saw Cheryl sitting in a rocking chair. For long moments he just stood and observed her watching the boys as they slept. She looked so natural sitting there, like a proud mother watching over her children. He wondered whether she had any idea how sensual she looked. She was wearing a bright red, oversized sweater with a cowl neck that fell off one shoulder, black jeans, and bare feet. One foot tucked under her bottom and the other barefoot gently pushed off the floor to move the rocking chair back and forth. Taking in the vision of her from head to toe, he noticed her red polished toenails; her hair was loose in an unconstricted style that framed her face. She wore no jewelry except a watch and no makeup. Her clear, clean complexion had a naturally healthy glow. When he moved to stand beside her chair, he inhaled the fresh scent of baby powder and soap. She was a picture of loveliness that captured his heart and stirred his soul. He wasn't at all surprised that the sight of her aroused him in other ways as well.

Following her gaze, he found himself watching Tommy and Eddie as they slept. He didn't know what she was feeling, but his feelings were crystal clear. He wanted a family. He wanted to wake in the morning and find his children eager to start a new day, a new adventure with him.

In that moment he knew he wanted Cheryl, too. It didn't take a genius to know Cheryl was happy doing exactly what she enjoyed. The poignant expression on her face spoke volumes. He noticed a little sadness in the depths of her eyes, a kind of wistfulness in her facial expression.

"You okay?" he asked lowly.

A sad smile crossed her face. "Yes, I'm fine." Then remembering why he was there, she said. "There are plenty of leaf bags on a shelf in the third garage bay. Help yourself."

Peter noticed she never took her eyes off the children, even when she spoke. He sat down on the end of the bed where Tommy was sleeping. He knew he shouldn't stay, but he was enjoying the sight of the two boys and Cheryl. Tommy turned over and his sleepy face slowly grew into a broad grin.

"Hi, Uncle Petey," he said around a yarn.

"Hey, Little Man," Peter smiled at the boy.

Tommy came from under the cover and crawled toward Peter who scooped him up in his arms and gave him a big hug. Then he sat Tommy on his lap.

"What have you been doing?" Peter asked, tussling the three-year-old's curly hair.

"I've been helping Aunt Cheryl take care of Eddie." He smiled broadly.

"How's she doing?" he asked the boy nodding toward Cheryl.

"She's doing great. She let us play video games, didn't you, Aunt Cheryl?"

"Only for a little while." She smiled at the boy. "Tell your Uncle Petey what else you did."

Tommy began the litany of things they did so far that day in detail with accompanying animation. Peter laughed at how excited Tommy was and the many things he said about being with Cheryl. She would make a great mother, Peter thought as he listened to Tommy.

Before Tommy finished his story, Eddie stirred and then woke up. Peter marveled at how well adjusted the boys were and how easily Cheryl handled them. He was having so much fun being with the boys he nearly forgot about the reason for his visit. When he did remember, Tommy wanted to help to bag the leaves. Cheryl agreed and bundled the boys in their lightweight jackets and then they all went outside together. The task took longer than it would have if Peter had done it alone, but he wouldn't have enjoyed it nearly as much. Tommy's little arms carried very few leaves while Eddie found it more interesting to taste the leaves rather than bag them. Cheryl was busy snapping pictures or capturing the scenes on video. Long before the task was finished, Ashton and Kristen returned to pick up their boys. Peter noticed the sadness in Cheryl's eyes as she smiled and waved goodbye to her little charges.

"They're truly something, aren't they?" he asked Cheryl.

"They're little golden nuggets," she said almost wistfully. Then she turned and shrugged her shoulders. "Well, now that your helpers are gone, I guess I'm elected to help you finish up."

Peter handed a bag to her. "The last one finished buys dinner tonight." He laughed and sprinted away.

Cheryl was so caught up in the challenge she didn't ask the questions that had been crisscrossing her mind since last night. The most important one was were they going on a date? Holding the bag in one hand and scooping the leaves into it with the other, her head came up to gauge Peter's progress and noticed Peter watching her as he worked. He was doing a lot of that watching stuff lately, she noticed. She smiled at him and worked harder and faster. In the end, she tied the last bag closed and tossed on the pile only seconds before Peter, and then she danced around the bags with her arms in the air as if she were **Rocky**. Peter laughed his amusement at her glee and graciously conceded she was, indeed, the champion leaf bagger.

"M'lady," Peter said with a courtly bow. "You have indeed won the day, but the evening is yet to come."

Cheryl registered the slightly veiled challenge and curtsied lowly as if wearing a ball gown. "Kind, sir, name your poison."

"I state before all the bags gathered before us, I will dance your feet off tonight," he said with a rakish grin.

"So be it, sir, yet need I remind you of the old days in Chicago when I won more dance contests than anyone, well except KC, and even got to appear on that popular nationwide dance show? We shall see who out dances whom tonight," she returned with a rakish grin of her own.

With a flourishing bow, he said, "Let the games begin."

Cheryl curtsied, hung her nose in the air in a playful air of nonchalance, turned on her heels, and sauntered away.

Peter stood watching her go. A grin lifted his mustache. Tonight promised to be very special. Very special indeed.

Chapter 9

Cheryl fussed and fumed as she discarded the twelfth outfit in her closet. What did she think she was doing challenging Peter? He was one of the best dancers she had ever seen, for goodness sake! She'd be lucky if she lasted through two dances with that man! He was no tap dancer, but his moves were as smooth as Gregory Hines and as precise as Hammer! Hell! He could have given Michael Jackson and Bruno Mars lessons! He was the one who choreographed the steps for his fraternity at a step off in his junior year in college—and they had won the competition!

Then suddenly she stopped.

What in the world am I doing? Why was she focusing on this when the real question was why is Peter acting like this? Challenging her? Peter hadn't done that since they were children and, when he did, he always had a hidden agenda. What she needed to focus on was what he up to? What she thought was a dinner with an old friend potentially to discuss a case was quickly turning out to be something completely different. Why was he looking at her with those mesmerizing, bedroom eyes of his . . . and why did she like it? Pacing the floor, deep in thought, she nearly missed the ringing phone.

"Yes," she answered.

"Hey, Kiddo, what do you know about a company called NICO Communications?"

"Uh, hi, Tina. You want to start with the amenities, like, how are you?" she teased.

Tina gave a long-suffering sigh. "If we must," she drawled. "Hi, Cheryl, how have you been since the last time I spoke with you around 9:00 A.M. this morning?"

"Mmm, that's better. Now, NICO Communications is a media company that's developing a new satellite to distribute digital television networks. It will be carried on cable television systems and LPTV stations, that's Low Powered Television stations, across this country and is scheduled to go global via live streaming on the internet. They're seriously looking at foreign markets. Nick Collins or Nico, as he's called by those who know him, owns the company that's scheduled to launch the satellite. The American Economic Empowerment Television Network is in production now. It's one of the few television networks I'll probably enjoy watching. It promises to be an interesting source of financial information and guidance. Why do you ask?"

"Nick Collins? Collins? Why do I remember that name?"

"Tall, dark, and gorgeous, that's why. He used to play professional football. Has a body that will make you forget your own name. As I recall, he got out of the game while he was still at the top, and started a company called NICO Enterprises about seven or eight years ago. His first company focuses on providing venture capital for big businesses. He, and people he knows in sports and entertainment, back struggling companies, but he's a corporate raider and not adverse to hostile takeovers.

"He's one of Alexander, Chandler, *et.al.'s* clients. Zackery Taylor brought him in when he joined the firm and handled his heavy lifting. Zack works almost exclusively as NICO's lead legal counsel. I think Zack and Collins went to the same private high school somewhere in Virginia and went to college at the same place. Collins is always in the business and the society pages. Ask KC's brother, George, about him. They played football on the same NFL team for several years. I believe they're still in touch. Now, are you going to tell me why you're asking these questions?"

"Just curious. His agents have been sniffing around Sweet Justice Productions."

"Maybe he's interested in having you move your show and production company to his new network or satellite."

"Mmm, could be, but I have two years before my contract is up with my current network and affiliates. I've already been offered a renewal contract." Then, as if an afterthought, "Oh, by the way, what's up with you and Peter?"

The question took Cheryl by surprise. "Huh? What do you mean?"

"What's this I hear about you two finally getting together?"

"Huh?" she asked again, confused. "Where in the world did you hear that?"

"I talked with Ashton and KC a little while ago. They were really excited about you and Peter starting to date."

"*Date? Each other?*" she squealed. "No, Peter may be dating again, but not me. I mean, we're going out to dinner tonight, but probably just to talk about a case or something. It's not really a date."

"Right. If you think I believe that, then maybe I can interest you in some swamp land in Arizona."

"Tina—," she drawled.

"Don't 'Tina me', Cheryl Annalisa Lawrence. I think it's great that you and Peter are finally coming out of the deep freeze. It's been a long, hard road for both of you and it's about time you two figured out you're attracted to one another."

"'Attracted to one another?'"

"Is there an echo in the phone? Yes, attracted, as in captivated, charmed or enchanted. I like that last one the best." She giggled. "Now, if you two would just get to the seduction part…"

"Hold it right there!" Cheryl flashed. "Peter and I are just friends, just like you are. We've all known each other since we were weaned off breast milk. Just friends. No more or no less."

"You need a hormone tune-up, Cheryl. Peter Brock ain't no baby no more! That man's a walking, talking, breathing dream come true! Those thick muscles," Tina swooned. "That physique," she swooned again.

"That baby has got *back*! Have you seen him in a pair of shorts? *Mercy!* And when he smiles, ooooh, he makes you wanna knock them boots to the ...."

"Hello?" Cheryl said knocking on the phone. "Hello out there in La La Land."

Tina exhaled audibly. "Sorry, Cheryl, but the man really trips my trigger!"

"Tina, are we talking about the same Peter Brock? Good friend of yours and mine? The one who used to dunk you in the pool when you thought you were dressed to kill? The one who used to take you on the scariest rides at the amusement park? The one who ...."

"I loved every minute of it."

Cheryl sobered. "Seriously? Have you got a love jones going on for Peter?"

"Look, Cheryl, I can appreciate a good brother without getting into a love thang, ya know? I'm not about to give up this heart to any man. That includes Peter Brock. What I'm saying is Peter is a woman's gift."

"Yeah, but you have to unwrap the present to appreciate the gift," she shot back.

"Not this one, you don't. You already know what's inside," she retorted. "Open the package, Cheryl. *See ya!*"

Dial tone.

Cheryl looked at the telephone as if she had never seen one before. What was that crazy Constantina Justice talking about? Open the package? Really, I worry about that sistah sometimes, she fussed. Just then the doorbell rang. Cheryl hopped up off the bed and traipsed down the staircase, fussing about Tina's craziness every step of the way. She didn't even bother to ask who was there. She just opened the door and froze in her tracks.

Peter was surprised to see Cheryl standing before him wearing a lacy, chocolate-colored teddy. His breath caught in his throat and his blood-streaked through his body like a lightning strike and settled in his groin.

She was so sexy, he couldn't believe his eyes. Although her hair was up in big, pink, hot rollers, she looked delicious. He leaned against the door jamb, folded his arms across his chest, and perused her sexy body from the bottom up.

"Hi," he said around a shit-eating grin.

Cheryl followed his gaze and looked down at her state of undress. Her eyes went as round as silver dollars. *"Eeeek!"* she squeaked, then turned and ran up the steps taking them two at a time.

Peter's laugh was deep, but his body was having a hard, *hard* time getting back from its aroused state. Watching Cheryl's long legs and perfect butt climbing the stairs was wreaking havoc on him. He took off his topcoat and hung it in the hall closet, took the handkerchief from his breast pocket and mopped the perspiration from his brow. The last woman he had been with was Denise a very long time ago, but even Denise's body in the near buff hadn't stirred him like that or even that quickly. Now, every time he thought about Cheryl, his body hardened. This was going to be a tough night, but he was going to make it a good one.

Cheryl thought she would die from embarrassment. Having Peter see her like that was never her intention. She simply hadn't been thinking when she opened the door. He probably thought she did that on purpose, she fumed. It was Tina's fault! If she hadn't been so undone by Tina's crazy, cryptic remarks, she would have been ready on time. Now she was late, something she rarely did. She was prompt to a fault, but now she wished she wasn't going out with Peter. She felt like she was all thumbs as she slipped into a rust-colored soft knit dress which hugged every curve of her body like sealskin and matching suede pumps. The neck was high in the front but dipped low in the back.

Snatching the rollers from her hair, she combed through the thick mass, tossed it to one side and secured it with a long, bronze decorative comb. She fumbled putting the dangling bronze earrings in her ears but steadied her nerves enough to apply her bronze-brown lip gloss. Checking herself in the mirror, she rolled her eyes to the ceiling and exhaled a quick breath. This will have to do, she said appraising herself. After all, it's not *really* a date.

Walking down the wide semi-circle staircase toward Peter almost made a liar out of her. He looked every bit as sexy as Tina said. His dark-brown, designer slacks, and ultra-suede jacket, a soft, cream-colored, knit sweater all combined to give him a Cosmopolitan look. What a look it was! she noticed. Her legs nearly buckled when he released that polar-ice-cap-melting smile of his. Tina was right. *Mercy!*

"Sorry I'm late, Peter. I was talking with Tina on the phone and the time just got away from me." She smiled, handing a matching sweater coat to him.

Peter took her coat and helped her into it. "Remind me to thank Tina for the distraction," he said at her ear. "You look lovely now and even better before you dressed."

Cheryl looked up over her shoulder at Peter and narrowed her eyes. "Uh, thanks?" she questioned around her confusion, "I think." What the hell is going on? she wondered. His face was a breath away from hers. She inhaled his woodsy scent and her toes began to curl. Her blood heated.

When seated in Peter's car and on their way to dinner, they talked easily. They never failed to have lively conversations. She realized she missed that aspect of their relationship over the past year. Because they were so engrossed in their discussion, Cheryl didn't notice where they were going until they pulled up in front of a restaurant and club in Annapolis, Maryland, with a canopy over the entrance. Two uniformed valets opened their car doors and she and Peter stepped out. When he came around the car, he held out his hand to her and she took it. He held her hand before when they were younger crossing a street or in a crowd, like at the grocery store or at the mall. Holding hands now seemed more intimate than they ever were with each other. Except for that dreadful night when he held her in his arms in the driving rain and rocked her while her body shook with emotional pain and anger.

She would never forget that night. Peter, even in his own pain, came to console her. To comfort her and help her through the worst ordeal she ever experienced. The memory of Wilbur and Denise deep into their passion on the table in her wine cellar was now a fading memory. The pain, thankfully, was gone. It was washed away that night at her waterfront home.

This time, when she took Peter's hand, she felt a revival of her spirit and new life in her soul.

There was a line waiting to be seated in the restaurant's dining room. They checked their coats and Peter, again holding her hand, walked past the other waiting guests and up to the maître'd.

"Peter Brock," he announced to the maître d'.

The man's face grew a wide smile. "Ah, yes, Mr. . . . and Mrs. Peter Brock? We're so pleased to have you with us this evening. We have your reservation. Welcome. Your table is ready. Edmund will show you the way. Have a wonderful evening."

Cheryl laughed. "Oh, I'm not—."

"Thank you," Peter said cutting Cheryl off. He knew she was about to correct the mistake in her being identified as his wife. He liked the way it sounded. Who wouldn't want a woman like Cheryl Lawrence as his wife? Certainly, Wilbur rued the day he lost her. He did everything he could to reconcile, but Cheryl was a strong, confident woman. Although Peter knew she took her wedding vows seriously, she was nobody's fool. She dropped Wilbur like a bad habit, never looking back, and moved on with her life. Peter was proud of her. She was truly a woman to be admired, cherished . . . and loved.

Cheryl gazed out of the ceiling-to-floor windows that overlooked the Naval Academy across the Severn River. It was a beautiful backdrop to the elegant, but cozy restaurant. The place was pleasantly packed with a mixed crowd. A pianist softly played in the distance. She and Peter had one of the best tables in the room. A candle array flickered on the table between them and reflected in the window beside them.

"Do you like it?" Peter asked. Cheryl had been quiet, just looking out of the window.

She turned to him and smiled. "Yes, I've never been here before. Have you?"

"No, this is my first time."

"It has a wonderful décor and I like the scent of food in the air. Considering the long line of people waiting to get in, it must be very popular. How did you find this place?"

"The owner is one of my clients. She's been bugging me to come."

"Oh, so that's why we got the royal treatment. I thought we'd be in line for a long wait."

Peter smiled. "My client promised that, if I came, she'd roll out the red carpet."

"She must be very grateful."

He shrugged. "I guess. I'm just glad you like it here."

She wondered why that was so important to him but didn't dwell on the subject. She was enjoying the ambiance and the company. Peter's hooded, tea-brown eyes were doing strange things to her. He was gazing at her with what appeared to be more than affection, bordering on desire in his eyes. She felt his gaze and couldn't discern whether she was breathing or not. Her heart skipped so many beats or was beating so erratically, she wanted to check her pulse. For long moments as they chatted, the world seemed to narrow to only encompass the two of them. When Peter put his hand on hers playing with her fingers and leaned forward on the table, heat pooled in her womanly core. Crossing her ankles and mashing her thighs together, she tried to think and talk with her mind, but her body was speaking an entirely different language. Her nipples plumped against her sweater-knit dress, the touch of his fingers playing with hers was sending sweet, tingling sensations up her arm and straight to her core. Unconsciously, she too leaned forward on the table.

Peter couldn't tell what he and Cheryl were talking about if his life depended on it. He was otherwise involved in watching how her sensuously plump lips were moving. Wondering how those lips would feel on his. How she would look when surrendering to their passion. How he wanted to lace his fingers through her long, thick, silky hair. How her dress would peel off of her. When she smiled at something he said, he felt his manhood go from half-mast to three-quarters. He had to touch her, so he reached across the table and held her hand.

Big mistake.

He couldn't let go with just a touch, he wanted more. Much, much more. She seemed surprised but didn't pull back. He was about to tell her he was interested in more than a friendship with her when a very breathy, sensual voice intruded on their conversation.

"Peter, darling," a tall, beautifully shaped, and very attractive woman breathed the greeting. Her blue eyes were sparkling. Then she bent and kissed him on the mouth, her reddish-bronze hair cascading around his face.

Cheryl sat back against her chair and removed her hand from Peter's ministration. Watching the ardent display between Peter and another woman brought back painful memories of similar situations when women kissed Wilbur like that in front of her. She was surprised how painful it was to see another woman kiss Peter as if she had a right to him. It didn't matter that the woman was his client. A southerner at that. She'd bet Texas, by the southern drawl in her voice. Suddenly Cheryl felt like an intruder on this passionate scene. She went still and looked away.

Peter was angrier than he had ever been. He avoided coming to the restaurant alone to evade scenes like this. Romaine Sanders was his client, but she had made it clear she wanted much more than an attorney-client relationship with him. In fact, she was explicit about what she wanted from him and it had nothing to do with his legal skills. He declined her offer to the point of threatening to drop her as a client, if she continued her sexually aggressive behavior toward him. He hoped they had put that issue to rest and Romaine wouldn't make a scene in her restaurant or in front of Cheryl. Still, he underestimated her and he was paying dearly for that *faux pas*. The look in Cheryl's eyes before she turned away screamed of a pain from deep inside. He knew what she was probably thinking. All he wanted to do was take Cheryl into his arms and kiss all of her pain away. First, he had to deal with Romaine. He stood and used his handkerchief to wipe her kiss from his lips.

"Ms. Romaine Sanders, this is my friend and colleague, Cheryl Lawrence. Cheryl this is my *former* client, Ms. Sanders."

"Ms. Sanders," Cheryl acknowledged, but Romaine didn't even seem to notice she was in the restaurant. She was too busy pawing Peter, who excused himself, and hurried Romaine from the table.

"Mmmm, I love the manly, take-charge type, but, darling what is this business about being your 'former' client? You're my attorney . . . "

"Ms. Sanders, I've warned you before that…"

"I know, I know, darling," she rushed in cutting him off, "but you shouldn't come in here looking so delicious," she purred, licking her lips. She rested her hands on his chest, moving so close their bodies touched.

Peter removed her hands and took a step back. "You won't have to worry about that problem again, Ms. Sanders. I suggest you immediately find another attorney to represent you. I won't be legal counsel for you anymore."

"But, daring," she cried, but it was too late. Peter walked away from her and back to Cheryl.

When he sat down, Cheryl didn't look up at him. Her face was buried behind the menu and the sensuous bond that held them together, suspended in time, was broken.

"Cheryl, I'm sorry about that. Ms. Sanders is—."

"It's getting late, Peter, and I'm hungry. I suggest that we order dinner," she interrupted.

Peter knew that tone of voice. It was purely business. He would have gladly rung Ms. Sander's neck. If Cheryl hadn't said that she was hungry, he would have suggested that they leave and find another restaurant. Her willingness to stay and eat bolstered his hope that the Sanders' incident hadn't wrecked his chances to save his first date with Cheryl. However, no matter how he tried to alter the atmosphere during dinner, they ate in near silence listening to the music furnished by the pianist. By the time coffee was served, Peter knew he had to find something to get them back to neutral ground. He focused on the most pleasant thought that came to his mind.

"Tommy and Eddie are a lot of fun to be around."

"Yes, they are, but they always are. I wish I had a house full just like them," Cheryl said absently looking out of the window. "KC and Ashton have every reason to be very proud of their sons."

She wanted a house full of children? Peter was surprised, to say the least. He knew so many professional women who, like Denise, weren't interested in parenting. Since Cheryl and Wilbur did not have children, he thought maybe she did not want children either. He was fairly certain Wilbur did not. Then he remembered the argument he and Denise had when she jumped to Wilbur's defense. In the heat of that argument, Denise claimed Cheryl was nagging Wilbur about starting a family. At the time, steeped in his own pain and disillusionment, he hadn't given Denise's comment about Wilbur that much thought. Now it blazed in his memory. Did Cheryl really want children? A house full? She must, otherwise why would she spend so much time with Tommy and Eddie? Why would she be volunteering with the young teens? Maybe she was just living vicariously through the children of others but had no desire to have children of her own. Yet, she had said it and he knew Cheryl well enough to know she didn't say things she didn't mean. Even in jest, there was always truth to her statements. If this was true and she did want to be pregnant, have children, and raise a family, an idea began to germinate in his all too fertile mind.

The thoughts were still zigzagging through his head when the waiter brought the check. Without glancing at it, Peter put his credit card in the black leather folder and handed it back to the waiter.

"Uh, Sir," the waiter cleared his voice behind his hand. "Ms. Sanders, uh, well, Sir, . . ." he said eyeing the leather folder and handing it back to Peter.

Peter's eyebrows bunched as he opened the folder. Inside there was no bill for the service, but a note from Romaine asking he forgive her behavior and consider remaining her attorney. Dinner, of course, was gratis. It was a nice gesture, but it wouldn't make up for the chasm Romaine caused to grow between him and Cheryl in the space of a few moments. He handed the leather folder back to the waiter with his credit card still inside along with Romaine note. The waiter, obviously sensing Peter's mood, simply slightly bowed, accepted the folder, and walked away. Moments later, the waiter returned. Peter signed the tab, pocketed his receipt, and then turned toward Cheryl who had been silently staring out of the window.

"Cheryl . . ."

"The food is very good here as I suspected. I enjoyed the music and the ambiance. Please tell Ms. Sanders I think she has a successful restaurant on her hands," she said shifting to retrieve her purse from the seat beside her and standing. "If you don't mind, I have an early day tomorrow and it's getting late."

He understood their evening was coming to an abrupt end. They weren't even going to have coffee or dessert. This was not what he planned to happen and he wasn't about to take it lying down. He stood and faced her. "So, you concede I'm a better dancer than you?" he said offhandedly.

The comment took Cheryl by surprise. Her head came around and her eyes locked onto Peter's smug smile. Her head tilted.

"Since you're no longer able to party all night and keep up with me, older woman that you are, it appears that I win by forfeit."

"I concede nothing," she said with a challenging, lopsided grin of her own.

"Then, it further appears that we have an impasse. There's only one way to settle this once and for all."

The smugness transferred from him to her and Peter relished the challenge he saw in her eyes. He didn't know whether he would be able to keep up with her on the dance floor, but once he had her in his arms, fit her body to his, he would feel triumphant.

Chapter 10

The country club, The Foxes Lair, at Havenhurst Estates was packed. The floor vibrated with the beat of the combo. Cheryl and Peter eyed the scene with enthusiasm, a throwback to their youth: blue lights in the basement, sweat streaming down their faces, and bodies gyrating to the latest music and dances. Hands in the air swearing that you just don't care, but, of course, they did. You had to look good, cool, nonchalant like it wasn't nothin' but a thang.

Cheryl stuffed her tiny purse in Peter's pocket, grabbed his hand and, simultaneously nodded to many of their friends and neighbors before they charged into the breach. When she got to the center of the hardwood floor, she abruptly stopped, dropped his hands, and struck a pose that screamed "show me what you're working with" with an attitude.

She had learned well from her friend, Tina Justice, how to throw down on the dance floor. In their youth, it was always Tina who learned the new dance steps first or created her own and everyone followed. Cheryl and Kristen always followed. Kristen trained in classical ballet; Cheryl in a jazzier form, but neither could quite get into the pop culture of the period the way that Tina could. Like her namesake, Tina Turner, Constantina "Tina" Justice, with an admiring audience, was always in her element on the dance floor. She was a teen icon on a popular, Chicago-based, nationwide television dance and music show at fifteen and still reigned as the best dancer in their peer group to this day. It was only a handful of years earlier when she and Tina hosted a surprise party for KC when she was voted into the federal court judgeship she recently resumed. The three of them cleared the floor at Tina's mansion with their energetic style that would have forced Beyoncé to take notes. *Single Ladies*, what? Ha! Cheryl learned enough in those youthful days not to embarrass herself. Now her group of twelve youngsters taught her the latest dances. She hadn't been dancing like this in years, but she wouldn't let on to Peter her bravado was tenuous at best.

He liked the glint of challenge in Cheryl's exciting eyes and even that smug grin on her pouty mouth. His own grin grew. He loved a challenge in the courtroom, but he loved to dance. He gave her a nearly imperceptible nod of acceptance of her challenge, which she returned.

Then it was on!

Peter knew every muscle in his body would respond to the Old School beat and they did. He let his body lead the way, follow the music. With his eyes locked on Cheryl's, they were jammin'. Heart thumping, adrenaline pumping, feet stomping, and shoulders locking and blocking. Fifteen minutes later and sweat slid down the nape of his neck ... still, he was kool with his moves. The DJ hadn't let up, moving from one popular tune to the next without letting the dancers miss a beat. No aerobics class worked the body any better.

Cheryl didn't know where the bursts of energy came from, but she had it going on. Her African-Cuban heritages came together through her blood, down through the centuries. Her movements were inspired. Had to be. She cleared her mind and her body took over. She didn't think about what she was doing. It was instinctive and innate the way her feet and arms moved in rhythm. Songs of yesteryear, golden oldies rocked the club and her youthful soul. It felt so good, so natural to be dancing with Peter. He hadn't lost anything over the years. If anything, he was better, smoother. No one would have guessed this long, tall, walking dream could hold a courtroom and even the judge in suspended animation with his mellifluous, succinct auditory. The gleam in his eyes was that of a randy teenager. Like days gone by, they hadn't sat down from the moment they walked into the club...and she was lovin' every minute of it.

When the music slowed, the lights dimmed and, like magnets, Cheryl and Peter molded together. Her hands rested on his hard biceps, her temple at his cheek. Inhaling as her heart rate slowed to a manageable level, her eyes drifted closed while Barry White's deep, melodious voice told the crowd how to love a woman in her secret garden. She sighed and somehow understood what it meant to exhale.

Lost. That was the sensation Peter felt with Cheryl in his arms. Lost in the fresh, clean, captivating scent of her hair and her skin. The responsiveness of her body, the movement, and the music. When her hands ascended in agonizing slowness up his arms to the nape of his neck, Peter exhaled. One hand between her bare shoulder blades, the other at the base of her spine pressed her closer to the length of his needful body. His hips and thighs rolled against her, his breath caught as she followed his movements precisely. When her soft hand palmed the back of his head and her other hand stroked the nape of his neck, his phallus went from half to critical mass.

Cheryl adjusted her body to Peter's, pressing her breasts into his chest. Her nipples hardened naturally. His unobtrusive, woodsy scent lulled her into euphoria, her mouth curving into a satisfied smile. Distantly, she felt his hard length against her, his strong thighs rubbing against hers, his long fingers massaging her back, his steel-like arms cocooning her. She liked the feel of his crinkly hair under her fingertips as she stroked his neck. Her breathing was quiet and serene, peaceful like the hushed garden in the song.

When the music shifted to four men crooning about how they would make love all night long, the same tempo remained encompassing the two forms that moved in such perfect symmetry they appeared to be one. Stretching her body slightly, Cheryl rose to her toes, her mouth and nose at Peter's neck, just below his jaw. Peter bent naturally, his breath at her ear as they swayed together moving slowly in sync. His muscles bunched, his chest hardened.

Peter's mind slipped to a memory of Cheryl's Jack and Jill Cotillion or was it The Links many years ago? Regardless, she had been a vision in white satin, Chantilly lace, and seed pearls. Her bronze-streaked hair piled on top of her head in a loose Georgian style. Her hair was longer then, just below her shoulder. Longer, perhaps, but not as alluring as the silky strands that curled around his fingers now.

He was Kristen's escort during that year of cotillion activities. One of Tina's six brothers, Bouchard Justice, escorted Cheryl while Kristen's brother, George, escorted Tina. There were so many occasions cementing the four families together, but the memory of Cheryl in the virginal wedding white lingered beyond that final night at the cotillion. Now the memory blossomed like the opening of a perfect white rose.

The music shifted again and someone tapped Peter on his shoulder.

"Mind if I cut in?" Zack Cooper asked, grinning.

Like two people coming out of a daze, Peter and Cheryl reluctantly shifted toward Zack's voice.

Peter cleared his throat. "Zack, I didn't know you were here."

"Why am I not surprised," he joked. "Hi, Cheryl, may I have this next dance."

Cheryl looked from Zack to Peter weighing her options. Zack's attention to her over the last year was growing since Tina's interest in him became nonexistent. She didn't want to be rude to Zack, but she much preferred dancing with Peter, especially while Whitney Houston crooned about loving a man and then having to let him go. Cheryl's indecision hung for a humming moment.

Peter let one woman he wanted slip through his fingers. He wasn't about to make the same mistake twice. "Get your own date, Zack," he said, laughing and spinning Cheryl back into his arms.

"Oh, it's like that, is it?" Zack questioned good-naturedly. "Next time, Cheryl." He smiled as he moved away in search of another conquest. His expression said there would be a next time.

Not if he had anything to do with it, Peter thought as he brought Cheryl back flush against him.

Chapter 11

"Well, that does it for the quarterly report," David Carter, one of the Founding Members and Managing Partner for Alexander, Carter, Chandler, Charles, Lightfoot and Towson, PA, finished. He looked around the long, U-shaped, mahogany, conference table at the bent heads of the senior law partners. Each was making notes. "Any questions?" he asked.

"David, I believe we could reasonably contribute more time and financial resources to a few political campaigns. There's an election coming and the firm should position itself with the right party," Celeste Maywood said, sitting forward in her high-back, executive chair.

"I disagree, Celeste," Cheryl interjected, pulling her stylish eyeglasses from her face. "The firm's clientele is diverse and heavily politic, as are we all. If we do anything, it would be my suggestion we support positions we can all agree on regardless of the political party affiliations. Otherwise, we should stay out of the political arena altogether and donate to national organizations, like Save the Children or cancer research or more generously fund our foundation to support educational programs."

There were a few heads nodding in agreement, while others pondered the ramifications. Cheryl pressed her point. "Since this firm was founded by you, David, Vivian Alexander Montgomery, and your law school friends, it never stood for one train of thought. Although Vivian is a Supreme Court Justice now, and many of the other founding partners are otherwise involved, your legacy has been the cornerstone of the firm's positions."

"Of course, you would take that position, Cheryl," Celeste said mockingly. "Were it left to you, we would all be spending most of our time representing indigent clients. Non-income producing clients, I might add."

"If that remark is meant to intimate I strongly support the continuation of this firm's helping-hand policy, I plead guilty. There are legions of young men and women who still need assistance. Our existing and potential clients have to understand what this firm stands for."

"Isn't it enough that you bring those twelve unruly street urchins of yours in here every opportunity you get? Really, Cheryl, haven't you heard? Charity begins at home. This is an office. We're about business here." She smiled smugly and then added. "If you want to be a social worker, there are opportunities available outside of this law firm."

Cheryl's smug grin belied the anger seething beneath her calm exterior. "Clearly, you're still out of step, Celeste. Our *'business,'* as you so aptly put it, is helping people and what we do is noticed both politically and socially. The firm's not-for-profit foundation has won many awards for our altruism. It's simply good public relations for what we do. Politicians notice and want to associate themselves with savvy, forward-thinking organizations such as this law firm. We have built a stellar reputation on our willingness to handle *pro bono* cases and changed history in the process. Moreover, my group of young women will grow up to be voters in the very near future. They may even go into businesses that will need solid, legal representation. We are paying forward. We wouldn't want to become stodgy and fail to keep in step with the times, would we, Celeste?"

There was no retort from Celeste, as Peter had expected. Celeste was out of her league trying to best Cheryl in a verbal sparring match. Many mistook Cheryl's clean, fresh, girl-next-door, sunny disposition as weakness. She could be tough, tenacious, and hard-nosed while still maintaining a gracious smile. He wondered only briefly whether Cheryl's work with the young women was politically motivated and then knew in an instant that it wasn't. Cheryl cared too deeply for her young charges to make her contribution to their growth and development seem contrite and shallow or superficial. She made her point, however, and her stock went up in his estimation. As he looked around the table, he noted he wasn't the only one of the founders and senior partners who saw the wisdom of Cheryl's arguments. His heart swelled with pride in the woman he had known all of her life.

"I've had it, Tina!" Cheryl fumed. "Some elements of this firm are becoming so conservative they're anal retentive. This is *not* what Vivian and the other Founders of this firm envisioned. I feel like I'm beating my head against a stone wall. Would you believe there are some of the new senior partners who want to cut back on the *pro bono* work we do through the firm's foundation to help mothers prosecute dead-beat dads? And the Youth in the Law program we started to help young people become responsible consumers? I can't believe this! And did I tell you they want to put more resources into mutual funds? This new group has no heart! Unbelievable! Un-friggin-believable!

"Why do some of them want to change our foundation's focus . . . wait for it. . . because they want a bigger slice of the law firm's pie! Some of us are bringing in bigger clients and larger fees, so some of the others want a slice of what they didn't work for. Some of us contribute more to the foundation. Others want those funds diverted to them."

Tina yawned loudly. "I've heard this all before, Cheryl. When are you going to get your act together and hit the road with my production company? You're restless because you're not using all of your talents. You've been complaining since you became a senior partner more than a year ago. Hell, kid, I've got a not-for-profit foundation. If you want to run it, it's all yours."

Cheryl laughed. "Oh, no you don't, Tina Rabbit. You won't have me hopping all over the globe with your company or your foundation. Insanity runs in my family. My parents epitomize the term. Unlike you and my globetrotting, thrill-seeking parents, I intend to live a normal life. You know, sleeping in the same bed I made night after night."

"How boring," Tina drawled, barely stifling another yawn. "Well, if you're not going to join Sweet Justice Productions or take over my foundation, what, may I ask, are you going to do?"

Cheryl leaned back in her high-back, office chair and propped her feet up on her desk crossing them at the ankles. "I'm going to open my own law office." She smiled triumphantly with dawning satisfaction and a hidden agenda. "And, if you want my legal advice, you'll have to pay my going rate."

"Mmm, there's a deal in there somewhere. I can smell it. Okay, Cheryl, let's have it."

"Geez, Tina, I thought you were going to make me work harder for it," Cheryl laughed.

"I'm a lawyer, so I was, but we're circling the airport and about to land in Denver. I'm scouting new locations for my call centers and I'm late for that first meeting. I hate when that happens. So, give me the CliffsNotes version before I have to turn off my phone."

"I'll handle your local *pro bono* work for you in this area, if you'll give paid summer internships to my girls who are interested in having a career in broadcasting."

"I can handle that," Tina agreed quickly.

"That includes room and board. Also, a chaperone and transportation, Tina," Cheryl cautioned. "My girls don't come from affluent family backgrounds."

"Yeah, yeah, yeah, I know. I've met them, Cheryl. My *pro bono* work will keep you very busy," she said, laughing. *"Deal! See ya!"*

Dial tone.

Cheryl stared at the telephone on her desk. Somehow that didn't feel as easy as it seemed. Tina's television show was carried in every major television market in the country. It was more popular than most other talk shows and soap operas combined. Her nationwide, toll-free, call centers operated twenty-four hours a day, seven days a week and were always busy. The call centers researched legal issues and dispensed legal advice on a whole range of topics, both criminal and civil. When legal intervention was required, Tina's legion of law students at her call centers in Washington, DC, Chicago, and Seattle, Washington, also matched people with practicing attorneys in their local areas. A prime list of legal talent around the country donated time and resources to Tina and her Sweet Justice Foundation. Cheryl sensed that very soon her telephone was going to start ringing off the hook with referrals from Sweet Justice Foundation to handle cases *pro bono*.

Not to mention Sweet Justice included a movie production company that released several, award-winning, feature-length films and had more in production. What had she gotten herself into? Cheryl wondered.

She took her feet off the desk and stood gathering her thoughts. Head down, squeezing her bottom lip between her thumb and forefinger, she was instantly deep in thought. One hand dug in the pocket of her tailored short skirt as she paced the expansive office. Could she really do it? Could she start her own law practice and take on a client like her friend, Tina's, Sweet Justice multifaceted business? Make a success as a businesswoman running her own operation? Why not? She represented female entrepreneurs, both big and small businesses who made a success of their ventures. She had the contacts to make her own law firm work.

She stayed with the Alexander law firm because of Vivian and their shared vision of how the law could be used to help people. Now that Vivian was sitting on the highest court in the land, and unable to intercede to keep the law firm on track, that vision was changing and there was nothing to keep Cheryl there.

Based on what her friend, Capri McAllister Kennedy said about how she started Kitt, Kenmore, and McAllister, she certainly had the initiative and the energy to run her own shop. She worked at the law firm since she stopped clerking for her friend KC, gained a lot of valuable experience and knowledge, and had a solid clientele who made her wealthy. She could financially afford to take the risk now since she recovered from Wilbur's claims to her income.

Surely, her parents would give her moral support. They were themselves the proverbial self-starters; both of them enjoying highly respected and successful careers as investigative journalists. They craved the challenge and, if the truth be told, some of their risk-taking, initiative, and investigative skills rubbed off on her.

Of course, things might be a little tight for a while, maybe a year, until she got established. She might have to work out of her home until she built her practice and could reasonably afford to hire a clerical and a paralegal staff. She had a carriage house she currently used as a pool house. She could have it renovated into offices. She wouldn't need to lease or buy office space somewhere close to her home in Maryland, right away, she thought. Maybe she could interest a few law school students into working with her. The space was definitely big enough. It was certainly worth a few inquiries with the law schools in the area like Howard, Georgetown, George Washington, American, and Maryland.

She could set her own hours. Initially, take only clients whose need for her services was the greatest. Throw in a few civil contract disputes and . . .

The telephone on her desk rang. Cheryl pressed the blinking light. "Yes?"

"Mr. Darrin Johnson on line three for you, Ms. Lawrence."

"Thanks," Cheryl said and then pressed line three. "Cheryl Lawrence," she answered.

"Good afternoon, Cheryl."

"Hello, Darrin."

"I just called to confirm dinner tonight. Are we still on?"

She checked the calendar on her desk. Was it time for their monthly planning session already? It seemed as if they just met to discuss this month's plans for the girls. She confirmed that indeed they were scheduled to meet that evening. "Yes, Darrin, our meeting is on my calendar. Shall I meet you somewhere?"

"No, I'll pick you up at your house at six. Just let the gate guard know that I'm expected."

"Sure, Darrin, and don't forget the girls' monthly progress reports and schedule for upcoming events. I believe there is a school board hearing coming up soon on a bond initiative to fund Internet access for the school and library systems. I want to make a presentation at that meeting. We can go over all of this during dinner."

There was a pause before he said. "Yes, I'll bring everything."

"Great, I'll see you at six."

She hung up the telephone, made a few notes in her portfolio, iPad, called the Havenhurst gate guard, and continued her thoughts on making a break from the law firm. A knock on her door again distracted her. Peter stuck his head in. It was the first time Cheryl and Peter saw each other privately for a week following their evening of dinner in Annapolis and dancing at the country club in their neighborhood.

Something was on her mind. He sensed it the moment he saw her. She was pacing her office. He came into her office suite just as her executive assistant answered the telephone and announced that Darrin Johnson was calling. He waited until she was off the telephone to knock. The little vertical furrow between her eyes told him something important was going on in that beautiful head of hers and wondered whether it had anything to do with Darrin Johnson.

He hadn't meant to let so much time pass between dates with Cheryl, but three of his major clients were simultaneously monopolizing his time. He worked for the last week from early morning until well after midnight. He finally had a breather and wanted nothing more than a quiet dinner alone with Cheryl.

She smiled. "You look exhausted, Peter."

"You look contemplative," he said giving her a tired smile. "How about grabbing a few bottles of wine from your extensive wine cellar and I'll cook dinner for us tonight."

"Can't," she said, her brows puckering.

"Oh," he said coming fully into her office and sitting on the arm of her sofa. "Client giving you problems?" he asked folding his arms across his chest.

Cheryl looked up at Peter as if noticing him for the first time. She stopped, stuck both her hands in her pockets, and looked at him quizzically. "Peter, what's your master plan?"

He grinned. "Helluva open-ended question to ask a man who just asked you to come to his home for a quiet dinner, Cheryl. You want to narrow my field of consideration for me?" he teased.

Cheryl rolled her eyes to the ceiling and smiled. "Never mind. Obviously, you're a little punch-drunk today."

"Yes, tired and hungry. Are you sure you can't have dinner with me?"

"Yes, I'm sure. I'm busy tonight."

"Oh, a hot date?" he questioned. "It can't be Tommy and Eddie again. They're in bed by seven o'clock."

Cheryl sensed Peter was probing for information the way that he did when they were younger and he played the role of her surrogate big brother. She was on to his ploy. "Counselor, the witness refuses to answer on the grounds she is old enough to go out without a big brother's intervention."

"Ah, so it *is* a hot date. Anyone I know?"

"Peter," she drawled. "Now, do I follow you around asking personal questions?"

He pretended to consider the question while lazily scrubbing his fingers over his five-o'clock shadow. "As I recall there was that time when I took Susanna Marcus ice skating. You asked her why I put two condoms in my wallet. Then there was the time Gigi Turner and I—."

"Don't remind me." Cheryl laughed, holding up a hand to stop the litany she knew would follow. She had tagged after him most of their lives questioning everything he did or said about dating. Particularly when his activities involved a girl he was acutely interested in. Even in those early days because of her interrogation techniques her friends and family predicted she would grow up to be either an attorney or an investigative reporter like her parents. "I was fourteen years old at the time," she proffered.

"Fifteen and a royal pain in my butt. You used to cross-examine my dates like a prosecutor. And I took it. Now I ask you a simple question, and what do I get? Evasion. Smoke and mirrors."

She gave him a Mona Lisa smile but did not answer.

"All right, counselor. Have it your way, but if you're not in by eight, I'm calling your father." He stood up, crossed the room, and without otherwise touching her, he took her mouth in a tantalizing kiss that left her vibrating with need. His tongue bathed her mouth and then his teeth gently tugged at her bottom lip. He pulled back slightly and grinned. "Then I'm coming after you." Another quick, feathery brush of his mouth against hers and he was walking out of her office, hands in his pockets whistling what sounded suspiciously like a rendition of **Uptown Funk**.

Cheryl stood mesmerized for the moment. Gingerly touching her mouth with her fingertips, she then licked her lips. She tasted Peter there and then blinked with a tingling sensation that skipped along her spine and curled her toes.

Amazing, she thought, *simply amazing*. She had kissed and hugged Peter before, but it never felt like the universe tilted. She shook her head as if to clear it. What was that strange electricity that lit her up like a Roman candle? *Mercy!*

Chapter 12

When Darrin showed up at Cheryl's door five minutes early, she grabbed her keys, purse, portfolio, and lightweight parka. She was wearing a pair of black ankle boots and thick socks, charcoal-gray, wool-gabardine slacks and a black, turtleneck sweater. She was dressed for the chilly mid-November air and comfort. Darrin, on the other hand, apparently had something else in mind. He looked like he just stepped off the cover of **GQ** when he handed a dozen, long-stemmed, white roses to her.

Confusion covered her face as she accepted the flowers. "Thank you, Darrin, but it's not my birthday." She sniffed the roses and smiled. "These are wonderful though."

"I thought you might like them," he said appraising her attire with a critical eye.

She followed his gaze, then again noticed how fabulously well he was dressed in a designer suit and long, black, cashmere coat with maroon wool scarf. "Did you come here from some other engagement?" she asked.

"No." He smiled sadly. "I got all dressed up just for you. I thought we might go to the San Souci for dinner."

"The San Souci?" She flushed. "Darrin, why in the world would you want to go there for dinner? Besides, you have to make reservations weeks in advance to get into the San Souci."

"I know." He smiled. "Two weeks in advance. Our reservation is for seven o'clock."

"Oh." She blinked again appraising her attire, then his. Obviously, Darrin planned well in advance. She really didn't feel like going to the upscale restaurant in Washington, but she didn't want to be rude. This was clearly very important to him.

"If you hurry and change, I'll call the restaurant and tell them we'll be a little late."

"We don't have to go there, Darrin. That place is very—," she was about to mention the expense, "busy," she finished instead. She knew that school counselors and social workers and even school vice principals weren't paid what they were worth, but she didn't want to embarrass him. She would assume he knew and understood what he was up against. She put aside her general fatigue. "I'll go change my clothes and be with you in a few minutes. Have a seat in the library. Help yourself to anything on the bar or in the cooler."

Cheryl dashed away to the kitchen to put the flowers in water and then up the winding back staircase to her bedroom suite. *This couldn't be a date, could it?* she wondered as she disrobed. If it was, she was really slipping. She recalled that Darrin asked her out once a few weeks ago, almost a month earlier, but she hadn't thought much about it. Tonight, she expected they were going Dutch treat to one of the family-style restaurants in the area the way they usually did. Someplace where they could spread out their calendar and reports. Then they could schedule events for the girls through the holidays. If she had her way, they could just as easily have stayed at her place and ordered something to be delivered.

As she stripped out of her clothes, she sensed no business related to the girls would be conducted tonight. Before she went into her closet, she looked at the beautiful flowers Darrin brought for her. Nope. This was definitely not a business meeting.

Fifteen minutes later, Cheryl descended the stairs wearing a forest-green, sequined, designer dress that fit like a seal skin over her shapely body. The high, cowl neck in the front dipped dramatically into a U shape to her waist in the back. She carried a matching purse and full-length, black coat made of some unusual fabric. Her hair was up in a French twist secured with a diamond-studded comb. Diamonds winked in her earlobes. She smiled when she saw the sparkle of appreciation in Darrin's eyes. His hand clasped in front of him as he rocked back on his heels. Darrin was a very handsome man she noted. She felt like a teenager on prom night.

"Better?" she asked while doing a slow *pirouette*.

"Much. Not that you don't always look great, but now you look spectacular." He smiled broadly reaching for the coat on her outstretched arm.

They chatted amiably on the drive into Washington, DC's Georgetown area. As they entered the posh restaurant and approached the maître d', who looked to have a Mediterranean ancestry, he smiled broadly.

"Ms. Lawrence, how nice to see you this evening," he said kissing her knuckles.

"Thank you, Robar. Your family is well?" Cheryl asked.

"Because of you, very well. Thank you for asking." He quickly perused his list of guests. "I don't see your name on the reservation list, but I'm sure we can accommodate you and your guest."

"The reservation is in the name of Johnson, Darrin Johnson," Darrin interjected.

"Of course, Mr. Johnson. Your table is ready. If you'll follow Kinard, he'll show you the way."

"Thank you, Robar," Darrin said shaking the man's hand which included a generous gratuity.

Robar looked at the gratuity, and then unobtrusively returned it to Darrin. "Thank you, Mr. Johnson. Ms. Lawrence and her guests are always welcome here." Robar gave Cheryl a broad smile. "Always."

Darrin accepted the return of the gratuity with a puzzled expression but had no time to ask why Robar returned it or why such a warm and familiar greeting passed between Cheryl and the maître d'.

What Darrin didn't know and what Cheryl would never reveal was that she negotiated terms to secretly get Robar's entire family safely out of Afghanistan. Her father interviewed Robar for an exposé on the condition of anonymity. Though he didn't use Robar's name as the source, the report was nevertheless traced back to Robar and landed him and his family in danger. Cheryl helped her father through Kristin Catherine's husband, Thomas Ashton Marshall and his friend Slade Richardson to change their identities and to purchase an interest and save Robar's family from certain death. Then Cheryl arranged for Robar position at the upscale restaurant and his wife's position as a registered nurse at Chuck Montgomery Hospital in Maryland.

As they followed the waiter to their table, Cheryl was stopped several times by notable people who knew her and her parents. Introductions were made, greetings exchanged, and quick confidences imparted before they were finally seated.

"Your usual, Ms. Lawrence," Kinard asked as he placed a napkin over her lap then removed the reserved sign from the table.

"Mr. Johnson will decide, Kinard." She smiled at Darrin.

"Then I'll send the wine steward to you, Mr. Johnson. Have a good evening." He smiled, bowed slightly, and moved away.

Darrin sat back in his seat, his eyes sparkling. "You're really something, Cheryl Lawrence," he said with awe. "I had no idea you were so well known. This is a very exclusive restaurant. Still, the maître d' knows you by name. The waiters know your tastes and preferences. That was the Secretary of State who stopped you to speak, the head of the White House Press Corp, and the Speaker of the House of Representatives. The junior Senator from Illinois, Mr. Briggs. Wasn't his son, Strickland, involved in a missing person's case?"

"Actually, yes, he was," she said, but she hadn't thought about Strickland's involvement with the missing attorney, Jillian Harris, in quite some time. Jillian just seemed to have vanished into thin air after a huge case involving her friends, Ashton and Kristin Bryant Marshall. They were all questioned by the local and federal authorities about Jillian's disappearance. Some even speculated that Kristen did away with Jillian because of her relationship with Strickland. That rumor died quickly when the news was released that Kristen and Ashton were married and expecting a child.

Cheryl had momentarily tuned out of her conversation with Darren, while he continued to mention the number of notable people in the restaurant and their acknowledgment of her. "A lot of people who know my parents," she said and smiled tuning back in. "I'm still the same person who enjoyed going roller skating with the girls and pumpkin hunting for Halloween or volunteering at a soup kitchen."

"Yes, but I'll bet you've been invited to the homes of the rich and famous and them to yours."

"Yes and no. Not so much lately, Darrin," Cheryl said shifting uncomfortably in her seat. The last time she entertained notables in her home was the night she found her husband and Peter's wife in the proverbial compromising position. "I don't do much entertaining anymore. I like spending time with my close friends, of course. You've met them, Tina Justice, Kristin, and her husband, Thomas Ashton Marshall. Vivian Alexander Montgomery. A few other people I went to school with or grew up with. Many of the acquaintances you met tonight seek my company because of my parents—."

"Perhaps. I've seen your parents on television, heard them on the radio, and read their commentaries in the newspaper. They're both very highly respected, syndicated columnists and television personalities, but I doubt that people want to be around you only because of your parents."

She didn't agree, but she didn't want to belabor the issue. She sought to lighten the topic. "They're still Mom and Pop to me." She smiled.

"Still, I thought that this would be something special tonight. Our first official date perhaps."

"First date?" She flushed. "Oh, Darrin, I didn't know you were interested, I mean, I'm flattered, but—."

"There's someone else, isn't there?" he asked.

Cheryl had to think about that question for a moment. Was there someone else? She thought about the way Peter kissed her earlier that day. Then, as if she conjured him up, he was standing by the table.

"Peter? It's still early yet. What are you doing here?"

Darrin looked up at the same time. Unconsciously, Cheryl looked at her watch. It was seven-forty-five.

The surprise on Cheryl's face was priceless. He knew she was remembering his threat to call her father if she wasn't at home by eight o'clock and to come after her. He let her stew for a humming moment. "I brought a surprise for you," he said stepping aside. Her father, Farrow Lawrence grinned at her.

He looked every bit the elder statesman, a respected member of the Fifth Estate, except for the long ponytail at the nape of his neck and the diamond stud in his left earlobe. His French Creole and Cuban heritages evident in his slick, black, wavy, long hair, green eyes, and fair skin tone. Tall with broad shoulders, hair graying attractively at the temples, he wore an impishly knowing smile on his still devilishly-handsome face.

"Daddy," she said rising to kiss and hug him. "This is a surprise. I didn't know you were going to be in town. How did you know where to find me? I didn't tell anyone where . . . oh," suddenly she remembered Darrin who had risen from his seat. "Dad, this is Darrin Johnson. Darrin, my father, Farrow Lawrence, and, of course, you already know Peter Brock."

"Mr. Johnson," Farrow extended his hand to Darrin who eagerly took it and shook hands.

"I'm honored, Mr. Lawrence. Cheryl and I were just talking about you and your wife. I'm an avid fan of your newspaper column."

"Thank you, son," he said graciously, "but my wife has all the talent."

"Where is Mother? Is she with you?" Cheryl asked.

Farrow laughed. "No, regrettably your mother is in London for a few days. Something about another political scandal in Parliament. This time in the House of Lords. Something to do with kidnapping young women for the sex trade, if you can imagine that."

Cheryl's instincts sharpened at the words her father spoke. Her friend, Tina Justice, was investigating the same issues and the disappearance of notable people; people like Jillian Harris. She was about to ask her father more when Darrin spoke.

"Won't you join us, Mr. Lawrence, Peter?" Darrin smoothly asked. "We were about to order wine."

"Don't mind if I do," Farrow said as he signaled the waiters who brought two more high, wing-back chairs to the table. When seated, Farrow turned his attention to Darrin. "So, you're the young man who my daughter has been telling me about? You're a counselor with the school system?"

"Yes, Sir," he smiled; obviously pleased Cheryl mentioned him to her father. "I'm a social worker by profession, vice principal, and school counselor. Cheryl and I have been working together with a group of twelve young girls for quite some time. She's very good with them and they love and respect her."

"Oh, and how do you feel about her, about my Cheryl Annalisa? Do you also love and respect her?" he asked with a raised eyebrow.

Cheryl turned to Darrin. "As your friend and legal counsel, Darrin, I suggest you not answer that question." Then her eyes slid to her father. "Father, you failed to answer my earlier question."

Farrow spoke to Darrin but nodded toward his daughter. "She calls me 'father' when she's annoyed with me." Then turning toward Cheryl. "What question, Kitten?" he asked and then winked at Darrin. "Her friends used to call her Cherry because her cheeks get pink when she blushes. Calling her Kitten ticks her off."

"Not enough to divert my interest in the answer to the question I asked."

To Darrin again. "She's really a very good attorney. Mind like a steel trap, like her mother."

"Father," Cheryl said, drawing out the word.

"Well, if you must know, I called your house to let you know I'd be in town for a few hours. I was going to take you out to dinner. You weren't at home and didn't answer your cell phone, so I called Peter. He made a few calls and *voila*, here we are." Turning back toward Darrin, he said. "Now, young man, should I be asking what your intentions are toward my daughter?"

"Don't answer that, Darrin," Cheryl quickly interjected again.

"I don't mind answering the question for your father, Cheryl." He smiled, took Cheryl's hand in his, and pointedly looked at Peter, "or for anyone." Turning toward Farrow, he said, "I'm very interested in your daughter, Mr. Lawrence. My intentions are honorable."

And shit out of luck, Peter thought amused as he sat listening to the conversation.

"Honest. Straightforward. Confident. Good home training. Serious-minded. Assertive," Farrow said nodding his approval and gauging Darrin.

Darrin laughed. "Are you sizing me up as a potential subject for your column or as a potential suitor for your daughter?"

"Excuse me, gentlemen. The lady in question is making a discreet exit to powder her nose." Cheryl eyed her father meaningfully and then rose from her seat.

All three men stood as well and re-seated themselves when Cheryl walked away. Peter watched her move through the thinly packed room. He loved the way she walked and enjoyed the full view of the curvature of her spine as her hips moved in an unpronounced, but very beguiling way. The slit up the back of her dress from the hemline gave a tantalizing, peek-a-boo view of her long, shapely legs and much of her thighs. He just bet she was wearing stockings with those man-killer kitten heels and not pantyhose. There was no panty-line, which meant that either she wasn't wearing any or what she was wearing was a barely there thong. She clearly wasn't wearing a bra and he liked that thought even more. Damn, she was stacked!

Give me strength!

"Wouldn't you agree, Peter?" Farrow was asking.

Peter had no clue what he was being asked to agree to. He caught the devilish gleam in Farrow's eyes and a lopsided grin grew on his face. He loved Cheryl's father as if he were his own. He knew the feeling was mutual. He, his father, and Farrow along with Tina's six brothers, and her father and grandfather, and Kristen's two brothers and sometimes her father spent many nights and sometimes an entire weekend talking trash over poker games, watching sports events or camping in the woods in Wisconsin. The father/son and multigenerational brotherhood bonds were secure and long-lived. He was an only child, but he had men around him who were as close as brothers. He wasn't the youngest male in the group; Tina's brother, Bouchard Justice, was and her grandfather, Reverend Ellis Justice was the most senior. Yet, the men constituted a solid and wholesome extended family.

"Perhaps you should expound on that thought further, Sir."

"Expound on perfection? How is that possible? You would agree our Cheryl is perfection personified, would you not, Peter?"

"Well, of course, there is Helen Kendall Lawrence, if we are to truly judge perfection," Peter smoothly said.

"Well said, Peter. You're right, of course. Cheryl's mother is flawless," a grin curling his lips. He was so proud of Peter and loved him like a son. There was a secret wish he and his wife shared, that one day they would welcome Peter more securely into their family as a son-in-law. Cheryl was an only child and Peter was always so protective of her, Tina, and Kristin. He knew Peter loved Cheryl like a sister and hoped someday love would move them into the same type of blissful euphoria he shared with his own wife Helen. Farrow believed Peter was the right man for his daughter.

He had good instincts when it came to people and a nose for news. He liked Darrin Johnson, thought he was a good man, but not for his daughter. Cheryl needed the love of someone who understood her, had known her for years and shared mutual experiences with her. Peter would fit and make his Cheryl very happy. Helen cautioned him about intruding in Cheryl's private life, but it was a father's duty to take care of his children, wasn't it? Cheryl was no longer a child, but he would do anything to keep her from undergoing the pain and disillusionment that came from loving the wrong man.

He stepped aside when Cheryl said she was going to marry Wilbur Hardy. He had to admit, from the beginning, he didn't care for the man, especially not with Cheryl, but he had held his peace. He wouldn't do that again. If Cheryl thought she could fall in love with Darrin Johnson, he would intercede, regardless of Helen's cautions. He hoped he wouldn't have to do that and Peter would finally take the initiative with Cheryl. If the gleam in Peter's eyes when he looked at Cheryl was any indication, Darrin would have insurmountable competition with Peter with which to reckon. Silently he prayed his daughter and Peter would soon come together and give him, Helen, Peter Senior, and Cassia the grandchildren they so dearly craved.

Daddy is up to something, Cheryl thought as she washed her hands in the ladies' room. He was a wily fox, but she loved him fiercely. As a little girl, her father spoiled her much to the consternation of her mother. Neither Cheryl nor Farrow could get much past Helen Kendall Lawrence though they sometimes tried. If Farrow was up to something, Helen would know what it was and Cheryl intended to peep his hold card. She and her parents would be spending Thanksgiving in Chicago with her friends, Tina and Kristin, and their families the way they did each year for as long as she could remember. Peter and his parents would be at the Thanksgiving dinner, too. Cheryl was looking forward to their annual get together.

She looked at her face in the mirror not really seeing herself. Her thoughts shifted to Darrin and Peter. Two men who any woman could be interested in, even love. Clearly, Darrin was making a move on her.

She wondered why having a handsome, virile man, like Darrin, interested in her didn't excite her the way it should. Darrin was warm, kind, and giving. He was in her age range and very mature, grounded, sound, and from a solid family background. Though she guessed their economic levels drastically differed, she didn't think that would be an impediment to a relationship between them. Some men found her income level and social standing to be too intimidating. She didn't think Darrin would be impressed, but she was in a marriage where her financial resources at the beginning did not seem to be an issue but did become one during and at the end of the relationship. She didn't want to be with another man where the balance in her bank account raised its ugly head again.

Those thoughts lead her to think about Peter. He was everything Darrin was and much more. She and Peter shared a common history as well. Their parents were the best of friends, she and Peter were friends to all the same people, and their goals and objectives were in sync. Peter's income was at least equal to hers and probably superior. He invested heavily in the stock market through one of Vivian's brothers, former basketball icon Gregory Alexander, and was very successful. However, did they know each other well enough to have an intimate relationship? Or did they know each other too well? That was possible. She and Peter shared so many things over the years, both good and bad. The heartbreak that came from their respective spouses' infidelities being the lowest points of their lives. They came through that though. They survived, but was Peter ready for another commitment? What if they did decide to have an intimate relationship and it didn't work out? They might lose the lifelong friendship that they shared. She wasn't sure she wanted to take that risk. Peter meant too much to her to lose him.

She knew she wanted a committed relationship, but not marriage. Someone who she could love and be loved by in return. Someone who wanted children as much as she did. Was that person Darrin or Peter? Or maybe someone else? The thought swam through her mind.

At one point in her life, she thought herself in love with Peter. He knew nothing of her feelings for him because it was clear to her Peter was in love with their friend Kristin Catherine. In fact, he almost married her. Cheryl knew the only reason Kristin ever agreed to marry Peter was because she was in a desperate situation. Kristin loved Peter like a brother, but she was never *in* love with him. Peter, on the other hand, was in love or at least he seemed to be. When Kristin was snatched from Peter, literally at the altar on their wedding day, Peter did not rebound easily. Still, Peter and Kristen remained friends beyond their ill-fated engagement and Kristin's marriage to Thomas Ashton Marshall. Peter's despair led him into an ill-advised and quick marriage to Denise. Then Denise betrayed him in the most cruel and elemental way. Cheryl was not at all certain Peter would ever want another woman as a permanent fixture in his life. Could Peter still be rebounding from his marriage to Denise? That uncertainty and her desire to move on with her own life caused her to give serious consideration to Darrin's affirmation.

Yet, there was something about the way Peter kissed her in her office today that still had her blood warming. This was a real quandary.

"Ah, here is my lovely daughter, at last," Farrow said rising from his chair. The other men followed suit.

"Have you finished your interrogation, Dad?" Cheryl smiled wryly at her father.

He stroked his chin grinning at her. "We've had an interesting conversation. Not all of it centered on you, Kitten."

"Darrin, we'll talk after my father is out of earshot. Then I'll give you the facts."

"I'll look forward to it." Darrin smiled at Cheryl.

Cheryl noticed the very male gleam in his eyes and knew they would have a lot to talk about.

"We took the liberty of ordering *Pouilly-fuissé* in your absence. I hope you don't mind, Cheryl," Darrin said.

Surprise covered her usually impassive expression. "That's my favorite wine. How did you know?"

"Peter mentioned it," Darrin muttered.

Cheryl sensed Darrin didn't like the fact Peter knew her so well, but, of course, there was nothing she could do about that. Peter *did* know her well. Too well, she thought. "Oh," she said eyeing Peter's smug, handsome countenance. She leaned forward crossing her arms on the table. "Do tell, Peter, how you knew where Darrin and I were having dinner this evening?"

Peter was comfortably leaning back in his chair trying to be as unobtrusive as possible. He wanted to watch the dynamics between Cheryl and Darrin and he was learning a great deal. Now a slow grin grew lopsided on his face as he leaned forward and folded his arms on the table. "Speaking of dinner, would you care to order now? After such a long day, a broken date, and a stimulating conversation in your absence, my appetite is ravenous."

Peter wasn't going to answer her question and she knew it. He was too good at being an attorney to slip up and reveal his sources. She would bet her salary her father knew. She'd find a way to get that information out of him.

"Are you suggesting conversations with me aren't stimulating?" she asked with one raised eyebrow.

Peter leaned closer, his voice dropped an octave. "On the contrary, being with you is always…uh, arousing."

Cheryl almost blinked her surprise and immediately flushed with heat. She knew her cheeks pinked proving her father's point. Peter's statement could have been interpreted in ways that were disconcerting. Thankfully, Darrin interceded by signaling the waiter.

Cheryl and Peter remained in a locked gaze, both heated. Hers from rising ire; his from rising desire. Either way, something passed between them that wasn't missed by their other dinner companions.

Their meal was interrupted several times as notables made their way to the table to speak with Farrow or sometimes with her or Peter. Her

137

father was congenial to all, but when they were interrupted again over coffee and brandy, Farrow's patience was running thin. He turned sharply toward the man and woman who interrupted them, and then his face softened into a genuinely brilliant smile. Quickly, Farrow got to his feet to hug the tall attractive woman and extend his hand to her much taller husband.

"Madam Justice," Farrow smiled into the attractive, brown-sugar colored face of a Supreme Court Justice, then hugged her, "and Doctor Montgomery," he said shaking the outstretched hand of her husband.

"Vivian, I didn't know you were here," Cheryl said rising to embrace her close friend.

"Oh?" Vivian said turning toward Peter who also stood and hugged her. "I thought Peter would have mentioned it. Shortly after you and Darrin arrived, Peter called my cell phone to ask me whether I knew where you were this evening. I told him I saw you come into the restaurant." Turning toward Darrin, she smiled and shook his hand. "Darrin, it's nice to see you again. I don't think you've met my husband, Chuck Montgomery. Chuck, this is Darrin Johnson. I might have mentioned Darrin and Cheryl counsel young women together."

Darrin stared in awe and swallowed audibly, pumping Chuck's hand. "You're Chucky P, aren't you? I remember when you played basketball in college and the NBA," he said with gusto and began to recall Chuck's stellar years as a sports icon.

Vivian turned a very inquisitive eye on Peter, as Chuck and Darrin chatted. "Peter, I'm getting the sneaking suspicion that maybe I wasn't supposed to mention where Cheryl and Darrin were dining this evening."

"It's my fault," Farrow interjected quickly, but smoothly. "I wanted to surprise my daughter. I asked Peter to keep it a secret."

Although it sounded plausible, Cheryl didn't believe her father for one minute. Peter wanted to find her for his own reasons. She knew from Vivian's statement that Vivian sensed it, too. What Cheryl didn't know or understand was why Peter would care one way or the other who she dated. *Dated.* It wasn't a date. Not a real one anyway from her perspective. Certainly not with her father and Peter unexpectantly in attendance as if she needed chaperones. Yet, at least, the mystery had been solved. Now she knew how Peter tracked her down. She made a mental note to check with Kristen and Tina to see whether Peter also called them looking for her.

Peter was right, however. He had good instincts that made him a very good attorney. If anyone knew where she was, it would be Vivian, Kristen or Tina. Although it appeared to be a stroke of luck that he found her, she felt something just below the surface of Peter's enigmatic smile. Darrin's expression wasn't mysterious at all, however. He was not happy with this turn of events. It was another indication of just how well Peter knew her, her friends and her movements. Still, her father couldn't have hidden his glee at the competition that appeared to be growing between the other two men, Peter and Darrin. She didn't have to ask whose side her father would take. Farrow loved Peter like a son.

"We're going to say goodnight, honey, aren't we?" Chuck smiled, kissing Vivian on the temple.

"Oh, couldn't you join us for a nightcap?" Farrow asked, smiling broadly at the couple.

"Sorry, not tonight, Farrow. It's date night for us. My wife and I are spending the night in town away from our children."

"I completely understand." Farrow said knowingly. "Not many people have twenty-six children."

"Twenty-seven," Chuck laughed. "We adopted a little boy, Craig, two weeks ago."

The fact Vivian and Chuck had so many children was at the top of the news reports for many weeks during the Senate hearings before she was confirmed as a Supreme Court Justice. If she were to be confirmed, one senator made the mistake of suggesting she would need to spend less time in the bedroom and more time in the courtroom. Political groups descended on the senior southern senator like avenging angels. Women's groups picketed both his home-state offices and his office on Capitol Hill day and night. Wealthy campaign contributors and corporate donors withdrew their support of the senator in droves. Bar associations whip-lashed the senator with cunning and avarice. Talk show hosts had a field day at the senator's expense.

Still, when their friend, Tina Justice, turned the all-too-seeing eye of her television show, **Sweet Justice**, on the senator's long history of questionable service to the public, the last nail in his political coffin was secured. Needless to say, Vivian Alexander Montgomery was confirmed at thirty-three, as the youngest, female Supreme Court Justice by a landslide Senate vote. It didn't hurt that Vivian's sister-in-law, JeNelle Towson Alexander, was the junior senator from California, her older brother, Benjamin, was a five-star general and astronaut. Even her younger brother, Gregory, a national basketball icon and two-time Olympic Gold Medalist was subpoenaed to testify before the US Senate's Judiciary Committee.

The disgraced senator tried to find something in her family history to use to deny her ascension to the Supreme Court. However, he couldn't dig up as much as an unpaid parking ticket to charge against Vivian. The senior southern senator was so soundly trounced in the last election that people barely remembered the many years he spent on Capitol Hill. He was last seen sitting on a molehill contemplating his navel.

"I'll speak with you soon," Vivian whispered as she hugged Cheryl again. "What I see shaping up between you, Peter, and Darrin ought to be interesting."

Chapter 13

"**I** had a lovely time tonight, Darrin," Cheryl said automatically while fishing in her small purse for her electronic door keys. She probably could have keyed the numbers into the panel faster, but she had a sneaking suspicion that, although she was ready to call it a night, Darrin wasn't ready to end the evening. She found her access key and stuck it into the lock. The lock flashed yellow. Keying in her code, she knew she had only ten seconds to disengage the security alarm. She wanted to get to the alarm but didn't want to encourage Darrin to come in.

"I'll just check the house to make sure it's safe before you go in."

He settled her warring concerns by brushing past her. Rolling her eyes to the portico above, she sighed and went in to reset the alarm in the hall closet. She had punched in the second complicated alarm sequence and was hanging up her coat when Darrin returned. She turned to lead him to the front door when he stopped her with a hand on her arm. Quickly she looked down at his hand and then back up into his warm smile.

"Do you mind if I have a cup of coffee before I go?"

She didn't want to be rude, so she smiled and shrugged. "Sure. Have a seat in the—."

"Why don't we just go to the kitchen together," he said, shedding his coat and hanging it in the closet. "We could talk while the coffee is brewing."

"Uh-huh, okay," she said, knowing this was leading somewhere, but not quite sure where. She turned and headed down the wide marble hallway toward the back of the house. Darrin followed close on her heels. When she entered the kitchen, the lights came on.

"How did you do that?" Darrin asked looking around the huge, professionally-designed, ultramodern kitchen.

"It's the security system. When I walk into a room, the lights come on. This is a Smart House. It was designed by my friend, JaiHannah Baylor and her husband's construction company built it. They've designed and built most of the homes here in Havenhurst Estates. Everything in the house and on the grounds is monitored. Vivian's brother, Kenneth Alexander, handles the smart house technology and the security system is handled by Richardson's Security." Cheryl went to the complicated looking coffee maker ensconced in its own cabinetry. She opened a cupboard just above it, which contained an impressive array of coffees and teas. She turned, leaned against the counter top, and folded her arms across her chest. "What would you like?" she asked.

Darrin approached and stared momentarily at the different types of both domestic and international coffees and teas in the cabinet above Cheryl's head. Then he moved to within a hairs breath of Cheryl and looked down into her eyes. He put both hands on the counter effectively locking her in.

"I'd like this," he said brushing a kiss across her mouth. "And this," he said deepening the kiss. His arms enfolded her in a warm embrace. "And this," he whispered against her lips. His tongue slipped into her mouth.

Cheryl permitted the intimacy out of curiosity. If she let herself, she wondered whether she could be interested in Darrin on an intimate level. He had a natural warmth about him she liked. He was certainly an attractive man, well built, and, if the vertical rod pressing against her abdomen was any indication, very well endowed. He certainly knew how to kiss a woman, she thought as she permitted herself to enjoy the moment, but he didn't make her toes curl or create a needful heat in her lower region. The universe didn't tilt and there was no nova. Certainly not the way Peter had set her on fire earlier that day in her office. Peter hadn't even touched her with anything other than his mouth. Maybe if she tried harder, Darrin could get her juices flowing. She circled his neck with her arms and leaned into the kiss opening herself more to Darrin's heat.

Nothing. Absolutely nothing stirred in her. What was wrong with her? Here she was with an attractive, healthy, straight man, and she couldn't get it up! *Oh, no,* she groaned silently. This was not a good sign. Not good at all.

Perhaps she was just tired, she tried to convince herself. It had been a long day and an even longer evening. Maybe she had too much on her mind. She was, after all, considering a major shift in her career, in her life. Maybe her timing was off. Any number of things might be affecting her libido.

Darrin was breathing hard when he loosened his hold on her. He closed his eyes and laid his forehead against hers. "God, I've wanted to do that for so long," he breathed a ragged breath. "You do something incredible to me, Cheryl."

She wished she could say the same thing to him because she really liked and respected him, but she couldn't. Inwardly she sighed. "How about that coffee? Maybe we should talk a bit." She turned in his arms and reached for an Amaretto blend coffee.

"Cheryl…" Darrin started.

"Have a seat at the breakfast bar," she interrupted. "This shouldn't take long to brew."

Darrin did as asked, but Cheryl could feel his eyes on her as she made the coffee. While it perked, she popped a few scones in the microwave to warm, then pulled the lemon curd and clotted cream from the frig. Turning, she leaned back against the counter again, crossed her legs at the ankle, her arms across her chest. Briefly, she looked up at the slowly turning ceiling fans gathering her thoughts. Then she leveled her gaze on Darrin.

"How do you feel about me, Darrin?" she asked not blinking.

Darrin looked puzzled for a moment, then returned her steady gaze. "Is this a trick question, Cheryl? If my kisses didn't tell you how I feel about you, I must be doing something wrong. I'm crazy about you."

"That's what I thought," she muttered briefly looking away. She pinched the bridge of her nose and momentarily closed her eyes. Then she returned to study his face. She needed to register his reaction to what she was about to say. Before she could speak, Darrin interrupted.

"It's Peter, isn't it?"

Cheryl blinked. "What?"

"Peter Brock. Something is going on between . . . "

"No, no." Cheryl held up her hands and shook her head in the negative to forestall his suggestion. She moved to the eight-foot-long, four-foot wide quartz center post counter and sat down on a bar stool across from Darrin. Taking his hands in hers, she held his gaze. "No, Peter and I are not involved. Yes, we are friends. We are both senior partners at the same law firm. We're neighbors, but we're not now nor have we ever been lovers," she said with conviction. She was telling the truth and she wanted Darrin to believe that.

She could see the relief in Darrin's face and feel it spread throughout his body when his tense hands relaxed in hers. He let out a breath that he had apparently been holding and gently squeezed her hands.

"I'm glad to hear that. You two had me worried for a bit."

"You know Peter and I have been friends since we were children. Our families are very close. We share the same friends and, unfortunately, for both of us, we shared the same tragedy when Peter's wife and my husband carried on a long-term affair with each other."

Darrin looked appropriately appalled. "I'm sorry, Cheryl. I didn't know. I mean, I knew you went through an ugly divorce, but you never talked about your marriage."

She shook her head and raised her hand as if brushing aside a pesky fly. "It wasn't worth talking about. We were hurt and humiliated because people knew about it before we did. It's over and done with now and properly put in the past. I'm not carrying any emotional baggage from that experience. The marriage was a mistake I don't want to repeat. It has nothing to do with now…with you or my future."

"Good. Then there's no reason why we can't have a more intimate relationship." Darrin beamed.

Oh, yes, there was, but how could she tell him? "Darrin, I could be intimate with you, have sex with you. I could even take you to my bed this very night and rock your world until you pleaded for mercy . . . ."

Darrin hopped up from his seat and started to round the counter. Cheryl held up her hand to stop him. "First, please listen to what I have to say." He stopped and returned to his seat across from her. "The only regret I have from my marriage is I didn't have children. Not that I should have had children with my former husband considering how our marriage ended, but I wanted children for me. He didn't share my need, but I have to be honest about this. I still want children. I want to feel a baby growing inside me, take a baby to my breasts, give a child or children all the love there is inside me . . . but," she halted him when he was about to speak. "I know that's a very selfish position, particularly in light of the fact I counsel young girls not to have children outside of marriage or not to have children they are unable or unwilling to care for. Nevertheless, it's what I want."

"If you're asking me to marry you, I'll have to think about it," he joked.

"No, Darrin, I'm not proposing marriage—."

"Don't look so frightened, Cheryl," Darrin teased. "I understand we need time to get to know each other better on a completely different level. Neither one of us wants to make a mistake. I want the chance to explore a relationship with you. For future reference, I love children. I'd have a football squad if I could or at least as many as your friends, Vivian and Chuck. I'm healthy and I can give you all the children you need or want. If that's what you want, then we're on the same wavelength."

She took his hands again and smiled at him. "I know you could, but I believe you'd also want marriage, a home, a wife, and a future."

Slowly Darrin withdrew his hands and stared at her. A frown crowded his handsome features. He folded his arms across his chest; always a protective gesture Cheryl noted. "What are you saying, Cheryl? That you don't want a marriage, a home, a husband, and a future?"

She nodded. "That's exactly what I'm saying. That's why I want to be honest with you at the very beginning. Over the next year, I'm going to make changes in my life. I'm leaving the law firm I'm currently with and starting my own practice. I may stay here or move back to Chicago or move somewhere else in the US or abroad. I'm still in the planning stages, but one thing is for sure; once I leave the law firm, I want to get pregnant. I've thought a great deal about this."

"Without a husband, how did you plan to manage to get pregnant?" The words were falling from his lip when the insight must have registered in his mind.

"Obviously, husbands aren't the only ones who can make babies, Darrin."

"You're talking about using someone like a stud!" Darrin said incredulously. "I can't believe this, Cheryl! What role would this stud play in your life or the life of the baby?"

Cheryl didn't answer. Darrin was a bright man. She knew he'd get the picture.

"None. That's it, isn't, Cheryl? You don't want a relationship. You want to use a man's seed, but not share with him in the fruits of his loin."

Again, she didn't answer. What could she say to that? It was the truth. He scowled at her, and with his hands on his hips, he paced the kitchen. Cheryl sat watching him until he stopped.

He glared at her. "I couldn't . . . no, make that, I wouldn't do that, Cheryl. Before I plant my seed in a woman, I want her to be my wife. I want my children to be a part of our lives. I want it all! Call me old fashion, but I want the dream. A home, a wife, a family, and a future of love, mutual respect, trust, and sharing."

"That's what I thought, Darrin. I'm not asking you to father children for me. I'm just telling you what's on my agenda. I've done a lot of research and contacted several reputable sperm banks around the country. It's not unusual for women in my situation to be artificially inseminated. When the time is right, sometime within the next year, I'm going to have the procedure."

"You're joking," he said shocked.

"No, Darrin. I'm very serious. I just thought you should know."

Chapter 14

"*What the hell...?*" Peter liberally cursed as he swung his Jaguar out of the way of a car that careened out of Cheryl's driveway barely missing him. He slammed on his brakes and glared through the darkness at the other car's rapidly retreating taillights. He recognized the vintage Camaro as the one Darrin Johnson drove. When he saw the lights on in Cheryl's house and her silhouette in the wide, glass front doors, he swung his car into her driveway under the portico.

Leaping from the car, he jogged up her steps. She opened the door to him and then turned pacing the wide marble hallway. He closed the door behind him and watched her for a moment. She obviously wasn't hurt, but whatever happened between Darrin and Cheryl had anguish written all over her face.

He didn't bother to ask the obvious question, but he wondered whether Darrin expected sex after such a lavish dinner, although he hadn't paid for the meal. Farrow insisted on footing the bill since he had crashed in on his daughter and Darrin. Peter wasn't worried though. He witnessed Cheryl emasculating unwelcome and pushy suitors without a qualm. She could cut to the quick most men, but the way she was pacing convinced him something monumental had happened. He wasn't leaving until he knew and understood what it was.

Peter smelled the fresh-brewed coffee and walked into the kitchen without a word. Eventually, Cheryl followed and resumed her seat at the kitchen breakfast bar workstation, raked her hands through her hair loosening the silky strands that cascaded around her face and shoulders.

He wanted to do more than rake his hands through her hair and peel that attention-getting sheath from her lush body, but he was there to listen to her if she needed to talk. Words were not always necessary between them. Somehow, they intuitively knew what the other needed. Just like the time he followed her to her beach home in the pouring rain on one of the worst nights of their lives. They sat on the deck, him holding her in his arms while the warm rain beat down on them until near dawn. They hadn't spoken that night either. He just held her against his body, happy they were there for each other as they always were. He realized with crystal clear vision they would always be together. Their friendship was one of the most important and precious things in his life.

"Thanks," Cheryl said as Peter slid the mug of hot, steaming coffee under her nose. She took a sip and closed her eyes. Then she looked across the kitchen bar at Peter, one of her best friends. "I may have lost a good friend tonight."

Peter shrugged and sipped his coffee. "I doubt it," he said. Then he opened a cabinet under the bar and brought out a bottle of brandy. Without first checking the label, he liberally poured some into Cheryl's coffee and then into his. Recapping the bottle, he left it on the countertop. "Good friends don't get lost."

Cheryl raked her fingers through her hair again, massaging her scalp. Then she sipped her coffee again. The warmth of the coffee and brandy spread calm through her taut body, causing her to slowly relax. Peter always knew how to make her chill out. He sat across from her patiently waiting for her to tell him what was going on in her head. Eventually, she would tell him. She could talk with Peter about anything, and she usually did. She wondered what he would think about her decision to be artificially inseminated. To bear and have a child without the benefit of marriage or even a man in her life. She was confident he would listen to her. He always did and she knew she could depend on him not to offer solutions unless he was asked. His opinion was very important to her and she trusted and respected it without question. So, she plowed ahead and explained the conversation she had with Darrin, excluding her plan to leave the law firm. She wasn't ready to discuss that yet with anyone.

"He thought I was rejecting him. I tried to explain it wasn't a rejection, but I wanted to put all of my cards on the table. If he was interested in having a non-platonic relationship, I thought he should know what I was going to do."

"Mmm," Peter intoned and pinched the bridge of his nose between his eyes. If he weren't so exhausted, he would have laughed. He could imagine Darrin's shock at hearing Cheryl was going to impregnate herself with some stranger's purchased frozen sperm when Darrin was more than willing to do the job for free. Well, it was Darrin's loss if he wanted to end his friendship with Cheryl over her need to be a mother. As he had earnestly listened to her plan, a plan of his own congealed in his mind. He'd be getting very little sleep over the next few nights thinking about what it was going to take to get Cheryl pregnant, but he wouldn't tell her yet. She was still worried about Darrin and whether she hurt his feelings.

"'Mmm.' Is that all you've got to say?" Cheryl asked, cocking her head to one side.

"No," Peter said, trying to stifle a yawn, "but I'm entirely too worn out to discuss it tonight. It was a long day, a longer evening, and an extremely long ride to take your father to BWI Airport to catch his flight." He stood up, took their empty cups to the dishwasher and put them in. Then he picked up his jacket hanging on the back of the bar chair and slung it over his shoulder, holding it with one finger. He walked around the center-post workstation to Cheryl, gathered her into one arm and soundly kissed her mouth letting his tongue send a message. A lifetime passed in a few seconds and then he was gone.

Cheryl blinked and stood in the same spot where Peter just left her. Putting her palms to her abdomen, she fought to take a deep breath. Then she looked down at her feet, willing her toes to uncurl.

"Mercy," she said aloud just above a whisper to the empty house.

She wasn't sure what had just happened. One minute she was telling Peter about her disastrous conversation with Darrin and the next minute she was in Peter's arms tasting a slice of heaven. She spied the bottle of brandy still sitting on the countertop. With shaky hands, she retrieved a crystal goblet and poured another drink for herself. When she drank it in one shot, she sat heavily on the tall barstool. Her fingers went to her well-kissed lips.

"Mercy," she said again. Then she shook her head, turned out the lights, and went to her bedroom via the rear stairs. It was going to be a long night.

Cheryl showered and was readying herself for bed when her phone rang. "Hi, Tina."

"Hey, kid, did you know that Jillian Harris hasn't been found yet?"

"Who is Jillian Harris?" she asked, her brain still fuzzy from Peter's kiss.

"You don't remember? She's the attorney who was second chair for Ashton's big case. The one that had Strickland Briggs representing the plaintiff."

"Oh, yes, yes, yes, I remember who you're talking about. In fact, I saw Strickland's father, Senator Briggs tonight at dinner at San Souci. Geezus, that was years ago. What brought that up?"

"I told you and KC I've been doing some research on missing people. Remember, Jillian went missing shortly after the case concluded. She was with Strickland on Martha's Vineyard when Kristen's father and Ashton's mother spotted them having sex in the parking lot of Lola's Restaurant."

"Your memory is phenomenal. I remember who you're talking about, but I have to admit, my memory is foggy on the details. Still, I'm sorry she's missing. Are the police still looking for her?"

"Not the ones on the Vineyard, no, but I've developed a theory about the abductions."

"Don't tell me what it is. My mind is too crowded with other things right now. However, this is right in my parents' wheelhouse. Have you spoken with either of them?"

"Not yet, but I plan to once I have more of my facts verified. They may remember a story several years ago about attempts to abduct the supermodels Angelique, Shannon, and Ardon."

"Yes, that I remember because Gregory Alexander was dating Angelique at the time. Wasn't Strickland rumored to be dating Shannon back then?"

"He was, yes, at the same time he was dating KC."

"Ugly business that."

"It was, yes. Still, Strickland was involved with one woman who would have been a kidnap victim and another one who I believe is a kidnap victim."

"Okay, now you're into the conspiracy theory realm of outer space," Cheryl said laughing. "Just don't tell me you think Strickland is involved in human trafficking."

"No, I don't believe he's involved, but my research shows there have been a number of abductions of both notable men and women in the past few years. I believe there is a criminal element dealing in human trafficking. It is the trade of humans, most commonly for the purpose of forced labor, sexual slavery or commercial sexual exploitation for the trafficker or others. This may encompass providing a spouse in the context of forced marriage or the extraction of organs or tissues, including for surrogacy and ova removal. It's trans-national, Cheryl. It's a crime against the person because of the violation of the victim's rights of movement through coercion and because of their commercial exploitation. It's a trade in people, especially women and children, and does not necessarily involve the movement of the person from one place to another.

"According to the International Labor Organization (ILO), forced labor alone, one component of human trafficking, generates an estimated one hundred fifty billion dollars in profits per annum. It's estimated that twenty-one million victims are trapped in modern-day slavery. Of these, fourteen million are exploited for labor, four million are sexually exploited, and two million are exploited in state-imposed forced labor.

"Cheryl, it's one of the fastest-growing activities of transnational criminal organizations."

"I know, Tina. It's condemned as a violation of human rights by international conventions. I've read my parents' commentaries. Almost three hundred thousand people are forced into the sex trade every year. The majority of them are girls like my Lawrence Twelve Crew who are between the ages of twelve and fourteen. That's why I added self-defense classes to our itinerary. I want my girls to have a fighting chance to protect themselves. Unsuspecting women have been led astray and ended up unwittingly becoming the victims of sex traffickers.

"Why do you believe it's what happened to Jillian Harris? She's not in the young age groups."

"Her body hasn't turned up on or near Martha's Vineyard."

"Gruesome thought, but a consideration. Again, she's not a young inexperienced woman. Why do you think she would be abducted?"

"Notoriety. She's a strong, prominent figure in the political arena; her parents own broadcast stations and never received a ransom notice. She was on television a lot before the trial as lead attorney for that big case Ashton represented. Some loony-tune would pay to get his hands on someone of her stature as a trophy."

"Careful, Tina. The same can be said about you, Kristen or me."

"I'm aware, so have a care. *See ya!*"

Dial tone.

Chapter 15

Cheryl fumbled trying to reach for the telephone. When she finally captured it, she knocked the lamp and clock to the floor. Her curses were muffled under a mountain of pillows as she dragged the cordless telephone into her warm cocoon.

"What?" she mumbled while trying to recapture the limited amount of sleep she had the night before.

"'What?' Is that any way to speak to your mother?" Helen Kendall Lawrence laughed aristocratically.

"Ma," Cheryl breathed drawing out the word. "It's not daylight yet. I'm still in bed."

"You were always a sleepy head." She laughed. "Now, sit up and talk with your mama."

Cheryl rolled over, her eyes still closed and pillows covering her head. "I'm listening."

"Oh, did I disturb you and Peter?" she asked.

That got Cheryl's attention. She bolted upright looking around her bedroom as if Peter might have been in the bedroom or her mother might have peeked into the erotic dreams she had about Peter.

"No," she drawled to her mother. "Why in the world would you think that . . ." and then it dawned on her . . . Farrow. "Ma, did you talk with Dad? Is that why you asked me about Peter?" she asked cautiously.

"Very early this morning your father called. He had that loud conga music going and he was singing into the telephone. He must have been dancing, too, because he was breathing hard."

"Ma, you and Dad ought to stop those obscene phone calls," Cheryl quipped as she lay back against her mountain of pillows and drew one hand over her face distorting her features.

"Not on your life, baby girl. Farrow is the sexiest hardbody I've ever had," she responded without embarrassment.

"I don't think I want to know about this, Ma," Cheryl said rolling her eyes. Her parents' outward display of affection was always hot and never seemed to cool. They were apart so often that when they had time together they seemed to go into hibernation. How she ended up being an only child had to be a minor miracle.

"Believe me, baby, I don't want to talk about it either. I haven't pinned that hunk in two damn weeks and I'm as horny as hell. I may have to end these interviews early and fly to California to get laid. I hate it when I have to do that."

"Mother!" Cheryl exclaimed. "TMI. Daughter here!"

"Oh, grow up, Cheryl." Helen laughed. "Speaking of getting laid, have you pinned Peter, The Black Adonis, to the mattress yet?"

Cheryl sunk deeper into the pillows and covered her face with several. Her mother must have been clairvoyant or something. After Peter left last night that's all she thought about until Tina called. "Ma, you're embarrassing me," she warned, yet she flushed to a warmth that spread throughout her body.

"Should I take that as a no?" Helen inquired.

"Ma, did you call me at this ungodly hour of the morning to talk about something important?"

"Talking about your sex life is important, Cheryl. It's probably been so long since you got laid that you could qualify as a virgin again." She verbally shuttered. "What a singularly horrible thought. Two weeks without your father between my—."

"That's it!" Cheryl interrupted cutting off her mother. "If you're going to turn this conversation into one of those 900-number calls, I'm hanging up, Ma."

Helen laughed at her daughter. "No, baby, don't hang up. I did call to talk with you about some other things, but I wanted to make sure you were fully awake first."

"Very clever, Ma," Cheryl deadpanned, trying to stifle the need to join her mother in laughter. "I'm awake. Now, what do you want to talk about?"

They talked for more than thirty minutes catching up on a few important things related to family and close friends, some property her parents wanted to retrieve from Farrow's Cuban ancestry now that they could, then the conversation centered around arrangements for the coming Thanksgiving holiday.

"Ma, I thought maybe I'd come home a few days early for the holiday," Cheryl said tentatively. "I want to talk with you and Dad about a few things."

"Oh, this sounds interesting. Isn't Peter coming home with you as usual?"

"Why do you keep bringing Peter into the conversation? Can't I just come home and spend some quality time with my parents? Geesus, Ma, Peter and I aren't joined at the hip, you know. We're independent. We just happen to work together and live together . . ." Cheryl flushed when she heard her mother's laughter and then realized what she had said. "I didn't mean that we *live* together. I meant that we live in the same . . . oh never mind . . . Why are you still laughing, Ma?"

Helen tried to compose herself. "Okay, baby, I will arrange my schedule to be in Chicago a few days early. Your father and I will see you there with or without Peter. How's that?"

Cheryl groaned. She sensed the amusement in her mother's tone. "That's fine," she said exasperatedly. "Bye, Ma."

"Bye, baby," Helen giggled as she hung up the telephone. Immediately, she dialed another number."

"McCoy Beverly Hills Hotel," the operator answered.

"Mr. Farrow Lawrence's suite, please."

Shortly, Farrow answered, Loud Mariachi music playing in the background nearly drowned out the conversation.

"Farrow, would you turn down that music? It's making my teeth rattle. I tried to reach you on your cellphone."

"Hi, baby," he crooned. "My cellphone battery died. I forgot to charge it. How's my rump shaker?"

Helen laughed. "Don't start, lover. I'm having a hard time sitting still as it is." Lowering her voice to a breathy whisper, she said, "I miss you."

"I'll be on the first flight out," he said seriously.

Helen giggled liked an experienced schoolgirl. "If you weren't interviewing the former president, I'd ask you why you're not here yet."

"President be damned. I want my wife in the worst possible way."

"Talk dirty to me, baby." She laughed . . . and he did.

A while later they were both breathless.

"All right, now that you've tripped my trigger, what did you find out about Cheryl and Peter?" Farrow asked.

"Not much. She's too good at deflecting questions, but they are going to be together for Thanksgiving as usual. We'll have a chance to observe them then."

"Peter's the same way. His lips are sealed tighter than a nun's thighs at High Mass. I wish we could move them along. I'm determined to get a grandchild out of those two next year."

"I'm with you, baby. So are Cassia and Peter Senior. We've got to have a plan."

Chapter 16

Cheryl pulled her stylish eyeglasses from her face and then palmed her face in her hands. She was tired, but she had to keep working. Her caseload was enormous. Even with the help of three law associates, five paralegals, and two very competent legal secretaries working exclusively under her supervision, she still had a lot of legal research and review to perform and she was running out of time. There were only ten days left before Thanksgiving and she wanted to leave for Chicago before the big holiday rush started. So, she had to keep at her work and try to get ahead of it so she could rest and relax with her family and friends during the holiday. She needed to speak with them about her plans.

Glancing at her watch, she noted it was nearly eleven o'clock at night. She took a quick break for Chinese food at six, but now as she sat in the firm's law library, she was fighting fatigue, eyestrain, and a growing desire for pistachio ice cream. Cheryl tried to stifle a huge yawn, but her jaw snapped causing her to utter an audible squeak in discomfort. Although there were many other employees in the library burning the midnight oil, no one seemed to give her any notice. Thick tomes opened or shut, papers were rustled or laptop keyboards clattered, but no one broke his or her concentration.

Stifling another yawn, Cheryl prepared to return to her notes. That's when she noticed Peter was sitting across from her at the same highly-polished mahogany table. She was so engrossed in her work she hadn't even noticed when Peter came into the library and sat down. Now she took a moment to study him.

A week passed since their late-night encounter in her kitchen. She barely saw him since then and only in passing. Peter had been in court each day litigating on behalf of one of his corporate clients and worked late each night. His teams of legal staffers were larger than hers were, yet he spent time working hard, if not harder than his staff members. Peter's reputation for excellence was well known throughout the large law firm and he was well respected in the legal community. Often called a gunslinger of the white-hat variety, other lawyers inside the law firm often sought his counsel and those outside the firm didn't want to tangle with him across a conference table and certainly not in a courtroom. At thirty-five, Peter was considered a corporate law expert.

Such an enigma, Cheryl thought. Twenty years earlier, Peter was a very popular high school sports jock with a cadre of young women at his beck and call. All through college, Peter was buck wild with seemingly no career aspirations. His social life was legendary. However, throughout his youth, Peter spent time working in his father's small laundry and dry cleaning business. Everyone expected Peter to join his father's business, but he stunned his family and friends when he announced he was accepted into one of the most prestigious law schools in the country. By the time Peter graduated from Stanford Law School, in the top one percent of his class, he had helped his father build his laundry and dry cleaning business into one of the largest chains in the State of Illinois serving restaurants, hotels, and communities. He may have been a randy teenager, but he wasn't stupid.

Peter felt Cheryl's eyes on him, studying him as if she was drawing a picture. He looked up at her over the top of his rimless glasses in silent query. She shook her head at him and went back to reading. So, did he, but when he stretched to reach for another book on the table, Cheryl was studying him again.

He sat back in his seat, took off his glasses, and briskly scrubbed his hands over his face. Then he looked at her and said, "What?"

She folded her arms on the table, looked quickly from side to side, and then leaned forward to whisper, "I want you to get me pregnant."

"Okay. Give me an hour to finish this brief. While you're waiting, you can look over this," he said pulling a blue covered file from his briefcase that sat on a chair next to him. He handed the file to her and went back to work.

Cheryl took the file but sat back in her chair with her face askew in confusion. *Surely, he could not have understood her statement. Otherwise, he would have had questions to ask her, particularly about the state of her mental health.* She didn't know or understand why she decided to ask Peter to father her child, but she knew it was the right decision as soon as the idea occurred to her.

What was even more perplexing was his response. If he did understand her statement, did he just agree to it? She tilted her head, biting her bottom lip, and looked at him silently trying to get his attention again.

Without looking up at her, he said, "Finish your research, Cheryl. I only have a few more points to cover and then write my summation."

She opened her mouth to comment, then noticing she didn't have Peter's full attention; she quashed the thought and went back to work.

Thirty-five minutes later, Peter saved his document on his laptop and sent it to his secretary. She would get it in the morning. He watched Cheryl as she re-shelved books and signed out of the library tracking system. When she stopped to speak with Zack Cooper, he began to sort through his briefcase. It didn't bother him overmuch that Zack was still trying to find a way into Cheryl's bed. If his plan worked, and it appeared it would, he would be the only man and the last one to share Cheryl's bed.

Smiling to himself as he began packing up his files, notes, and laptop, he recalled the confusion on Cheryl's face when he agreed to father her baby. What she didn't know, but would soon find out, was there was going to be more than one child.

Cheryl shook her head as she walked away from Zack Cooper and his continuous attempts to date her. If they weren't in the library she probably would have laughed out loud at his inability to attract her interest. She knew his reputation, but even if she didn't, he would not be under consideration as a potential father for her child. She was confident the thought of getting her pregnant would scare him silly.

She chuckled to herself as she walked back toward Peter. He was standing up and closing his briefcase. When he rolled down his shirt sleeves, inserted his cufflinks, and reached for his suit jacket, he looked up at her approach with a curious smile on his face.

"Ready to go?" he asked.

"Yes," she said as she hung her purse and briefcase on her left shoulder. "Did you need for me to read that contract tonight?"

"You can read it when you get home."

They grabbed their overcoats and headed for the parking garage chatting amiably all the way. They reached Cheryl's car first. She put her purse and briefcase in the trunk and then turned to Peter. "I asked you to father my baby, but I'm not sure you—."

His kiss took every thought out of her head. When he released her, he said. "I'll follow you home."

She was so stunned by his kiss she could only nod and get into her car. She sat thinking until she saw Peter flash his headlights. Then she pulled out of her parking space and drove to the exit. The garage door climbed up into the ceiling.

Traffic was very light on the drive out of the city and she was pulling into her garage thirty-minutes later. She used the drive to think about Peter's uncharacteristic behavior and his kisses, which she was beginning to enjoy. She left her garage bay door open after she retrieved her purse and briefcase. Peter was pulling into her driveway when she closed the trunk.

She waited for him to join her in the garage before she closed the bay door and entered the house through the mudroom. The lights flipped on as she went to the panel to disarm the security system. Then together, they walked into the kitchen.

"Have you got anything edible?" Peter asked as he walked to the side-by-side refrigerators. "I haven't found time to order groceries this week."

"Mmm," Cheryl hummed, as she checked the mail on the desk in her kitchen. "Mrs. Brown made roast beef yesterday for dinner. I told her I wouldn't be home for dinner tonight, but there should be some leftovers; at least enough for two sandwiches.

Peter found the roast beef, horseradish cheese, lettuce, tomatoes and rye bread, washed his hands, and began building sandwiches. Then he put loose tea into an oval perforated infuser and in a blue porcelain pot and added hot water from the water cooler. He found a bag of chips in the pantry and a jar of kosher dill pickles in the refrigerator. When all was ready, he put it on the round banquet table in the solarium adjacent to the kitchen. Cheryl placed a large white napkin in front of Peter and then grabbed two large mugs. She took honey from the refrigerator and popped it into the microwave and then washed and quarter-cut a fresh lemon from the fruit basket on the bar. There was French apple pie left and hand-dipped pistachio ice cream she picked up from Greenfield Brothers Bakery and Ice Cream parlor. She put that on the table too for dessert.

They certainly seemed like a domesticated couple the way they worked together to prepare a late-night snack, Cheryl thought as she opened her briefcase to retrieve the contract Peter wanted her to read. She sat at the table with him and, after saying grace, she took a bite of her sandwich.

"Mmmm, that's good, Pete. Thanks," she said, then began to read. That was the first and last bite of the roast beef sandwich she had. As she read the contract, her eyes widened in disbelief. When she finished reading, she sat back against her seat and stared at Peter.

He was reading sports' articles and scores on his iPad. When he picked up his sandwich again, he noticed Cheryl staring at him. Then he noticed the contract in front of her. "Questions?" he asked and took another healthy bite of his sandwich.

"How did you know I wanted you to father my baby?"

He wiped his mouth with a napkin and swallowed before he answered. "I didn't know until you told me about your plan to be artificially inseminated. I knew I wanted a child of my own and planned to ask you to be the surrogate. So, what do you think?"

"Let me see if I got this right. We are going to get married over the Thanksgiving holiday. We sell or lease our existing homes, move in together in a new house. Then, initially, we contract for two children, in two years for a total of four children in the next five years? Two children for you and two children for me?"

"There are a few clauses that allow more than four children, depending on your agreement and health." He eyed the other half of her unfinished sandwich. "Uh, are you going to eat that?"

Cheryl placed the uneaten half of her sandwich on his plate. "I don't want to get married."

"Nonnegotiable."

"We could live together anyway."

"No."

"Why not? We don't need a piece of paper to keep us together."

"No, Cheryl. I respect myself, you, your parents, and mine too much to do this any other way. It's a deal breaker. We get married or no contract."

"So, you're going to ejaculate into a cup so that I can be inseminated and then store the rest of your sperm?"

He looked at her, his brow wrinkled. "Uh, no. There will be nothing artificial about your insemination, pal-o-mine, each and every time. I haven't had sex since my divorce. I'll be making up for lost time."

She flushed and felt her blood warm. She knew she couldn't penetrate Peter's iron-clad will on this issue. "Okay, but the contract expires in five years."

Peter thought about it momentarily. "Insert a renewal clause at five-year intervals."

"Expiration at say, twenty years?"

"Twenty-five. By then our children should be in college. We can write a new contract then."

Tentatively, she asked, "Suppose I want access to your body when we're not trying to get me pregnant?"

Peter was about to take another bite of the sandwich but thought better of it. He put the sandwich down, sat back in the banquet, and stretched his arms out along the seat back. He looked at her cautiously. "How often might that be?" he asked.

"How should I know, Pete? Less than hourly, more than daily? I've read that some pregnant women want sex frequently. If my parents are any indication, sex is synonymous with breathing or a midlife crisis."

He grinned at her and resumed eating the rest of the sandwich including bites of the pickle and chips. "That can be arranged," he said and shrugged. "Amend the contract to provide unlimited access to my body, but of course the same goes."

Cheryl's brows beetled. "How often?"

"At least daily," he said and took a sip of his tea before starting in on the dessert.

"You may not find me desirable when I look like a whale," she said, concerned. "If we are married, I don't want you sharing your body with someone else."

"I expect the same from you. We will have an exclusive relationship, Cheryl or the contract is off."

"Agreed."

"Good. Any other questions?"

"Not at the moment."

"Okay. Think about it over the weekend. Tomorrow, I want to look at a house on the other side of the lake. It has six bedrooms, six and a half baths, two offices, a library, family room, sunroom and balcony off the upstairs master bedroom suite. There's also a four-car garage with house staff apartments above. It's another JaiHonnah design, much larger than your house or mine. We will probably have to get some help for Mrs. Moore," he said polishing off the pie and ice cream.

"I've seen the outside of the house you're talking about. I like it because it has nice curb appeal, but you're right, it's very big. Sarah Brown still works for me. We'll need the additional help. We'll bring her on board in the new house. What time do you want to take a look?"

"I'll call you early in the morning, sometime after my run," he said rising from the table and taking the dishes to the dishwasher. "Thanks for the snack. It hit the spot." He pulled her into his arms and kissed her soundly. "Sleep well," he said as he headed for the garage door.

Once Peter was gone, Cheryl sat and reread the contract two more times. Picking up her cell phone, she speed-dialed Tina.

"Yes?" Tina answered on the first ring.

"Hi, Tina, it's Cheryl. I need to use your Sheridan Road home to get married on the Saturday after Thanksgiving."

"Okay? Who are you going to marry this time?" Tina asked, her voice bored.

"Peter."

There was a pregnant pause before Tina asked, "Our *Peter?* Our own personal long, hot, sip of chocolate, *Peter Brock?*"

"The same," Cheryl said and laughed.

"Well, hell yes!" Tina said no longer disinterested. "It's about time! Since we don't have a lot of time to work with, I presume we're talking family only and close personal friends?"

"Yes, Tina, but that's easily a hundred people, but everyone should be home for Thanksgiving anyway. Ask your grandfather whether he will perform the ceremony."

"Will do, but I'm confused," Tina said. "You never mentioned that you and Peter were even dating. How come?"

"We weren't dating," Cheryl supplied.

Skeptically, Tina said, "Okay? So, he just popped the question out of the blue?"

"Uh, no. We were talking last week and I told him about my discussion with Darrin Johnson." Cheryl briefly explained the conversation she had with Darren. "Tonight, we were in the library at the office working when I propositioned Peter to get me pregnant. Like some magic trick, he produced a prepared contract detailing the terms and conditions under which he would agree to my proposal. I was shocked, to say the least. Nevertheless, we ironed out the details tonight and I have the weekend to think about it. Still, we're starting house-hunting tomorrow."

"Unbelievable!" Tina said demonstratively. "Well, whatever works. I'm calling Kristen. This deserves a three-way discussion."

Cheryl sighed. She wouldn't have to think about it over the weekend. She resigned herself to the fact she was going to marry her best friend and have babies with him.

Chapter 5

On Monday morning, Peter and Cheryl signed their unconventional contract to marry before a notary public at the bank they both used and was owned by one of Cheryl's clients, Jackson Chase, in Mitchell County, Maryland. Next, they signed the settlement papers for the purchase of the newly-built house their friend JaiHonnah Hawkins Baylor designed and her husband, Roderick Baylor, built. The Baylors provided the electronic keys for the new place and they were set. Peter called a moving company to pack and move their household goods to the new house before their return on the Sunday after Thanksgiving. Their housekeepers, Mrs. Moore and Mrs. Brown, arranged for a cleaning crew to come in and do a thorough cleaning of both the new house and their former residences from top to bottom and supervise the placement of their furniture in the new property.

By late Tuesday afternoon, they were on an Adventurer Executive Airline, non-stop flight from a small Maryland Airport near their home to Chicago's O'Hare. When they arrived at the private jetport Baggage Claim, they were surprised to see Cheryl's parents, Farrow and Helen Kendall Lawrence, waiting for them.

"Dad? Mom? What's going on?" Cheryl asked, giving them both a hug and kiss.

"Just thought we would meet your flight and give you a lift to Peter's house."

Peter laughed. "What? You thought I forgot how to get home?" he asked as he hugged and kissed Helen's cheek and shook Farrow's hand with a manly embrace.

"Uh, no, of course, not," Helen said snaking her arm through Peter's. "Farrow and I just arrived, so we thought we would share the ride into town."

Peter and Cheryl cut their eyes toward each other and then shrugged. Whatever was going on, they would know about it soon enough. A private car service owned by one of Tina Justice's brothers, Keenan Justice, a Chicago police detective, was in the driver's seat waiting at the curb as they left Baggage Claim. Once the luggage was loaded, they were off to the Southside Jackson Park area of the city while catching up on each other's travels. They arrived at Peter's parents' home, a four-story brownstone that was converted from an eight-unit apartment building into a single-family home before Peter Junior was born. The place used to house both Peter Senior's and Cassia's parents, but they were long dead now. When they entered the house, it came alive with a surprising number of family and friends all yelling, "Surprise!" Paper wedding bells were hung from the high ceiling, along with doves and wedding rings.

Tina Justice stood in the midst of the melee grinning at Peter and Cheryl. "You didn't really think you were going to get away without a party, did you?"

"I should have known. You took the news too calmly," said Cheryl.

"You didn't give us much time to work with," Cassia Brock said beaming at the daughter of her heart.

Cheryl hugged the woman who was a second mother to her and wiped away Cassia's tears. "You know your son better than anyone. Once he makes up his mind, it's full steam ahead."

"When he called us to say you and he were getting married on Saturday, Peter senior and I were shocked."

"Also thrilled," Helen Lawrence added joining Tina, Cheryl, and Cassia. She put her arm around Kristen Bryant Marshall who also joined the group of women.

"We had to hustle to get dad to sign the marriage application," Kristen added about her father, Clarence Edward Bryant, an Illinois State Supreme Court Justice.

"Then we're all set?" Cheryl asked.

"A 7:00 P.M. wedding on Saturday in the chapel at Tina's Sheridan Avenue home," said Marguerite Alonza DelaVega Justice, Tina's diminutive Argentinean mother. "The reception is to follow immediately with a buffet dinner at the main house. I just have to work out the musical selections you and Peter want during the wedding."

"Also, the dresses," Cassia added. "We have an appointment for 7:30 A.M. at a bridal boutique. The owner is Peter Senior's client and she's opening up hours early just for all of us. So, we have to be on time."

"Do you really think we can find wedding dresses on such short notice," Cheryl asked. "I could just wear almost anything…"

"Oh, no," came the simultaneous rejection.

"With all of us pulling together, this is going to be a wedding to remember."

He always had a need for family, Peter thought; a big unruly brood and a couple of loopy dogs to chase around a yard. His family was small, just his parents and him with one aunt and one uncle and a male cousin living in North Carolina who he barely knew. Still, he had Cheryl, who was more of a sibling throughout his life, Peter thought, as he watched her talking with his mother and hers, Tina and her mother, and Kristen, in the circle around his fiancée. They all still mourned Kristen's mother died tragically. The Lawrences, Justices, and Bryants were his family all of his life, he reflected as he leaned against the bar in his parents' family room. Then there was Tina's father, grandfather and six older brothers and Kristen's father and two brothers, men he counted as his best friends. Now they accepted Thomas Ashton Marshall, Kristen's husband, who was also an only child, into the fold and he fit like a glove among them. All totaled, as a family unit, they were legions.

"You stepped into some good luck, Son," Redmond Justice, Tina's father, said clamping his big, heavy hand on Peter's shoulder. "I don't have to tell you I love that girl like a daughter, do I?" Tina's father was a huge man who looked like he could bench press the entire Chicago Bears football team.

"No, Sir. I know how you feel about her."

"That's good to hear," said Reverend Ellis Justice, Tina's paternal grandfather, the minister of one of the largest congregations in Chicago; a man almost as big as his seventh son, Redmond. "Two down and one to go before any of us can take a deep breath. Maybe my only granddaughter, Tina, will take the hint and find a husband, too. Seven grands out of Redmond, one a girl, and not one great grand in the crew."

"We'll have to live vicariously through Kristen and Cheryl," added Redmond Justice. "You are planning on having a family soon, aren't you, Pete?"

"Oh, yes, Sir," Peter said and smiled at Tina's father and the good Reverend, Tina's paternal grandfather.

"Good. Good. When I heard the news about these speedy nuptials, I suspected you two had gotten a head start on the family planning, but my Anna Lettie tells me that's not the case."

"No, Reverend Justice, it is not," Peter said, his hand covering the grin on his face. Truth be told, he hadn't laid a hand on Cheryl in all the years they had known each other. Moreover, there would be no premarital sex before the wedding, Peter thought wryly. Given his youthful reputation, it was likely no one would believe that he and Cheryl hadn't been intimate. However, as he looked at his bride-to-be, he intended their wedding night would be an event to remember.

Her wedding dress was the one she wore for one of her cotillions, Cheryl realized, amazed it looked as if it were brand new. She turned in a circle on the raised, platform before three mirrors and viewed it from three sides and the rear. It still fit after nearly fifteen years.

"I can't believe you kept this dress, Mom."

"You were a vision that night and loved this dress so much," said Helen Kendall Lawrence, her smile beatific, her eyes moist. "Cassia and I kept it in storage and Peter senior cleaned it each year. We believed it was such a special dress you would want to consider it as your wedding gown."

"It's perfect," said Cheryl who, after giving it another critical appraisal, turned and hugged her mother and Peter's. "Absolutely perfect. Did you save the shoes too?"

"Of course," said Cassia producing the box from a shopping bag, "and the headpiece."

"Amazing," chuckled Cheryl. All she needed was a fresh, fragrant, white gardenia to wear in her hair behind her left ear, she thought.

Amazing is what Peter thought on Saturday evening when he first saw Cheryl coming up the Chapel aisle toward him holding her father's right arm and a bouquet of white gardenias in her hand and one in her hair. She looked absolutely amazing. He couldn't imagine how he could be this lucky when she looked up and smiled her beguiling smile at him. The beatific fresh-faced, girl-next-door smile had his heart doing somersaults in his chest and caused his blood to warm. He released the breath that backed up in his lungs and returned her smile. She was radiant with the seed pearls and sparkling diamond-like stones cascading over her hair and framing her face in an ancient Egyptian style reminiscent of one of her cotillions. The gardenia tripped his memory of that long-ago evening when he came home from college just to be her escort. He gave a bouquet of gardenias to her then as now and she broke off one to wear in her thick hair. It floored him she now wore the same dress she wore that night. It was covered with Chantilly lace, sequins, and seed pearls overlaying her bare shoulders and arms. Her breasts were still full, firm, and plumped just enough to crest the top of the satin bodice that tapered to a narrow waist, then flared out over rounded hips.

He looked magnificent, thought Cheryl as she was squired to Peter in the chapel on the grounds of Point of View, Tina's Sheridan Road mansion and grounds. He wore a black tie and designer tux that looked as if it were designed just to celebrate the contours of his fine physique. She tingled a bit at the thought that, before the night was over, she would have her hands on Peter's body and, after a two-year hiatus from sex, ride it to nirvana. She licked her suddenly dry lips in anticipation and noticed that Peter's eyes dropped to her mouth following the action. She released a smile of pure joy she felt from the bottom of her feet to the top of her head. It seemed as if her feet never touched the ground until she stood before Peter, their collective families and closest friends listening to Tina's grandfather perform the ceremony making them husband and wife. Through it all, she never took her eyes from his. Somehow, she knew her best male friend would be her forever man and relaxed into the comfort that feeling brought to her soul.

"By the power vested in me, I pronounce you, Peter Linwood Brock, Jr. and you, Cheryl Annalisa Lawrence, to be husband and wife. You may now salute your bride," Reverend Justice finished to the roar of the crowd and the applause raised to the Chapel rafters.

Neither Peter nor Cheryl heard the clamor as she rose on her toes and he bent to join in their first kiss as husband and wife.

Snow was falling when, hand-in-hand, Peter and Cheryl led the way from the Chapel across the grounds of the Tina's Sheridan Road estate to the brightly-lit, main mansion with its turrets and balconies that rivaled European castles, such as Downton Abbey. Years earlier, while the building was abandoned, in foreclosure, and ready for the wrecking ball, developers wanted to get their hands on the forty-acres of land to turn it into one-acre McMansions. Though Tina had no need for such a large home or to spend such a huge amount of money it took to renovate the place, she found the concept of forty acres and a mule prophetic nevertheless. So, she out-bid everyone else, bought it, and named it Point of View. She enlisted her college friend and former classmate, JaiHonnah

Hawkins Baylor, to redesign the interior into a new functionality and Jai's husband, Roderick Baylor, put his crews to work breathing new life into the nearly two-hundred-year-old shell. Now it sat on the shore of Lake Michigan as a crown jewel and was on the registry of the top one hundred landmark homes in America. Though it was not open to the public, as so many others were, the Justice, Lawrence, Brock, and Bryant families often spent memorable occasions there, sometimes sleeping in its many bedroom suites several times a year.

When Peter and Cheryl entered the mansion's massive ballroom, the live band swung into action. As cotillion tradition required, Peter twirled Cheryl into his arms and waltzed her around the expansive space as others looked on. Midway thru the waltz, others joined in to begin the partner exchange. Men moved to their right as did the women. Soon, all were in sync without missing a step while they exchanged partners around the circle until Peter and Cheryl danced with everyone in the ballroom. They were again in each other's arms and everyone was with their original partner.

They then led the way to the extensive late supper buffet in another opulent hall nearly the size of the ballroom, populated with round tables and chairs dressed in traditional holiday colors. Thanksgiving dinner had been held there only days before. With Tina's capable hands steering the arrangements, it was now decked out for Christmas with festive live pine trees perfuming the air, sparkling tiny lights, and beautiful ornaments. The party carried on even after Peter and Cheryl slipped away just after midnight.

"Well, we did it!" crowed Farrow Lawrence. "We finally got those two married."

"The way they were looking at each other, I'm not sure we had anything to do with it," said Cassia Brock.

"Let's synchronize our watches. Nine months from now we should have our first grandchild," boasted Peter Brock, Senior.

"I'll drink to that," said Helen Lawrence raising her glass to toast with the others.

Chapter 18

Someone had done a very good job readying Tina's dome-shaped, one-thousand-square-foot hideaway on the grounds of Point of View for his and Cheryl's first night as husband and wife. That was Peter's thought as he was balls deep and stroking her erogenous zones with regularity. That is when he could think at all. Most of the time, they were in a state of heightened bliss.

When Cheryl engaged the mechanism to raise the Murphy bed and the padded floor separated, Peter was surprised to find an exercise pool full of warm, churning, fragrant water. Underwater lights mimicked the music filling the air from hidden, surround-sound speakers. They slipped naked into the five-foot-deep water some time ago and were about to shrivel up to prunes if they didn't get out of the pool soon.

Cheryl was about to crest another orgasm. She lost count of the number she already experienced, but keeping her thoughts lucid with Peter . . . her husband . . . between her thighs was an exercise in futility. The man knew how to make love to a woman.

He had stamina galore, Peter realized while in Cheryl's arms. Her heady scent, the touch of her fingertips on his needy body, the sound of her voice, the catch in her throat coalesced into an impossibly difficult task of trying not to hit his limit. He felt her lock in around him, so he hiked her thighs up higher around his waist and came continuously until he felt nearly boneless.

"Oh, yeah," Cheryl breathed in his ear.

He chuckled at her sound of satisfaction as she collapsed around him, her head lolling on his shoulder and his on hers. "Remind me to thank Tina again for the use of her sanctuary."

"Will do, if we have the strength to get out of this pool before we drown," she said and sighed. "We need to add an indoor spa and exercise pool to the new house."

"Check. On my to-do list. I'll call JaiHonnah. Maybe she can fit us into her schedule before she and JRock leave to visit her family in Texas for the holidays. Now, hold on," he said lifting her warm, wet body up until she sat on the pool deck. He then hoisted himself up to sit beside her, their feet still dangling in the warm, churning water. The music played and the mood lights changed colors in the water and on the white, domed ceiling like an aurora borealis.

Cheryl leaned her head on his shoulder, his arms coming up to cuddle her close.

"Are you all right?" he asked.

"More than," she said, sighing. "Thank you for making me see that marriage is the right way for us to go. Your parents and mine, everyone is so happy for us. I know we did this as a way to have children, but," she said, shifting her head and looking up into his mesmerizing eyes, "because of your crystal clear persuasion, we had a beautiful, impromptu wedding. I'm going to work hard to make this work for you, too, Peter."

He kissed her delectable mouth. "For us, Cheryl. We're both going to work hard to make our marriage work. You, Tina, and Kristen have always been my BFFs."

She had to ask, "Do you still have feelings for KC?"

"Only as a brother might feel for a sister. Nothing more. However, I feel lucky and honored you agreed to marry me and become the mother of our children."

"Me, too, Peter. I feel lucky and pleased you are my husband."

"I know we haven't talked about this, but no more residual feelings about Wilbur?"

"No, none what-so-ever. How about your feelings for Denise?"

"None. It was a relationship that never should have happened."

"Then we're starting with a clean slate."

"We are, yes. We're not bringing any emotional baggage into this marriage."

"I may have to alter our contract slightly, though."

His brows bunched. "Oh, how so?"

She kissed him, mounted him forcing him to lie back on the carpeted, heated floor. "Now that I know what you're working with, I need to increase the number of times per day I can have you hot and ready under me."

He chuckled and shot his member home. "Consider it a welcomed amendment to our agreement."

On Sunday morning, Peter and Cheryl weren't surprised to learn the Justice, Brock, Bryant, and Lawrence families spent the night at POV. Breakfast was just getting started when Peter and Cheryl trudged through seven inches of fresh snow across the lawn from the dome-shaped hideaway to the main mansion.

Of course, there were ribald jokes both Peter and Cheryl had snappy comebacks for. Laughter continued until they were ready to leave for the airport and journey back to Maryland.

Three hours later, they were pulling into the driveway of their new home. They got out of their car in the garage.

"Let's leave the bags. I'll get them later," said Peter beckoning Cheryl to join him outside the four-bay, side-load garage.

When she did, he closed the garage door, took her hand, and lead her around to the front of the house where the tall, impressive, glass-and-wrought-iron, double doors stood framing the entrance to their home. He unlocked the door, lifted her in his arms to carry her over the threshold. Cheryl delighted in the old-fashioned gesture and smiled broadly as he carried her up to bed to christen their new mattresses.

Hours later, they sat in the sunroom finishing a late lunch prepared by their housekeepers and left in the refrigerator with a gift bottle of wine from Châteauneuf-du-Pape, a Rhône region of France. As they culled through their mail, they engaged an electronic wall calendar imputing events and due dates for the ones they wanted to attend and household bills that needed to be paid.

"Here's an invitation to a holiday party from Chuck and Vivian," said Peter. "I'd like to make time to attend this one."

"Agreed," said Cheryl as she typed the info into the calendar. "I've been kicking around an idea to have a summer or fall cotillion for the Lawrence Twelve Crew. I want to discuss it with KC, Tina, Vivian, Savannah, and JaiHonnah. What do you think?"

"You, Tina, and KC enjoyed your cotillions, didn't you?"

"We did, yes. Getting dressed up in beautiful clothes was so special. Cotillions were for us like a Bat Mitzvah; a sort of coming of age party, a turning point from being girls to becoming young ladies. I don't imagine it's practiced as much anymore, but I think it adds a certain amount of balance."

"As juxtaposed to the martial arts classes you have the Lawrence Twelve Crew taking now, I suppose?"

Cheryl chuckled. "Self-defense is a necessary part of building self-esteem. Our parents had all of us enrolled from the time we were five years old. I wear my third-degree black belt in Taekwondo and Shotokan Karate, proudly."

"I bow to your superior skill, Grass Hopper."

She grinned, palmed her hands together, and bowed over them. "Any time you would like to test my skills, Sensei, we have mats unloaded in the downstairs gym."

He mirrored her pose and said, "Babe, I'd much prefer to pin your phine ass to the mattress of our brand new bed."

"We'll see who pins whom, Sensei."

"You're on, but I agree, the Cotillion is a great idea. Have you spoken with Darrin about it?"

She shrugged one shoulder. "I haven't, no."

"Why, what's…you haven't told him we were married, have you?"

"We did this rather quickly, Peter. I really just haven't had time, but I will on Tuesday. We usually have our regular planning session twice a month at a local restaurant."

"Do you think I should come with you, at least to explain?"

"I'll handle it. This is hard only because I'm aware he is/was interested in taking our relationship to a completely different level. He may be disappointed, but I still would like to keep his friendship. We've done good work together over the recent past."

"You're good with people, babe. He's crazy if he wants to sever your friendship because you're unavailable on an intimate level."

"Thanks. I hope he sees it that way, too."

"Let me know if I can help. Now, if that's all of the mail we need to sort through and the household bills that needed to be paid, how about going through the house room-by-room and deciding what, if any, changes we want to make. Combining two households even in a much larger home, we're bound to have duplicates of everything we may not be able to use."

She grinned at him, stood up, and dropped her robe. "It will only take me a few moments to set the kitchen to right . . ." and giggled as Peter scooped her up in a fireman's hold over his right shoulder, slapped her naked bottom, and sprinted up the back staircase two steps at a time with her laughing all the way.

Much later, following the instructions in an Angelique cookbook, Peter sautéed jumbo shrimp with garlic, butter, Shitake mushrooms, and Brussel sprouts cut into halves. Cheryl put the finishing touches on a pineapple upside down cake; another of Peter's personal favorites, then popped it into one of the ovens to bake. Peter served the shrimp over seasoned, brown rice with a bottle of Coles du Rhône.

Though the sun was down, and because the dining and breakfast rooms were not yet set up, they again sat in the sunroom directly off the kitchen to eat.

"I love this wine. Where did you find it?'

"I bought a case of it from Vivian's brother, Gregory Alexander."

"He's a sommelier? When he retired from professional basketball, I thought he became a stockbroker."

Peter laughed. "He is a stockbroker, my stockbroker in fact. He also buys vintage wine cellars for investments through a hook-up he has in the business."

"A female, of course," she said, laughing.

"Why not? Women make great sommeliers."

"Greg would know. He's one of the most eligible bachelors according to last month's issue of *Stallion*."

"I, for one, don't envy him that position."

One disbelieving eyebrow hiked up on Cheryl's face. "You don't?"

"No, I've only had sex with Denise a few times without a condom. Look at the money I save now that I never have to wear another one for the rest of my life. Gregory, on the other hand, still has to buy stock in a condom company to keep up with the demand on his body."

Cheryl burst out laughing at Peter's deadpan delivery until tears leaked out of her eyes. Being married to Peter Brock was going to be a lot of fun. Once the kitchen was cleaned for the second time that day, it was Cheryl's turn to pin Peter to the first available horizontal surface she could find in the family room . . . the floor. She lit the gas log fireplace with a remote control device, stripped him bare, and proceeded to pin him while she had her wicked way with him for the rest of the night.

The next morning, after their morning run through the golf-cart paths, and an exuberant bout of shower sex, they decided to take the day off from work. Showered, dressed, and expecting their housekeepers to arrive from their two, two-bedroom and two bath apartments above the four-car garage by nine, they had breakfast and began their room-by-room survey. Over lunch, they searched the web for pieces to complete their home's décor. Not surprisingly, they were in agreement with most of their selections. Those pieces that didn't fit were tagged to be donated to Habitat for Humanity. They arranged for a moving company to pick up the furniture, carpets, and boxes of pots and pans, dishes, silverware, towels, linens, and other household goods and deliver them to the Habitat Home Store. The charity welcomed the gifts and promised that needy families would receive the donations before Christmas.

Satisfied with their choices for replacement pieces, they placed their orders and set about designing where the new additions containing the indoor pool and spa would be sited on the property.

"I like it over here on the other side of the house. It would mirror the garage and motor court with the servants' quarters above."

"I agree that makes sense. Then the house will resemble a capital H instead of a lower-case h that it is now. If we put the addition there, we're forming a three-sided courtyard in the back, but it won't obstruct the view of the lawn, the gardens or the lake."

"How about putting a pool in the courtyard and providing access thru an underwater viaduct to the indoor pool?"

"I like that idea, but I want to retain as much green space as possible."

"We can do that by just having a few feet of concrete or stone pavers as an apron around the perimeter of the pool."

"Yes, that's good," said Cheryl making the adjustment on the CAD program JaiHonnah recommended they use to start the preliminary planning for the new additions and renovations to their new home. No one knew the home better than JaiHonnah since she designed the original eight-bedroom structure.

"This will be great with the gym in the lower level and the pools when we can't run in the winter because of snow or ice and too hot in the summer."

"It will be a great place to teach our children how to swim, too," Cheryl said with a wishfully beatific smile.

He kissed her mouth. "It will, yes. Now that's settled, where did you want to go on our honeymoon?"

Cheryl shrugged, her brows beetled in thought. "I didn't think about it, but now that you mention it, how about Japan? We've never been there before."

"Good call. Then I'd like to do the Greek Isles in mid-summer."

"About that, I want to open my own firm, Peter, particularly if we're pregnant. How do you feel about that?"

"I was thinking we could give notice together the first of the month, finish up any open cases, take the rest of the month off, and then open Brock, Lawrence, and Associates around the first of the year."

"Can we do that, Peter? Financially, I mean?"

"We can, yes. I believe we have enough combined resources to sustain us for about twenty-four to thirty months before we have to dip into our savings. That will give us plenty of time to rebuild our clientele. We can bring on young associates as time and resources permit."

"That's good. I'm going to need the extra hands. I agreed to handle Tina's *pro bono* work in the DC metropolitan area in exchange or her taking members of my Lawrence Twelve Girls into her production company. She'll hold up her end of the deal so I have to step up on my end.

She kissed Peter and hugged him tightly. "This will work out perfectly. Yes, let's give notice to the firm and our current clientele, honeymoon in Japan for two weeks, and open our new offices the first of the year. While we're off, we need to lockdown office space before we go to Japan and file articles with the state."

"Done. I did that when you agreed to marry me. I still own the twenty-unit office park complex where Denise had her practice. Each unit is a duplex and spacious enough to start. As the practice expands and we add associates, we may have to do some renovations down the road."

"That's a perfect location. It's only a few miles from here."

"An easy, ten-minute commute using mostly back roads. Now, with these major decisions made, I'll make arrangements for transportation on Friday night. We can sleep on the plane and be more alert when we get to Japan. We'll be back home two weeks before Christmas. Our parents plan to come here for the holidays. Do you feel up to doing a New Year's Eve party this year to kick off the new practice?"

"Yes, definitely. This is the perfect venue for that. We may even have some good news by then."

"I think we need more practice to make sure we have a perfect baby."

With that, they snuck off for a quickie while the housekeepers finished emptying boxes in the kitchen.

Chapter 19

"Wake up, sleepyhead," crooned Peter. "We'll be landing at Narita Airport in about forty minutes. I'm going to take a shower."

"Mmmm," Cheryl moaned burying herself under more pillows.

Peter laughed at his wife's antics and marveled at how much he enjoyed being her husband. They were together all of their lives. He could not recall enjoying any woman as much as he did Cheryl. She was naked and warm under the covers. He opened the shade over the portal windows on Cheryl's side of the bed. Sunlight streamed in.

The Adventurer Executive Airline jet had four bedrooms and small attached baths in the aft sections of the aircraft with seating forward, for meals and lounging. Initially, on the first leg of the trip, they shared the jet with two couples from Washington, DC, who deplaned in Denver, Colorado, and afterward made another stop in San Francisco, California, to pick up two businessmen and a family of four headed to Hawaii. They were chasing the sun across several time zones and the International Dateline for the seventeen-hour flight. After Hawaii, they were the only passengers with a crew of four and now they were landing at Narita International Airport in Japan.

His back was to the shower door of the tiny area, but somehow Cheryl managed to inch her way inside and, with a mischievous smile, proceeded to rock his world.

"Welcome to Japan," said US Air Force five-star General, jet fighter pilot, and astronaut Benjamin Alexander, "Benny" to his family and friends.

"Benny, it's great to see you again," said Cheryl giving him a warm embrace. "We're especially happy that your recent space flight with Tate Kennedy was so successful."

"Thanks, Cheryl. Peter, congrats, man. You and Cheryl make quite a team."

"Thanks, it's only been a week since the wedding, but we're doing fine for newlyweds." He was remembering his wife's antics in the shower just before the flight landed.

"Let's get you through customs and into Tokyo. You don't have much luggage."

"Mostly jeans, T-shirts, and tennis shoes. We understand Tokyo is a walkable city." "Although Japan is about the size and shape of California, only an area the size of Los Angeles County is habitable. It's about an hour from here into the city and the traffic is crazy."

"We appreciate you for meeting us at the airport. We haven't seen you since the party at JRock's and JaiHonnah's home several years ago."

Benny flashed his military and embassy credentials at the security area and they were ushered into a separate space where Peter and Cheryl's passports were stamped and approved. "We only get stateside for special meetings of the Joint Chiefs of Staff, and twice a year for a month of vacation time around Juneteenth and then the Thanksgiving, Christmas, and New Year's holidays."

"Then you should have been on your way a week or more ago."

"Here we are," Benny said, as they stowed what little luggage there was in a waiting chauffeured military car. They climbed in and got comfortable while they were driven away. "We would have been, but Stacy is dealing with a sticky problem involving twenty, young, female refugees."

"Oriental refugees?" asked Cheryl. "When Vivian suggested we contact you and Stacy, I thought she said you are serving as the Air Force Attaché to the Japanese government and that Stacy is serving in the same capacity as the US Naval Attaché."

"The refugees are African, but you're correct on Stacy's and my roles here in Japan."

"How did these girls end up here?"

"A long story, much of which is classified. My wife is trying to get the girls relocated to the states."

"What's the holdup?"

"A faction in their country of origin is claiming these girls, who are all preteens, are rightfully the brides of Jihadist in their home country."

"Bull!" exclaimed Cheryl heatedly. "From what I've read, these terrorists are despicable, misguided bullies. They misinterpret the Koran to fit their sick, perverted views."

"Agreed. These girls are African royalty. Their families have been murdered and their villages decimated. Stacy, through her office, is working on emancipating the girls. There have been two attempts to kidnap them here in Japan. Although the girls have been living and going to school on the American military base here, where they are relatively safe, they do go off base from time to time to sightsee and attend events. The second attack occurred yesterday while they were at an afternoon concert. Several Japanese citizens were injured, so now the government is demanding the girls leave the country."

"What does the US Ambassador have to say?" Peter asked.

"That the matter is not within his purview because these girls are not American citizens. He's suggested the girls be returned to their homeland."

"Un-friggin' believable! Does he not know or understand what will happen to them if that happens?" asked Peter.

"Sensitivity isn't his long suit."

"We'll just see about that!" fired up Cheryl said digging her cell phone from her purse. She speed dialed her friend, Thomas Ashton Marshall, Esquire. He answered on the second ring. "Hi, Thomas, it's Cheryl. Sorry to wake you up, but I need your advice."

"Who did she call?" asked Benny.

"Thomas Marshall."

"KC's husband?"

"Exactly. He's an international law expert and he has negotiated the release of prisoners on the international scene several times. He and the US Ambassador to the United Nations Nathan Flack, Savannah Logan's husband, have worked together successfully. If anyone knows how to quickly solve this matter, they do."

Benny and Peter continued to talk while Cheryl took notes on what she needed to do. At some point, Thomas woke up Nathan Flack and conferenced him into the call.

By the time the military car arrived at the McCoy Tokyo Hotel and Resort, several wheels were set in motion.

"So, we'll see you for dinner?" asked Benny as the hotel porter unloaded their luggage from the military transport.

"That works for us," said Peter.

"Great! We'll send the car for you at six."

"We'll see you then," said Cheryl with a warm hug. If she hadn't been so enamored with Peter back in college, she really could have fallen head-over-heels for Vivian's brothers, Benny or even Kenneth. They were both older than Vivian and drop-dead gorgeous men. They, as well as their twin cousins, Donald and James Dixon, often used to visit Vivian on Spelman College's campus in Atlanta. They would treat Vivian and her close friends to dine at great restaurants and shows whenever they came. She, Tina, and KC were always included along with JaiHonnah and Savannah.

Cheryl remembered that Benny could dance his behind off. For a tall, solidly-built man, he had some moves that could rival the professionals. The fact he was not only an astronaut and an Air Force jet fighter pilot, with a rank of a five-star general, but also the US Air Force Attaché, essentially a diplomat, to the government of Japan, added to his appeal all these years later. He raised his now-teenaged daughter, Whitney Ivy, alone for her first five years. Whitney's mother, Stacy Greene, was deployed where no one knew where she was. When Stacy returned, she married Benny and in recent years, they had two sets of triplets; girls and then boys. That fact alone confirmed that Benny Alexander was happy with the life he now led.

"You've been quiet since we got into the suite. Are you okay?"

She smiled at her husband, her best friend, and did not regret she never hooked up with Benny, Kenneth or his twin cousins Donald or James Dixon. She was quite happy with where she was in her life. She palmed his jaw. "I'm fine. You worry about me too much." She kissed him; her hands rubbing his chest.

"I'm entitled. You're my BFF and wife. What did Thomas and Nathan have to say?" he asked enjoying Cheryl's fondling.

"They're working on a solution through back channels to arrange for the refugees to be permitted to immigrate to the United States. Thomas agreed to act as their legal counsel. He and Nathan should have some things worked out by tomorrow," said Cheryl.

"You're not going to solve those situations today."

She palmed his face again. "You still look concerned."

Peter kissed the palm of her hand. "I'm thinking about Jillian Harris and other high profile men and women who have gone missing and never found. Their families are wealthy, but no ransom demands have been made. This situation with these girls makes me believe there is more to these abductions than what's on the surface."

"You're right. Tina said the same thing a few weeks ago. In the meantime, I'm starving and we have a lot of hours before we go to Benny and Stacy's for dinner. Let's eat and do some sightseeing. Later, once they are awake, I'll call Dad and Mom and ask them to dig up whatever they can on the Jihadist group. Then, I'll see if I can interest Tina in doing a special or an exposé on the plight of young girls and women in certain Third World countries," said Cheryl. "She's already doing research on women at risk."

"I'm proud of you, babe," said Peter, sincerely.

"That means everything to me, Peter. When we have children of our own, I want them to grow up to be socially conscious of the world around them."

"They will be. We'll see to that."

"How do you do it, Stacy?" Cheryl asked truly perplexed as they lounged before dinner. "Seven children and a busy military and diplomatic career, too?"

She chuckled. "I have absolutely no idea. Benny and Whitney Ivy run the household. They're a team; always have been. Both sets of triplets adhere to whatever plans my husband and daughter put in place. Whitney tested out of most of her high school and many of her college courses. She wants to go to law school in the states and, with her aunt a US Supreme Court Justice, I have no doubt she'll have her pick of law schools. When she leaves to attend law school, I have no clue what Benny and I will do," she said laughing.

"You have a great home, a wonderful husband, and exciting career. Your girls are beautiful and the boys are handsome. They are bright, energetic, and curious children. You couldn't possibly go wrong."

"Thank you, Cheryl. Benny and I are very proud of our children and their accomplishments. We are also pleased with where we are professionally. He sacrificed a great deal to follow me into the military diplomatic corps when his true calling is as a jet fighter pilot and astronaut."

"He still does that too, doesn't he?"

"Yes, but for him, family has always come first. It's something I had to learn. He's a great teacher though. He knows how to reel me in when I'm working too hard. Like with these twenty girls. They are older than our triplets and a few years younger than Whitney Ivy. You couldn't imagine what I would do to protect them from what these terrorists intend to do to them."

There was something undefinable in Stacy's demeanor, Cheryl noticed. She had fierceness perhaps, but definitely an edginess Cheryl recognized from her life in Chicago growing up. Stacy was a Chi-town girl, too, just as were Cheryl, Tina, and Kristen, but they clearly didn't run in the same circle of friends. Stacy grew up in the old Cabrini Green tenements on the near north side of Chicago; a neighborhood that was now turning around thanks to Tina and Stacy who were working to make homeownership in the revitalized community affordable for its residents. The renovations would result in upscale, high-rise, and row houses for a mixed-income neighborhood. They had established The Greene Crew, a group of property owners who policed their community and reported any dangerous or unlawful incidents to the proper authorities. Roderick and JaiHonnah Hawkins Baylor were at work refurbishing the apartment units into condos and rehabilitating the overall appearance of the buildings and their surroundings into a city showplace instead of an eyesore.

Cheryl remembered Stacy when she was a local basketball athlete and championship city and state title holder, but lost track of her when she graduated high school and went into the Naval Academy in Annapolis, Maryland. Apparently, Stacy and Benny met after Stacy graduated with honors from the Academy and was assigned to the staff of Admiral Gordon. He was head of the Joint Chiefs of Staff now. Stacy was on his staff as an advisor to and for the Pacific Rim and was the primary diplomatic contact for intergovernmental exchanges among the Asian and African countries bordering the Pacific Ocean.

What was not known was that Stacy was also a covert agent, Code Name: Explorer One; the one who led the incursion to root out terrorists in certain Third World countries and stumbled across the girls who were widely reported as having been abducted before she and her teams' arrival.

"You were in Chicago recently?" Stacy asked.

"Yes, in fact, Cheryl and I were married there over the Thanksgiving holiday. As usual, it was a cold as a witches' tit," joked Peter. "Still, it's always good to visit the city. Of course, Tina and her family and Kristin and her family were there."

"Our families usually spend Thanksgiving together. We have a basketball game the day after Thanksgiving."

Stacy laughed. "I remember you have a touch football game around Labor Day, don't you?"

Peter nodded, laughing. "We hold a baseball game at Easter and a tennis match on Memorial Day. It's a tradition our great-grandparents started. They used to block off the street and have street games and cookouts."

"Now that Tina purchased that forty-acre property on Sheridan Road we go there. You ought to join us sometime," suggested Cheryl. "It's a lot of fun."

"Cheryl's right, it is fun. The Justice family refurbished a sixty-foot sailboat that was a working fishing boat in the many years of their ancestry. Tina's home backs to Lake Michigan and they dock the boat there. When we were all young kids, we'd sail to Mackinac Island for the day."

"If we're in the country the next time you're in Chicago, we'd love to join you," said Benny. "Stacy loves to sail."

"I do, yes," agreed Stacy. "Although I grew up around The Lakes, I never learned to sail until I was in the Navy and stationed in San Diego. I took sailing lessons."

"How about you, Benny? Do you sail?"

"I've gone out with Stacy, but she mostly uses me on the gunwale for the weight factor," he joked.

"I would really like to sail in a regatta," said Stacy.

Cheryl nodded. "That's what we do. We've participated in the boat races. We're planning to practice for bigger races as soon as Tina can wrap up her current exposé on missing women."

Peter thought he noticed a slight shift in Stacy's demeanor at Cheryl's mention of Tina's current initiative. "I don't suppose you can watch much American television her in Japan."

"Certainly not everything, but we do receive American news stories. Tina's exposé has received a lot of attention everywhere," said Benny.

"It's a growing concern among some of the Pacific Rim countries. We've had to work with a number of military bases to ensure that our own personnel aren't targeted or abducted. We've had a few Air Force women go missing."

"I hadn't heard that," said Cheryl. "We know of a woman, an attorney, Jillian Harris who went missing a while back. She hasn't been found either."

Peter was correct in his assessment of Stacy as he watched her avid concentration on the topic of missing women. Perhaps her attention stemmed from her responsibility for the twenty young girls, but somehow he thought it went beyond that…far beyond.

The topics changed to discussions about the college NCAA games and the NBA season. Apparently, now that Benny's younger brother, Gregory, retired from professional basketball, he was in the midst of starting a new basketball league for semi-pro players who didn't make it into the NBA. It would be like farm teams in baseball, but they would be located outside the top one-hundred major metropolitan areas in communities without large college or NBA teams.

Too soon it seemed it was time to go. They bid the Alexanders good night and were returned to the McCoy Hotel.

Peter and Cheryl were enjoying their honeymoon thanks to Benny and Stacy's recommendations. The Alexanders made themselves available as often as possible, but their duties both as military attachés and parents of seven healthy, energetic, happy children didn't leave much time to play tourist guide. So, the newlyweds, armed with a map of the city and tennis shoes, found their way around the many segments mostly using the very efficient subway system. Each night they dined at a different five-star restaurant in one of the nine unique quadrants of the city. They even took the bullet train to Kobe and toured that city with Benny, Stacy, and their children on a rare day they were all free.

A few nights before Peter and Cheryl were scheduled to return to the states, Benny and Stacy again invited them to dinner at their home.

Their children were a delightfully animated bunch. The triplet girls were almost identical at five years younger than Whitney Ivy and the triplet boys just out of the toddler stage.

When Whitney Ivy and Benny trotted the youngsters off for baths, bed-time stories, and bed, Peter and Cheryl helped clear the dinner table and clean the kitchen. Once done, Benny joined them again while they sat with an after-dinner aperitif.

"I hope you enjoyed your time here in Tokyo," said Stacy.

"I believe we did. We certainly hit all of the high spots on our itinerary," said Peter. "We'll have to come again for another tour. When will you be in the states again?"

"If all goes as expected and the girls are free to travel, we'll be on our way before the end of the week. I won't leave until they are safely away from here," said Stacy. "We've secured private transport for them and Ashton Marshall, Nathan Flack, and I arranged for passports and visas. We should be in DC before Christmas."

"Great," said Peter. "I hope you'll join us for a New Year's Eve gala at our home."

Benny looked at his wife and extended his hand to her. She took it and nodded her acceptance. "Consider us there," said Benny smiling.

"Now that I know the girls will be safe, I will breathe easier," said Cheryl.

"That's the plan, but there are still risks to their safety. Those who tried to abduct them are still on the loose. We've tried to keep their location and movements a secret. However, the press and news media are still hot on the story. We have to be very cautious about their location."

"They don't stay in the same place two nights in a row," said Benny. "They are here on base, but they are scattered so they are not bunched together and easy targets."

"Even on this military base?" asked Cheryl.

"Yes, because we have locals who come to work here, there is no guarantee any one of them could have been bribed to disclose where the girls are."

"That is no way for them to have to live," remarked Peter.

"That's why it's imperative we get them out of the country as soon as possible."

"Please let us know if there is anything else we can do to help," said Cheryl.

"You've done a lot already, Cheryl."

"It still doesn't feel like enough. I think about Jillian Harris and whether she's been kidnapped like someone is trying to do to these young girls.

Chapter 20

It wasn't altogether a surprise when, shortly after Cheryl's call, without notice, Thomas Ashton Marshall, Esquire, showed up in Japan to represent the young girls. After all, this issue was in his wheelhouse. However, when someone with the exalted stature of former Ambassador Emeritus Jefferson Alden Logan comes out of semi-retirement and puts in an appearance with his similarly notable and extremely wealthy wife, LaiLoni Skai Hawkins, Peter was duly impressed. Their arrival in Japan was tantamount to having the President of the United States and First Lady come to afternoon high tea; it was an event.

The Japanese government's leadership and their royal family capitulated on their position about the plight of the twenty young girls so fast Peter's head swam with the one-hundred-eighty-degree turn of events. The red carpet was rolled out and immediately a state dinner in Jefferson's and his wife's honor was held. Peter and Cheryl, as well as Thomas Marshall, and Benny and Stacy Greene Alexander were on the honored guests' list. Cheryl wished one of her BFFs, Thomas' wife, Federal DC Appellate Court Judge Kristin Catherine "KC" Bryant could have also been in attendance, but she had a heavy court calendar and was pregnant and due within the month with her and Ashton's third child.

Years earlier, Cheryl, Tina, Kristin, and LaiLoni Skai attended Spelman College at the same time. Cheryl, Tina, and Kristin were freshman while LaiLoni Skai was a senior known then as Dakota Sinclair. Though they were not friends *per se*, Cheryl's, Tina's, and Kristen's classmate, JaiHonnah Hawkins, was one of the loner, Dakota Sinclair's, few friends. Perhaps the relationship developed because it was apparent both LaiLoni Skai and JaiHonnah were a mixture of African American and Indigenous American ancestry. As it was later discovered, Dakota, as an infant, was a kidnap victim from a Texas clinic within a day of her birth. She grew up in a Native American orphanage, Sinclair House, in North Dakota; hence the names, Dakota Sinclair, she was given.

As an adult, on a trip to Africa as a member of the US Vice President's wife's entourage, she attended an American Embassy reception hosted by Ambassador Jake Hawkins and his new wife, Kelly Baylor, the sister of J. Roderick Baylor the former basketball icon. JaiHonnah Hawkins, the daughter of Jake Hawkins and her husband, Roderick, were also in attendance with their children. When JaiHonnah and Dakota were renewing old acquaintances about their days at Spelman College while in the receiving line, Jake Hawkins recognized Dakota's resemblance to his deceased wife, Skai Littlefeather. Within a few hours, it was confirmed Dakota Sinclair was, indeed, LaiLoni Skai Hawkins, the kidnapped daughter of multibillionaire, Jake Hawkins, the titular head of BlackHawk Global, a *Fortune* five-hundred conglomerate. Although Jake has two sons, both of whom serve as officers of the BlackHawk Company, it was now being headed by his son-in-law and daughter, J. Roderick and JaiHonnah Hawkins Baylor.

Though the serendipitous Hawkins family reunion was widely publicized, what few knew was that Dakota Sinclair, Code Name: Wind Breeze, then in her thirties, was a member of The Nursery, a super-secret organization, created by the G8 and authorized to operate covertly with impunity in nearly one-hundred percent of the stable, democratic countries worldwide. Dakota was recruited from Spelman College by a then young Navy Lieutenant, Stacy Greene, to join her twelve-person team of women and secretly trained as SEALs and Mossad operatives. Dakota, an excellent, Olympic-quality, long-distance runner, was actually on a mission to free a group of American industrialists and government officials, including Nathan Flack, being held hostage in Africa when her father claimed her as his daughter.

To ameliorate the incessant intrusions by the press and news media clamoring for details of the phenomenal Hawkins family reunion, LaiLoni Skai reached out to her schoolmate, Cheryl Lawrence, to enlist her illustrious father, Farrow Lawrence, to write the exclusive story of the discovery and reunion. Though a renowned investigative journalist and television personality appearing on many world affairs talk shows, Farrow agreed, but no mention was made of the covert nature of Dakota's missions.

Cheryl's efforts, to bring media attention to the plight of the twenty, young girls, were successful as well. Both of her parents focused their newspaper columns, television appearances, and considerable influence on different aspects of the matter. However, Tina Justice's **Sweet Justice** television show's exposé layered on optics when she took her cameras on location into some of the most dangerous areas where militant and radical Jihadists murdered entire villages, kidnapped the women and female children, and made the young males soldiers in the Jihadist army.

For two weeks, Tina and her camera crews shot live footage of the devastation and carnage and were hot on the heels of the fleeing terrorists. People were riveted to her twenty-four seven and her television show's ratings shot through the roof. Members of the audience blogged and her show went viral. She hired what she thought was a reputable special operations and helicopter company to protect her people and move swiftly.

The company, unbeknownst to Tina, was actually a front for The Nursery and her efforts galvanized human rights organizations and the United Nations into action, sending in troops to root out the militant Jihadist, rescue the women and children, and bring those responsible for the massacres to justice. The Special Operations, known as the Spec Ops' team, was led by an outlier, Slade Richardson, Director of Investigations and Security for the law firm Marshall and Marshall, Thomas Marshall's Portland, Oregon-based law firm. Slade, Code Name: Cobra Kahn was a dead ringer for the actor Sendhil Ramamurthy and could easily infiltrate any Arab or East Indian or North African group. He spoke many languages and dialects fluently, making him a very valuable asset for The Nursery.

By the time Peter and Cheryl returned to America from their honeymoon in Japan, Cheryl's parents' names and Tina's name were being bandied about among the Pulitzer Prize nominating community. The effect of Cheryl's action of making that one phone call was tantamount to tossing a pebble into a pond and watching the rippling consequence it produced. Worldwide laser-beam attention was focused on the plight of women led by former Ambassador Jefferson Logan and enhanced by his brother-in-law and protégée, UN Ambassador Nathan Flack. Cheryl's friend and Nathan's Special Assistant at the UN, Capri McAllister Kennedy, took on the women's rights challenge and spearheaded the US efforts. Cheryl and Peter were pleased by the fact that the twenty young girls were finally safe in an undisclosed location in the United States.

"It's good to be home," said Cheryl, yawning. They had just arrived from their honeymoon on a jet that landed in the wee hours of the morning at a small county airport not far from their home.

"Are you hungry?" asked Peter as he culled through the mail that accumulated.

"I could eat. What would you like?"

Peter's eyes salaciously scanned his wife's body and she noticed.

"Fuel, babe," she said, smirking. "Fuel first, then fun."

"If you insist," he said going to the refrigerator for eggs, cheese, and more ingredients for a Spanish omelet.

"What time will our parents be here?" Cheryl asked while shredding white potatoes for home fries.

"Sometime this afternoon. I'll check and make sure their rooms are ready after we eat.

"I'll need about an hour to go through my office and personal e-mail. Are the decorations finished with the Christmas and New Year's themes, do you think?"

"What I saw on the outside before we pulled into the garage looked impressive, but the lights weren't on. We'll have to wait for nightfall to see the full effect."

"I hope the Christmas gifts we had shipped from Japan arrived already."

"I'll check on that and make sure they're well-hidden before the parents arrive. You know how your father is about sneaking a peek at gifts."

Cheryl chuckled. "Mom always puts jingle bells on their bed to alert her if he tries to sneak a look on Christmas Eve."

"Does that work?"

"Every time."

"So, what do you think?" Cheryl asked her parents and Peters.

"I think a cotillion for the Lawrence Twelve Crew is a great idea," said Cassia Brock. "It would be a lot of work though."

"Do you think you'll have time once you go back to work?" asked Farrow Lawrence as he got another slice of roast beef and a scoop of creamy potatoes au gratin from the buffet before returning to his seat at one of the dining tables in a smaller salon.

"Cheryl and I have decided to open our own office here in Maryland, so we'll be able to fit it in easily enough."

Their parents stopped eating and stared.

"Well, hell, son," said Farrow. "Talk about burying the lead story. Congrats!"

"Oh, I'm so happy for you," exclaimed Cassia.

"Great move," said Helen Kendell Lawrence. "I think you should have a blowout party to celebrate."

"Way ahead of you, Mom. We're planning it for New Year's Eve," said Cheryl.

"So soon?" asked Cassia. "Why that's only a few weeks away."

"We gave notice to the founding partners and our current clientele already before we left for Japan," said Peter and then reached for another dinner roll. "We were asked not to leave the firm, so we agreed to be 'of counsel' to the law firm for a year. After that, we'll re-evaluate where we are."

"We had invitations printed for the party and Betty Jones, Peter's personal assistant, addressed, and mailed them while we were away."

"Isn't Betty Jones the receptionist who used to work for Denise?"

"She is, yes."

"You kept her on after Denise left?" asked Cassia.

"I was already paying her salary and she's very efficient. She now manages the office complex for me."

"Doesn't she have a son?"

"She's a single mother, yes. Her husband was a soldier. He died in Afghanistan years ago when her son was very young. David is fifteen now."

"The perfect age for a cotillion," remarked Cassia.

"You're right," said Cheryl. She got up from the dinner table to make a note of it and distribute warm apple pie with clotted cream for dessert.

Peter poured coffee for everyone except Cheryl. She was having herbal tea. "After the New Year, I'll be working with twelve at-risk young male teens and a female school counselor."

"The surprises don't stop with you two!" exclaimed Farrow. "Turning the tide of world opinion, opening your own law offices, and mentoring law students, etc. Now working with at-risk youth? You are allowing time for making our grandbabies, aren't you?"

Everyone laughed at Farrow's worried expression.

"Dad," Cheryl said, her tone a warning.

"I'm just saying . . ."

"He's not the only one," said Peter Senior. "Don't you two get too busy to get busy, if you know what I mean."

Everyone chuckled.

"So, you seem happy," observed Helen of her daughter as they sat with Cassia in one of the salons. They had their feet up enjoying a relaxing after dinner aperitif, but Cheryl stuck with her herbal tea.

The men were clearing up after dinner and stowing the leftovers or nibbling on them as the case may be.

"I am, we are. Peter and I have always been close."

"Still," Helen said significantly, "You two went into this rather quickly."

Cheryl laughed. "I'll say. We only had one official date."

"It takes time for love to grow. I know you two love each other, but, still, are you able to fall *in love?*"

Cheryl shrugged. "We have a better chance of that happening, we think, than most people do because we have always been close friends. We enjoy each other."

"I don't want either one of you to regret taking this step," said Cassia.

"So far, we don't regret making this move. We went into this marriage with both eyes open. We know each other completely and there isn't anything we dislike about the other."

"Best friends, I'd say are like that," added Cassia.

"I agree, but only time will tell whether we're good for each other over the long term. That's because we, the Bryants, and Justices are such great friends. You raised all of us together; particularly me and Peter. Cassia, you were the stay-at-home, go-to mom to all twelve of us."

She laughed. "Having to babysit for my son and the eleven of you children while your parents worked was a handful, but I'm proud of each and every one of you. If I could, I'd do it all over again."

"Still, it wasn't easy, Cassia," said Helen. "Especially when I was always out chasing a story, Marguerite was working in the community medical clinic, and we lost Lydia."

"No, Lydia was in semi-retirement and you both helped out when you could. Anna Lettie volunteered for field trips when she didn't have church business to attend to, but that was a very sad time for all of us for a long time."

"Lydia was very young when she was killed, wasn't she?" asked Cheryl.

"Younger than you are now," sighed Helen. "She was the youngest of us all, yet such a shining star on the stage and big screen. She began ballet in Canada when she was six years old."

"I remember when she started teaching dance to me, Tina, and Kristen."

"She did, yes. I think you girls were four or five years old. She had a wonderful way with children," said Helen. "I wish Clarence hadn't closed Lydia's school. She intended for it to be a legacy for her daughter, Kristen, and for you, and Tina, too."

"I do, too," said Cassia, "but he took Lydia's death so hard."

"Well, KC has a dance troupe of her own now and her father seems happy enough now married to Ashton's mother."

Helen chuckled. "It seems Clarence Bryant and Sheila Duckworth Marshall were an item back in Howard's law school long before Clarence met Lydia. Sheila dumped Clarence and married Thomas Marshall, II. Thomas, the III, was born less than nine months later."

"I didn't know that," said Cassia, surprised.

Helen nodded sagely. "So, this is the second time around for both Clarence and Sheila."

"That was quite some feat you and Cheryl pulled off in Japan," remarked Peter's father. He took a long puff of the Cuban cigar Farrow supplied, glad there was no longer an embargo in place.

"More Cheryl than me. The plight of those twenty girls really got her Cuban blood boiling."

"Indeed, it did," said Farrow. "Woke me and Helen up before dawn hot as a pistol. As soon as Helen heard how angry our daughter was, she hit the record button on the phone, so she could get some more sleep," he said laughing. "We were out the night before at the Correspondents Dinner in Washington. We flew back to Chicago after the dinner and didn't get home until almost four in the morning. It was nearly noon before we surfaced, but Helen got right to work."

"Apparently, so did you. I liked your columns," said Peter Junior.

"You said a mouthful on Face to Face, too. Told that African representative he ought to be ashamed of himself. His position about women was indefensible. If he had said those things to any one of our women, she'd have handed his balls to him on a silver platter," said Peter Senior proudly.

"He was a real tool, that's for sure," added Farrow, "but our Tina is the one who put the proverbial nail in the terrorists' coffin. She scares the living daylights out of me sometimes with what she's willing to tackle with her Sweet Justice show."

"There isn't anything she isn't willing to expose. She keeps it simple, though. There are good guys and there are bad guys and never the twain shall meet according to her."

"Big Red despairs sometimes about how fearless Tina can be," said Peter Senior of Tina's father Redmond Justice, aka Big Red.

"No doubt all fathers feel that way about their daughters," offered Peter.

"You'll find out soon enough when you and my daughter have a houseful. From their first breath, you'll worry."

Peter Junior chuckled. "Not exactly a houseful, Farrow. We plan to have children, maybe even adopt the way Chuck and Vivian have."

"Wow, talk about a houseful!" exclaimed Farrow.

What Peter Junior didn't say was the Alexander-Montgomery household had increased by twenty for a short period of time until the additional guests could be relocated to Vivian's very close-knit family in Goodwill, Summer County, South Carolina. Former Ambassador Jefferson Logan was now the Dean of Summer County Academy there.

When his own three young sons' lives were in danger, Summer County proved to be an extremely safe haven for them, particularly because one of The Nursery's secret units was based there. Any strangers showing up anywhere in the county with a dangerous intent would immediately be spotted and severely dealt with.

"You and Cheryl certainly have the home for it, and Helen tells me you're adding more square footage."

"Mostly on the rear, we're adding two pools; one indoor connecting to an outdoor pool, and spas for both. On the front, Cheryl wants a *porte-cochere* and a stair-step water feature signifying climbing up a ladder to success. That's mostly for the Lawrence Twelve Crew's benefit. Each step will have words of encouragement."

"Very creative."

"It is."

"Okay, son, we've danced around this elephant in the room long enough. Are you and Cheryl pregnant yet or not?"

Peter laughed. "What, do you have money on the table?" At his father's and father-in-law's chagrin, Peter laughed louder. Though Cheryl missed her period and the home pregnancy test proved positive, they were waiting to have her friend and OB/GYN specialist, Dr. Savannah Logan-Flack confirm it when she and her husband, UN Ambassador Nathan Flack, returned from visiting her brother, Jefferson Logan and his family in Summer County, South Carolina.

Chapter 21

"**Y**ou're Mr. Peter's mother?" asked Soledad, one of the more outspoken members of Cheryl's Lawrence Twelve Crew. They were at Cheryl and Peter's home on Sunday before Christmas for high tea and a gift exchange. Each girl saved five dollars and Cheryl and Darrin matched each girl's savings with another five from both of them. The girls were encouraged to make a gift with the fifteen dollars or purchase something and wrap the gift in holiday paper that Cheryl supplied. Cheryl taught her crew to knit and crochet just as Cassia Brock, who loved handcrafts, taught her, Tina, KC, and any of the boys she could get to sit still long enough. Cheryl expected there might be a few knitted caps or tops in the gifts.

"I am, yes," said Cassia smiling.

"Wow, he's so handsome and you look so young," Soledad said, swooning. "Does he have a younger brother?"

This time Cassia chuckled. "Uh, no, he was my only child and thanks for the compliment, I think."

"He married Ms. Cheryl, Soledad," Cookie, another Lawrence Twelve Crew member, piped up, exasperated. "You can't be lookin' at Ms. Cheryl's man like that."

"Yeah, Sole," said Lena the oldest, but smallest girl, "that's just wrong on so many levels."

Cheryl discretely listened to various conversations going on in one of the salons in her home, pleased her girls were learning a sense of proper decorum. She had successfully enlisted twelve of her female friends to mentor each girl through the myriad of social events each month leading up to the cotillion. She recognized the costs could escalate, but each of the "sponsors," if necessary, would bare most of the costs involved including the costs of the cotillion gowns and accessories. The girls had a group of tickets to sell for the big event to their family and friends. Cheryl also had a few surprises up her sleeves and a few surprise events for the girls and their escorts. Also, in the room were more than twenty boys, twelve who potentially would be the girls' escorts.

Her girls looked well-groomed considering some of their homes were a challenge to exist in. For the last two years both she and Darrin worked with them, Cheryl saw a marked improvement in nearly every aspect of their deportment. They trusted both her and Darrin enough to come to them with any personal problems they were ill-equipped to handle on their own.

One potentially very dangerous situation involved a male relative's attempt to molest Shenesca, a fourteen-year-old. She was perhaps the most physically well-endowed of the twelve. Using the self-defense techniques Cheryl taught her, she successfully protected herself and then called Cheryl. Cheryl called the police and immediately went to Seneca's home. The police arrived shortly after Cheryl and arrested the inebriated man who showed signs of still being in serious pain and discomfort from the beat-down Shenesca delivered.

The girl lived in a single-parent household with her father, a German immigrant, who worked construction jobs. He paid for his cousin to come to the United States to work as a favor to a favorite aunt in Germany. As it turned out, the cousin was a ne'er-do-well, losing every job Seneca's father arranged for him.

With Cheryl's help, the man would spend a considerable amount of time as a guest of the state's penitentiary system and then be deported to Germany where the punishment for child molestation was more stringent than in the American justice system.

Peter and Cheryl purchased their holiday gifts while in Japan, including small gifts for the Lawrence Twelve Crew. They also sent boxes of gifts to Jefferson and LaiLoni Skai Hawkins Logan in Summer County, South Carolina. They never explained to anyone why they sent so many boxes filled with new clothes and shoes to Vivian's South Carolina home.

"You're really getting on my last nerve," Tina Justice snapped out into her cell phone, her tone threatening.

Cheryl turned to regard one of her oldest friends. "Okay, someone took you out of your happy place."

"Claude," Tina said jamming her cell phone in her pocket. "He doesn't seem to get the concept he's my publicist, not my lover."

"Remind me again. This is December, right? Do you *have* a flavor of the month this month yet or did I miss the announcement?"

Tina rolled her expressive dark eyes. "Just because you and KC are off the market, everyone thinks I should be, too."

"You haven't met the man brave enough to scale the Justice fortress walls and I'm not referring to your Sheridan Road estate."

"You and Peter didn't do badly yourselves. This is a great home, and speaking of great things, how is Peter as a husband?"

"Nice sidestep, but I'll allow it *sine qua non*. Still, that's a topic that's rated 'R' for Restricted. However, suffice-it-to-say, I have no regrets.

Tina smiled at her friend. "I'm truly happy for you and for Peter. He's one of the good guys. You two deserve each other."

"I'll drink to that," added Kristen Bryant Marshall. "That is if I could drink anything, but water these days," she said rubbing her rotund belly.

"How is little Lydia Martine today?" asked Cheryl, patting Kristen's abdomen.

"She learned the River Dance, I'm sure. She's been doing every dance move my mother ever taught us."

Tina and Cheryl both laughed.

"Thomas is over the moon because you're having a girl. After two boys he was beginning to despair a daughter wasn't in his future," said Cheryl.

"I imagine he'd keep practicing until he got it right," joked Tina.

"It's almost as if history is repeating itself. Your parents had two boys and a girl," Tina pointed out to Kristen. "Your mother taught us to dance. You did the same thing starting your dance company."

"Thankfully, the dance company is doing well without me. I may go back to it, but I need to stay put while the children are young. Touring the world each theatre season was fun and exciting. However, going back on the bench is one way to stay put."

"Well, this looks like old home week," commented Supreme Court Justice Vivian Alexander Montgomery as she joined the group of women.

"It does, doesn't it," commented Tina. "Even more so for the country-and-western ball you're planning for Christmas Eve. So many more of our classmates will be there."

"You're right. Chuck and I have received about eighty-five percent acceptances. The RSVPs are still coming in."

"Then the next week, Peter and I are hosting a New Year's Eve party."

"It's going to be a stellar event," commented Helen Kendall Lawrence, also joining the group.

As her eyes passed over the crowd of debutants, their potential escorts, and sponsors, Cheryl stalled on the sight of Darrin Johnson talking with Betty Jones . . . because they were both smiling at each other. She admitted, at least to herself, she liked them together. Just before her stare was noticed, she turned away and looked at Betty's boy, Clay Jones, chatting with Soledad and the little exchange of cell phones which obviously was for the exchange of phone numbers.

She was letting nature take its course with the girls having the pick of the litter, so to speak. Vivian graciously served up her teenaged sons as potential escorts. The boys may not have been gung-ho about all of the events they would have to attend leading up to the cotillion, but Vivian's word was law in the Alexander-Montgomery household. So, the boys capitulated and were putting the best face on their forced participation.

They were on parade for the girls' selection and they knew it. After the high tea, the girls would make the selection of their first, second, and third choices. Once all details were decided, the boys would be notified via mail and formally invited to be an escort for a particular young lady. It was all going rather well, thought Cheryl.

Chapter 22

"Would you believe our parents have money riding on how soon we give them grandkids?" asked Peter as he climbed into bed. He sat up with his hands laced behind his head and watched Cheryl ready herself for the night. His chest was bare and his pajama bottoms tented around his arousal. The sight of Cheryl in his pajama shirt and bare legs hardened his body.

Cheryl shook her head and laughed. She was putting lotion on her hands and face. Her hair was up in a messy top knot. "I had a feeling they were up to something. What did you say to our dads?" When Peter didn't answer, she looked up and found him staring at her. "What?" she asked.

A lazy grin covered his mouth. "You are one sexy woman, Cheryl."

She grinned at him in return, padded barefooted to his side of the bed, then climbed onto his lap facing him.

"Is that what you told the dads?" she asked while she lifted her bottom and fished his hardened member from his pajamas. Slowly she eased on to him before lacing her fingers with his behind his head. She leaned in close until her hardened nipples graced his and whispered in his ear. "Talk about sex appeal? Babe, there are times when just the thought of getting you naked causes me to orgasm. You don't even have to be anywhere near me when it happens. It's a little embarrassing to have to change my thong several times a day."

Peter's head fell back against the stack of pillows, his eyes closed while Cheryl bit his earlobe and rocked as if on a hobby horse. His penis twitched and hardened more as her inner muscles gripped tightly around him.

"Just because they're betting on how soon we give them a grandchild, we should hold off telling them that I've missed my period."

Peter's eyes opened slowly and searched hers. "Geezus, Cheryl, did we do it? Did we make a baby?"

"I've been riding you like it's my regular nine to five since our wedding night. I'm usually as regular as a Swiss watch. I can't imagine we're not pregnant by now. I haven't been on any form of birth control since before the night we caught Sheila and Wilbur together. According to my last check up, I'm as fertile as a freshly plowed field. I think we did it, Peter. I think we're pregnant. At least that's what two different home-pregnancy tests indicate."

He brought their joined fingers from behind his head and kissed her palms. Still holding eye contact, Peter unbuttoned the shirt Cheryl wore until her rosy-colored nipples came into view. He then shifted his hands from her high breasts to her flat abdomen rubbing the spot where he fervently hoped a baby had taken root. From her waist, Peter's hands smoothed down to her thighs. He carefully lifted her just enough to lower her to her back without pulling out of her. Again, joining their fingers, Peter began a methodical rhythm that had Cheryl's breath catching in her throat. Still, they looked deeply into each other's eyes as Peter's thrusts and Cheryl's counter moves intensified.

Peter's vision blurred just as Cheryl's eyes went opaque. It took a while after they reached nirvana for their lazy thrusts to subside. Still, their breaths hitched until sleep claimed them.

The sun was just coming up over the lake at the back of their property when Cheryl opened her eyes. Ice crystals sparkled on the still green grass and lit up the expanse with the sun's glow. A smile graced her lips as she watched the ducks and geese lead their young on an early morning forage for breakfast. Then she moaned long and deep and held a death grip on the bed linen. Her mouth opened, but her eyes slammed shut when she came violently at her husband's instigation. The man's clever fingers and mouth were lethal weapons on the chilly morning.

He wasn't finished with her yet.

The fireplace was lit in the sitting room and the teapot was starting to whistle on the credenza, but Cheryl only recognized the sound as if in some distant dream. What her husband was doing to her body under the comforter had her transfixed. She felt like all of her nerve endings were sensitized and exposed. Before she rebounded from the last orgasm, another more potent one was upon her. This time she couldn't quite control the long, keening sound that emanated from her throat signaling her unbridled release.

"Good morning," Peter said coming out from under the covers. He fit himself between Cheryl's limp thighs and inch by inch secured himself deep into her body.

"Good morning," she moaned and grinned. She tasted herself on his lips as he rhythmically began to arouse her anew.

Later, in the shower, Peter rinsed the conditioner out of Cheryl's hair and fashioned a towel around the springy mass. "What's on your agenda today?" he asked.

"I thought I'd go by to see the office space this morning and do some measurements for furniture placement.

"Good, but I have client meetings in town or I would join you."

"Betty said she would be there," said Cheryl patting more water from her hair. She watched Peter as he soaped himself again and then stood below the rain shower and before the body sprays.

"She will be," he said and shut off the waterworks. "She's very dependable."

Cheryl turned on the oil warmer when Peter stepped toward the mirror on his vanity. Dipping her hand into the warm, fragrant oil, she stepped behind him and began to smooth it over his back and bottom. He did the same for her and then they patted each other dry.

"Did you notice Darrin and Betty spent a great deal of time together talking?"

Peter shrugged, "No, not necessarily, but then again, I wasn't watching her or them."

"I think he likes her."

He chuckled. "What's not to like?" he asked. "She's a bright, attractive, and personable woman. She's doing a good job raising her son alone." He looked over his shoulder at her, eyeing her curiously. "Are you playing matchmaker?"

"Well," she said on a windy sigh. "Maybe just a little."

He shook his head on a wry smile, turned her into his arms for a warm hug. "You're still concerned about Darrin's feelings about you?"

"A bit. I mean, our marriage blindsided him. He's a good guy."

"Betty is a good woman. They've been introduced. If it's to be, let them find a way to each other."

She looked up into his amused eyes, kissed him quickly, and sighed. "You're right. They're two grown adults."

"Yes, they are." He turned her back toward him. "One of the things I love about you is your genuine compassion for people," he said as he started to dress.

One of the things, he had said, thought Cheryl. She wondered what other things he might *love* about her. Moreover, did they simply love each other as friends and now as husband and wife or could they have fallen *in love* with each other? She really didn't know the answer to that question.

In their headlong rush to have children, they never talked about whether their relationship could reach new levels as both his and her parents had. It was clear their parents were still very much in love with each other. She wondered, not for the first time, whether she and Peter might move beyond a loving friendship to actually being *in love* at some point in their lives together. Or was a loving friendship enough to sustain them?

"Hey, babe, where did you go?"

She snapped out of her fugue state and then smiled up at Peter. Looping her arms around his neck, she rose up on her toes to kiss his mouth. "I'm right here."

He looked at Cheryl, curiously. She was just in deep thought, but he sensed it had nothing to do with her match-making efforts where Darrin Johnson and Betty Jones were concerned. He wanted to explore her thoughts more, but he had clients to meet and he didn't want to be late.

He realized today would be the first day since they married, they would spend an appreciable amount of time apart. He enjoyed Cheryl and her company. They never failed to have a multitude of things to talk with each other about on so many levels. They were very much attuned to the other, yet he felt they still had universes to explore about the other. They were a good match. Over the years to come, he hoped they were a match made in heaven.

Chapter 23

Betty Jones was already in the business office working when Cheryl arrived. It was really cold outside and the air turned her breath visible just before she entered the warmer building. She shivered and appreciated the heat she felt when she went inside. Her parents and Peter's were at the breakfast table that morning plotting what gifts they wanted to give her and Peter to round out their home's decor. She and Peter really didn't need for much, but at their parents' insistence, she left her and Peter's iPad of household accoutrements for them to pick over and select as gifts. Their parents were well into the selection process when she followed Peter into the garage for another warm kiss before they parted ways for the day and got into their respective cars.

Cheryl had been in the office for a while when Betty tracked her down in one of the many empty back offices.

"I have to run out to the store for a few office supplies, Cheryl. I'll be back in a few minutes," said Betty.

"Take your time. I still have several offices to measure and figure out how to furnish."

"Okay, so that you won't be disturbed, I'll turn on the answering system."

"Thanks, Betty," said Cheryl as she continued to take measurements and jot down the results.

Shortly after Betty left, Cheryl heard the front office door open and close again. "Did you forget something?" she called out. When there was no answer, Cheryl left her schematic in one of the offices and walked out into the common area. She was brought up short by the sight of three, physically imposing men, obviously of African descent. Something about them made her feel decidedly uneasy. Yet she stood her ground and asked. "May I help you?"

"You have place here?"

Her brows bunched at the thick dialect. "Place? You mean available space in the complex?"

"This you have?"

"I do not know. The business agent for the complex will be back shortly. If you don't have time to wait, I can give her contact information to you."

One of the men stepped forward into her personal space, looked her over critically, and inhaled deeply.

Cheryl wanted to step back but instead stepped sideways behind the desk where she spotted a baseball bat beside the chair. She felt as if she might have need of it but took a business card from its holder on the desktop instead. "This is who you need to contact about available space in this business park," she said holding out one of Betty's business cards. It's a wonder her hand did not shake, she thought. Then again, she was a woman who grew up on the south side of Chicago. She knew not to show fear, though fear she did. After all, there were three of them and only one of her.

The man nodded to one of the other men who stepped forward and took the card from her fingers. An awkward silence followed as the first man ran his obsidian gaze around the office as if drawing a map and then back onto her face. Again, he stepped toward her and inhaled deeply as an animal might scent another.

Cheryl was still a bit shaken from her encounter with the three African men when she, Peter, and their parents, arrived at Chuck and Vivian's ranch. Nevertheless, the party was in full swing when they entered the ballroom. Chuck, garbed in Western gear, complete with cowboy hat and boots with spurs, was on the dance floor with his and Vivian's children leading the group in doing a line dance, the Down N Dirty, with a host of other dancers. For a big man, nearly seven feet tall and a doctor, owner of Physicians' Hospital, he had a smooth move with the Stetson pulled low over his pretty eyes and his thumbs looped in his low-riding jeans, thought Cheryl.

He usually wore his hair in a ponytail at the nape of his neck, but this time it was loose framing his face and highlighting the diamond stud he wore in his left earlobe. He could pass for a tall, well-built Johnny Depp, long hair and all.

Everyone wore Western-style clothes, cowboy boots, and Stetsons. The hats were gifts the guests received upon arrival. Peter pointed out Vivian's parents and former mother-in-law, and Chuck's father among the line dancers not missing a beat. She and Peter joined the line, enjoying the shouts and calls as the live band and singers gave the dance a real country flavor.

Cheryl also saw Vivian and Chuck's multitude of family members, Kenneth and JeNelle, Benny and Stacy, Gregory Alexander and the youngest of Vivian's siblings, Aretha Grace Alexander. She also spotted Vivian's cousins, the twins, Donald and James Dixon, with their wives, Cecile Jordan Dixon and Janice Atterly Dixon.

Her and Peter's pals, Kristin, Ashton, and Tina were also there. It surprised her to see Tina's parents, Redmond and Marguerite Justice, and their six sons also in attendance.

"Hey, Tina," Cheryl greeted giving her friend a hug. "I didn't know your parents and brothers were coming to the party."

Tina returned the embrace. "Your parents didn't mention it?" Tina asked.

"We plan to, yes. You know our parents live for holiday parties."

"Peter and I will have to do a better job of planning for our law firm's events," she said grinning.

Tina's eyes widened. "You're going to do it? You're going to open your own firm?"

Cheryl nodded gleefully. "Peter and I are opening Brock Lawrence and Associates. We're making the official announcement at our party next week."

"When did this happen?"

"Peter and I made the final decision some time ago. I was in our new offices today working out some of the details." She craned her neck searching for Betty Jones. "Let me introduce you to our office manager," she said guiding Tina to where Betty stood talking with Stacy Alexander.

"Hi, Stacy," Tina greeted her with a hug before she turned while Cheryl made introductions.

"Betty Jones, this Tina Justice, one of my best buds from Chicago."

"A pleasure to meet you, Ms. Justice. I've been a fan of your television show since it first aired."

"Thank you, Betty, but please call me Tina."

Betty nodded, the smile on her face indicative of her pleasure.

"Cheryl tells me you're going to be the new firm's office manager. So where are your offices?" Tina asked Betty.

"We're in a beautiful business park that Mr. Brock owns in the county, not far from here. Until today, I would have said it was safe too, but Cheryl had a scare."

"Wait, what happened?" asked Stacy Greene Alexander of Cheryl with noticeable concern. They were chatting when Betty mentioned the encounter.

"Well, nothing really. They just gave me a creepy feeling. That's all," said Cheryl.

"You were more than creeped out, Cheryl, when I got back to the office an hour later. You were in fight mode when I came in," said Betty.

"Just shaken up a bit."

"What happened?" asked Stacy again.

"I went to the store to pick up supplies and left Cheryl in the office alone. It's a relatively safe area, so I didn't lock the front office door when

I left because I knew she was inside. When I got back the door was locked. I didn't think anything of it, but I had a lot of packages in my arms. When I finally got the door opened, Cheryl was standing behind it with my son's baseball bat in her hands ready to take a swing. Scared me half to death. She told me about the three men who came to the office, but I remember seeing them around the complex before. I didn't know they were looking for space in the office park. They just seemed to be hanging around. Since they didn't bother any of the tenants, I didn't think it necessary to call the complex's security team or the police."

"What did they look like?" asked Stacy.

"Warriors," said Cheryl spontaneously before Betty could answer. "I mean they were wearing suits, but they looked like they weren't comfortable wearing clothes like that. The suits were too tight over their frames. Their English was not native to them and they had a myriad of old scars on their faces. They were big men, well over six-foot-five and very muscular."

Though she did so unperceptively, Cheryl noticed Stacy's eyes searched the crowd and appeared to land on Vivian's cousin, Donald Dixon and friend, Bill Chandler, who were talking together across the ballroom.

When Stacy seemed to have caught her starring, Cheryl looked away.

"Do you think you could describe them to a sketch artist?"

Cheryl shrugged. "I suppose, but . . . something is wrong, isn't it?"

"Maybe, maybe not, but I want to be cautious and identify these men."

"You think this has something to do with . . . ?"

"Let's not jump to any conclusions, Cheryl" Stacy interrupted quickly. "One step at a time."

Cheryl nodded her understanding, but she felt uncomfortable with the revelation.

"What's your time like on Monday?"

"I have a few returns to make, but nothing that can't wait."

"Good. I'd like you to meet me in town at the brownstone around ten on Monday morning."

"I can do that."

"You, too, Betty."

"Yes, okay. I can do that, too, but where is this brownstone?"

"Georgetown area of DC," Stacy said and rattled off the address.

"I'd appreciate it if we didn't mention this to anyone else," said Cheryl. "I don't want to cause unnecessary concern over something that might turn out to be nothing at all."

"I don't know, Cheryl. I usually keep Peter appraised on anything unusual that occurs at the business park," said Betty. "After all, he is my boss and he owns the business park."

"If anything comes of this, I'll tell Peter about it," said Cheryl, though she felt uncomfortable about keeping this incident from her husband. She was so accustomed to handling everything herself. She and Peter had only been married for less than a month.

Though seemingly still skeptical, Betty nodded in agreement.

"Then I'll see both of you at ten on Monday," said Stacy.

It continued to bother Cheryl more than she thought it would to keep Peter in the dark about her encounter. They were snuggled spoon-style in bed when Peter asked, "What's going on, Cheryl?" He pulled her more securely into his embrace. "You seem to be a million miles away."

"It's nothing, really, but three men came into the office complex," she began telling him everything and played down the encounter. It just spilled out of her.

Peter turned over and hit the lights on a remote control device before sitting up in bed.

Resigned to not getting to sleep right away, Cheryl sat up, too. "I know what you're going to say, Peter. I should have told you about this incident right away."

"I trust you, Cheryl, to know what is relevant and what isn't. However, if it has anything to do with your safety, all bets are off."

"You have always had my back. I know that."

"If our roles were reversed and someone might be out to do me harm and I didn't mention it to you, what would you think?"

She exhaled, resigned. "That you didn't trust me."

"Exactly. We can't have it both ways, babe. We're a team now. What affects me affects you and the reverse is true."

"I know, I know," she said hastily. "I have always trusted you."

"I trust you, too, Cheryl, so let's make sure we never let anyone or anything threaten the trust between us."

She nodded her understanding and leaned into his open embrace. He enfolded her in his arms, kissed the top of her head, and when she looked up at him, kissed her mouth. Shortly thereafter he slipped into her.

"Good morning," Benny Alexander said when he opened the front door to the brownstone just shy of ten on Monday morning.

"Good morning," Cheryl and Peter chimed. Cheryl almost didn't recognize Benny in a USAF T-shirt and jeans with his feet bare. He looked fantastic in his uniform, but there was something about a well-built man dressed down for no specific occasion that enlivened the imagination. She felt the same way about Peter when he chose to wear comfortable old clothes and no shoes while they worked around their home together. Peter's sex appeal was enormous and caused her to christen nearly every room in their new home.

"Everyone's in the kitchen," Benny said while taking coats to hang in the closet.

Cheryl spied the massive Christmas tree in the front parlor to their left. The fireplace was lit and fragrant wood smoke permeated the air. To the right was a large library filled with books and another decorated tree. The sweeping staircase looked like it came straight out of the film *Gone With The Wind*. It was elegant and the railings were trimmed with green, gold, and red garland and big red bows. It didn't look stodgy with its fine-grained wood.

On the way back through the long, wide hallway to the kitchen, Cheryl noticed the dining room which easily sat twenty or more at the fine, mahogany-wood table. In the kitchen, the back wall opened up to a panoramic view through curved glass windows of the covered wood deck and spectacular sight of Rock Creek Park. Adjacent to the eat-in kitchen was an expansive family room where yet another fireplace crackled and snapped at large logs. Two potted and dressed Christmas trees stood sentry at both ends of the fireplace with gifts neatly arranged around the base of each.

Two additional people Cheryl didn't expect to see, Donald Dixon, Benny's cousin, and Bill Chandler, one of Vivian's friends and founding law firm partners, were in the kitchen. She had met Donald before and, of course, Bill Chandler was both her and Peter's former boss at the law firm. Both Donald and Bill were lawyers and both were very handsome. Bill, however, could have passed for the actor Matt Bomer.

Betty sat at a long, kitchen, trestle table with a man who was sketching a picture and then transferring it to a laptop.

"Good morning," they all greeted in unison.

"Peter, Cheryl, I don't think you've met my brother, Russell Greene," said Stacy.

"No, we haven't," acknowledged Peter with a handshake, "but we've certainly seen your work in art museums and magazines. You're a fine artist. We saw you at the party but didn't get a chance to speak."

"Thank you," said the young man who appeared to be in his early twenties.

"Coffee?" asked Stacy as she got up from the table with her cup in hand.

"Thank you, yes," said Peter as he moved to assist Stacy.

"Herbal tea for me, if you have it," said Cheryl, as she watched Russell work and chatted with him praising his talent as an artist.

"We do, yes," said Stacy, eyeing Cheryl critically.

"This is a fabulous house."

"Thank you," said Benny. "My great-grandaunt, Hanna Ivy Benson, sold it to me years ago. My father, brothers, various other family members, and I renovated it into a multi-unit home. Then Vivian and her law schoolmates, including Bill, rented it from me while she and they were in law school."

"I still live here most of the time," commented Bill.

"I remember," said Cheryl. "When Vivian married Chuck and moved to the farm, Kristen Catherine rented it for a time when she was on the appellate court, Peter was KC's chief of staff and Tina and I were her law clerks."

"I was traveling most of the time while she was living here until she and her husband, Thomas Marshall, moved to Vivian's Watergate property," said Bill.

"Since then, various family members have lived here," said Benny. "When JeNelle is in town for work on Capitol Hill, she lives here. Vivian and Chuck's children attend school not far from here and stop in after class if they don't have afterschool activities. Then Vivian and Chuck pick them up from here when they're ready to head to their ranch.

"Are your children here?"

"They're still at Chuck and Vivian's ranch with the grandparents," said Stacy. "Donald's wife, Cecil, his twin brother, James, his wife, Janice, along with their children and parents and grand aunts and uncles are at the ranch too.

"Stacy and I become *persona non grata* or second-class citizens when the grandparents are around." He continued to talk with Peter, Bill, and Donald while the Keurig coffee brewed and water heated for Cheryl's tea.

"Pregnant much?" teased Stacy quietly of Cheryl.

She shrugged and grinned. "Maybe. Hopefully. How did you know?"

"First, it's the golden glow you're wearing. It wasn't apparent when you visited us in Japan. Then it's the tea. Each time I was pregnant, I couldn't get enough of the stuff. Otherwise, I'm a coffee junkie."

"Peter and I have our fingers crossed."

"Congrats, Cheryl. I know what family means to newlyweds."

"You have seven children. That's a house full. Neither Peter nor I had biological siblings, but we had each other, the Justice, and Bryant families as surrogates. We're looking forward to having at least three or four children of our own. We may even adopt."

"As Chuck and Vivian have proven, there are a lot of children in the world who need loving parents and a stable household, especially those who are hard to place because they have health challenges."

"I've known Vivian since undergrad, but I don't know how she and Chuck do it."

"Teamwork," said Benny joining Stacy and Cheryl putting an arm around his wife at the ten-foot-long, center-post, and breakfast bar. He put a box of three dozen Greenfield Brothers' pastries on a platter and plucked up one of the glazed donuts for himself.

Peter, Bill, and Donald watched the drawings as Betty and Cheryl refined their memories of the three men.

Within two hours, reasonable facsimiles of the three men were prepared. While facial recognition programs were run, Stacy gave instructions on how to proceed should the men be spotted again.

"If these men are after the African girls, how do you think their search led them here?" asked Cheryl.

"The media attention. Tina Justice brought the plight of the girls to the spotlight. Your parents did several articles about young girls in certain African cultures. Thomas Marshall, Jefferson Logan, and Nathan Flack were prominently displayed in connection with this story. You and Peter were also the focus of media attention in Japan. The stories all went away when you left Japan. These men just connected the dots. If they are who I think they are, they're trying to figure out who you are in relation to the girls. They don't understand Americans or our culture. While they are bumping around trying to get the lay of the land, it should give us time to locate them."

"How will you find them?" asked Betty.

"They'll gravitate toward people of their own culture. They'll look for restaurants that serve their native foods, housing in neighborhoods where others speak their language; things that are familiar to them."

"The embassy?"

"No, not likely. The embassy officials will not want to be associated with terrorists for fear the association will affect their standing in the world community. Although the officials may privately support the practice of kidnapping young girls and may even have a role in the child trafficking, they would not say so publically."

"Is there anything else other than what you've told us we should do in the interim until you find these men?" asked Peter.

"Just be vigilant. They want the girls with as little fanfare as possible and may try to find them through you."

"I don't know the girls or where they are," said Betty, concerned.

"Since we know they are hanging around your office, that's one of the primary places we'll start looking."

"My parents and Peter's are still in town until after the New Years," said Cheryl, concerned.

"You have excellent security at your home, but not so much at your cabin in the mountains or oceanfront home at the beach. We'll take care of that whether you or they are here or in Chicago."

After returning from their honeymoon in Japan, they spent ten days at their mountain chalet with their parents and were surprised to learn Ambassador Jefferson Logan and his wife, LaiLoni Skai, aka Dakota Sinclair, were also vacationing at the same mountain retreat across a wide, deep, clear water lake from one another in a cabin owned by LaiLoni. Jefferson Logan's sister, and Cheryl's doctor, Savannah, also owned a cabin at the same mountain lake community with her husband, Nathan Flack. The area offered excellent skiing and hiking. They just had to be careful not to stumble onto Camp David, the Presidential mountain retreat a few miles away.

"This is the type of incident the CIA and/or FBI handle, isn't it?" asked Cheryl. "You're a US attaché to the Japanese Embassy in Japan and on the Joint Chiefs' staff."

"This crosses several enforcement organizations. It's a joint task-force effort."

Although Peter believed Stacy, he sensed her involvement went much deeper. He also wondered why Donald Dixon and Bill Chandler were present but didn't ask.

Chapter 5

One week before Valentine's Day, Cheryl sat on the sidelines watching her girls go through their Taekwondo exercises with a martial arts master who would evaluate their progress and certify their standing. She was nearing the end of her first trimester of pregnancy and was not taking part in the exercise routines. Though she participated with Tai Chi, she didn't want to jeopardize her delicate condition or cause Peter to banish her to their bed for an afternoon nap.

Her pregnancy, which they announced during their New Year's Eve party, was not a particularly easy one with daily bouts of nausea which caused her to be dehydrated. That was pretty much over, but her friend and OB/GYN specialist, Dr. Savannah Logan Flack, was keeping a close eye on her. This caused Peter to become overly protective and hypersensitive about her health and safety of late. Their law offices were up and running, but they were only taking on a limited number of new clients, in part, due to her morning sickness. They were still handling a substantial number of old clients from their days with Alexander, Carter, *et.al.*, but Peter made sure they had stress-free time to be together. They shared breakfast and lunch each day and dinner by six, usually at home.

They made time to socialize with close friends, particularly for birthdays and anniversaries or stay-at-home get-togethers for cards, pizza, and beer. This particular Saturday morning, the Lawrence Twelve Crew was in Cheryl and Peter's home gym.

It was nearly two months since the encounter with the three African men, but Cheryl felt for some reason they were still in the area. Benny and Stacy returned to Japan, but Cheryl still felt a presence wherever she went. Betty Jones shared her feelings of discomfort but had not sighted the men in the office complex. Their relationship was closer now and with the law office and the complex management separated, at Peter's request, Betty would usually accompany Cheryl when she left work early to meet her crew. Cheryl, however, sensed Betty had an ulterior motive when Darrin Johnson showed up and smiled brightly at the single mother. It was apparent, from what Cheryl overheard of one of their conversations, Darrin introduced Betty and her son, Clay, to his brothers, Trevor and David Johnson. To Cheryl's way of thinking, Darrin and Betty seemed well-suited.

Still, though Cheryl appreciated Betty's company and Peter's attempts to make sure she was never alone, she was more concerned about the twenty young girls' safety than her own. Daily news reports recounted military operations in Africa geared to keep the Boko Haram and AQIM terrorists from getting their hands on government-educated, school children. Attacks had intensified due to training the terrorists received from al-Qaeda. The Islamic Jihadists were opposed to western-style, modern education. The Boko Haram targeted and killed hundreds of students, frightening thousands of parents into not permitting their school-aged children to get an education. Girls were targeted and kidnapped because the terrorists believed they should not be educated at all. Cheryl thought it was the height of stupidity.

She felt movement in her abdomen and despaired at what families, and particularly children, were suffering at the hands of terrorists. She felt her baby move again and placed her hand on her abdomen rubbing soothingly. She knew she would fight to her dying breath anyone who threatened her child. She imaged the absolute terror the Boko Haram caused.

"Did you see me, Ms. Cheryl?" asked a very excited Lena.

"Uh," Cheryl sighed, caught off guard. She was staring at the activity, but her thoughts were on the other side of the globe.

"I think you did extremely well," commented Darrin cheerfully to the child while coming to Cheryl's aide.

"The question, young lady, is how do you feel about your accomplishment?"

Lena beamed a broad smile. "I did it! I did really well! I took down someone bigger than me!"

"You certainly did," boasted Darrin.

"I'm going to do it again!" she said and ran back to the group who were taking a break.

"Thanks, Darrin," sighed Cheryl.

"You're welcome. Betty and I noticed your attention isn't quite here today. Is everything all right?"

"It is, yes. Just a little distracted."

"I can't imagine how you do it with all the construction going on around your house, getting your law firm up and operational, mentoring this crew, working on the cotillion events, and then planning for a baby in August."

"Fortunately, I'm not doing any of those things alone," she said and chuckled.

"You seem happy, Cheryl. I realize now I didn't handle our discussion all those months ago very maturely. You were trying to discuss with me what you needed and all I could see was what I wanted. Every day I regret not being more open to your needs. Maybe I could have held out long enough for you to fall in love with me as you have with Peter. Now with your marriage and pregnancy, you have what you needed. I'm happy for you and even for Peter."

"Thank you, Darrin. It wasn't your fault we didn't move to a more advanced level in our relationship. The chemistry between us, from my perspective, just wasn't right."

"I'm sorry for that. It will always be one of my biggest regrets."

"Cheryl?" asked Mrs. Brown.

"Yes?"

"We need you upstairs."

"What is it?"

"There is a truck at the guard's gate claiming to have a furniture delivery for you and Mr. Brock."

Cheryl's brows beetled. "I wasn't expecting anything." She rose from her seat. "Excuse me, Darrin. I need to see to this." Though she was glad of the interruption, she hurriedly took the stairs closest to the kitchen where the wall monitor connected to the estate's security system showed the truck with no furniture store markings at the gate to the development. She shook her head feeling uneasy. "Officer Hankman?" Cheryl said into the phone. "I understand there is a delivery for us, but I'm not expecting a delivery of furniture. I'll check with Peter, but in the meantime, does the deliveryman have paperwork?"

"Yes, ma'am, he does."

"Would you fax it to me please and a copy of the driver's license?" she asked while simultaneously dialing Peter.

"Hi, babe, I was just thinking about you. I may be a little late for lunch."

"That's okay, but, Peter, did you order furniture?"

"Furniture? Uh, no, I wouldn't have done that without talking with you. Why?"

"There is a truck at the gate claiming they have a delivery for us. Hold on a moment. I'm getting a fax." When she saw the paperwork, she was surprised it appeared to be Peter's signature on the invoice, but when she looked at the driver's license, her breath caught in her throat.

"Cheryl? Cheryl?" Peter anxiously asked. "Babe, I'm on my way!"

"Ms. Lawrence? Are you there, Ms. Lawrence?" Officer Hankman asked.

"I'm here, officer. I've checked with my husband. We didn't order anything."

"Not to worry. After I returned the driver's paperwork and license, they left in a rather big hurry. Do you want me to follow up? I have the license plate number."

"Thank you, Officer Hankman. I don't think that's necessary."

"Okay, but I'll still make out an incident report. Good day to you."

"To you, too," she said and then disconnected.

Later, when Peter arrived, he found her sitting in the kitchen with the papers spread out before her. He hugged her and cuddled her in his arms before looking at the papers. "I stopped at the gate and spoke with Officer Hankman before I came home. He wanted to report the incident to the police. He said you told him not to bother."

"I did, but I do want to get a message to Stacy. Peter, I'm sure this is one of the men who came to the office," she said showing the picture of the license to him.

"Then why not notify the police?"

"Of what? Three men of African origin come to a business office and ask for information. I see a man who I believe was one of the men attempting to deliver what he claims is furniture you ordered. I don't have evidence they attempted to do anything. For all I know, the man has a job delivering furniture."

"I agree. This is circumstantial, but I'm not risking your safety because I may be paranoid." He got up from the table taking the papers with him and went into his office. Cheryl followed him in and waited while he faxed the papers to Stacy in Japan with an explanation and a copy of the guard's incident report. Though it was nearly midday in the states, it was midnight in Japan, so they didn't expect a response immediately. "There, that should do it," he said once the fax machine verified receipt. He then pulled Cheryl onto his lap and kissed her. "I saw the school van outside. Are the girls here?"

She wrapped her arms around his shoulders and rested her head against his. "They are, yes. They get their certifications today." She looked at her watch. "The girls should be finished by half eleven. Mrs. Miller and Mrs. Brown will have lunch set up shortly. Betty was giving them a hand."

"Darrin is with the girls?"

"He is, yes."

Peter was about to say something when the house phone rang. He answered, not waiting for either housekeeper pick up. Then he noted the call's origin and was somehow not surprised with who was on the other end of the call.

"Hello, Stacy."

<<<<>>>>

"Delta, how do you read?" whispered the team leader into a face mic.

"I'm reading you five-by-five, Explorer One. What's your ten-twenty?"

"On target."

"Sitrep."

Chapter 25

"Ms. Lawrence, your 10:00 o'clock appointment, the Mitchells have arrived."

"Thank you, Mary Kay. I'll be right out," Cheryl said, as she slowly and carefully rose from her chair. Walking was a little more difficult these days with six weeks left of her pregnancy before she was due to deliver. She finally made it to the reception area just as Peter came in the office front door. He had an early court schedule that apparently hadn't gone well she judged by the frown on his face.

When Peter and two of their junior law clerks came into the office, he couldn't help the smile that changed his mood considerably when he saw Cheryl coming into the reception area. She had such a beautiful glow even though she waddled a bit when she walked. He wanted to kiss her right then and there, but the reception area had clients waiting. Still, he approached her and took her hand. "You are going home for lunch, aren't you?"

She smiled up at him. "I am, yes. I only have one appointment today. Aren't you supposed to be in court this morning?"

"Opposing counsel asked for another continuance. This is the third one and, according to Judge Blayney, the last one. So, since I didn't expect to be in the office, I think I'll go home and have lunch with my very beautiful partner."

She gave him her Mona Lisa smile, winked, and whispered, "Be prepared, handsome. Lunch with you isn't the only thing I want." Then she squeezed his hand before going to her new clients.

"Mr. and Mrs. Mitchell?"

"Yes," they both answered and rose to greet her.

"I'm Cheryl Lawrence Brock," she said extending her hand. "Please come this way."

Once comfortably seated across from each other on double settees in her office, Cheryl asked, "How can I help you?"

"We are planning to open a travel agency in Mitchell County, Mitchell Travel and Tours. We understand there are certain state and federal requirements which need to be met," said Robert Mitchell.

"You're correct, local requirements, too, but may I ask why you didn't consult a law firm closer to where you plan to start your business?"

"My parents' families are very influential in the county. In fact, Mitchell County is named for the Mitchell ancestors. My parents and grandparents, both paternal and maternal, are still opposed to my decision to marry someone they didn't hand pick for me and to start a business that does not fit into their plans for my life. Most of the attorneys in the area owe their livelihood or allegiance in one way or another to my family and want to stay in my families' good graces. So, they won't take us on as clients."

"Ah, you're related to State Senator Julius Mitchell?

"My father," answered Robert.

"I see and your mother would be Norah Barkley, a member of Barkley family of Anne Arundel County?"

"If your questions mean you're unwilling to represent us . .?"

"Not at all. I'm not intimidated or impressed by members of your family. So, let's get to work." Cheryl took them through the myriad of local, state, and federal requirements and nearly an hour and a half later, they were wrapping up their meeting. By then, they were on a first name basis.

"Cheryl, thank you for agreeing to represent us."

"You're welcome, Robert, Jackie," she said shaking the young couple's hands. "I should have all of the paperwork ready for your signatures in a few days."

"That would be great."

Cheryl gathered her things and walked the Mitchells to the Accounts office before she went to find Peter.

Less than two hours later, Peter and Cheryl woke from a nap when the phone rang. Mrs. Miller announced their lunch was ready. Peter got up, slipped into a warm up, and went to the kitchen to pick up their lunch. He brought it back to their master suite and set it up on the sun-filled sitting room adjacent to their bedroom.

"Who are your new clients?" asked Peter as they ate.

"Robert and Jacqueline Conner Mitchell."

"Any relation to the Mitchell County Mitchells?"

"Yes, Robert is one of Julius Mitchell's sons."

"Ah, yes. The oldest son is Julius Junior. I believe the middle son is Robert who is a twin to Rachel. The youngest boy is Brian Mitchell."

"How do you know so much about them?"

"Denise. She dragged me to many events hosted by the Mitchell clan. State Senator Mitchell's father is a businessman with his hands in several different businesses. Denise was a supporter of State Senator Mitchell's campaign."

"You voted for him?" she asked incredulously.

"No, I voted for the other guy."

Cheryl's laugh was infectious. "Whew! You had me going there for a moment."

"What do your clients need?"

"Articles of Incorporation," she began and filled him in.

"They seem rather young."

"I sensed they're under twenty-five. They both gave me Power of Attorney to handle their legal affairs, too. They're both very smart and energetic. I predict they will do well. I'm willing to help them meet their goals."

"We agreed you wouldn't put in too many hours. You have staff for that."

"I know," she said sighing. "This is pretty much routine. It should only take a few days."

Peter kissed her and rose from the table. "I think we should go to the beach house for an extended weekend just to make sure you don't overdo it."

"That's a great idea. Maybe we can drive down later today. What time do you have to meet the Brock Boys?"

"Three-thirty. They're coming here for swimming lessons."

She looked at her watch. "Well, nothing says we can't start on that long weekend early," she said rising from her seat and discarding her robe, smiling at her husband, and heading for the king-sized bed.

Peter rapidly peeled off his warm up.

Cheryl giggled when Peter scooped her up in his arms.

Chapter 26

"It's a girl," announced Peter, enthusiastically, his face wreathed in a huge smile.

His and Cheryl's parents were just returning from breakfast in the hospital cafeteria and engulfed him in a big, five-way, group bear hug.

"How is Cheryl?" asked Helen and Cassia almost simultaneously.

Peter grinned. "She's a little tired, but she and Kendal Cassia Brock are both fine. She wants all of you to come meet your granddaughter."

Their parents were in a near jog down the Physicians Hospital halls to the birthing room. They donned white gowns, masks, and hats. They and Peter had taken the Tdap vaccine to guard against the pertussis virus as did Tina and Kristin who were also in attendance. Still, they were taking every precaution with the newly born grandchild.

"Oh, my, she is just beautiful," crooned Helen.

Tears stood in all of the grandparents' eyes. Peter stood at the foot of the bed beaming a satisfied smile at his wife and daughter. Kendal Cassia was such a tiny thing, thought Peter, and wide awake taking in her universe. Cheryl acknowledged his smile with one of her own. Their little golden nugget was two weeks earlier than expected, but no one regretted being roused at one o'clock in the morning to spend the ten hours in the hospital waiting room. The hospital was small but was very comfortable and well appointed. The food in the cafeteria was delicious and furnished by contract with the Greenfield Brothers. Their staff also served the meals.

A few days later, they were oohing and awhing over little Kendal Cassia, before Farrow, still wiping tears from his eyes, said, "Okay, it's settled. We're buying your previous homes and moving to Maryland."

"You're what?" asked Peter.

"Helen and I are buying Cheryl's former home and Peter Senior and Cassia are buying yours."

"Why?" asked Cheryl. She had just finished breastfeeding Kendall.

"That should be obvious," remarked Helen. "We want to see our grandbaby grow up. So, we were considering buying your former homes. We'll keep our homes in Chicago too for times when we need to be there. Now it's settled. Since the houses are next door to each other and fairly large when the Justice family is in town they can stay with us. Thomas and Kristen Catherine already have a home here in Havenhurst Estates; we can use our homes for family overflow. Your father and I can fly out of Washington, Maryland or Virginia just as easily as we fly out of Chicago."

"Plus, it doesn't get as cold here as it does in Chicago," commented Cassia.

"There is that," remarked Farrow. "So, this is a win-win situation all around.

"We can use golf carts to drive to your home from ours or even walk in good weather," commented Peter Senior. "I don't have to go away to play a round or two of golf."

"This is a very walkable community. We can take Kendal Cassia for long walks to the park and around the lake," stated Farrow. "I'm not much of a golfer, but taking my granddaughter for a walk will let me stretch my legs. Plus, I like the park-like atmosphere here."

Peter looked at Cheryl and they both shrugged. It was a good idea, and they would have ready access to babysitters.

"You've convinced us," said Peter with Cheryl's nod of agreement. "We hadn't put either home on the market yet. When do you want to take possession?"

"Today is Monday," said Peter Senior. "How about next Monday?"

"Works for us," Farrow agreed with Helen's agreement.

"For us, too," said Cassia. "I'm going to love decorating that house!" she exclaimed.

"Oh, boy," Peter Senior sighed.

Everyone laughed.

The following Saturday, Cheryl watched one of her best friends, Kristen Catherine, lead her Lawrence Twelve Crew and their escorts in a waltz for the cotillion. They had their routines from the introduction of their parents to the closing ceremony down to a fine science. Though the event was still a few months away and would be held at the Washington, DC, McCoy Regent Hotel and Conference Center, they were doing the dress rehearsal in Peter and Cheryl's ballroom. Peter Senior had donated abandoned wedding gowns from his dry cleaning business for the girls to wear and keep after the cotillion.

Cheryl's friends agreed to pay for any alterations for the gowns and the tuxedos.

Ardon, the supermodel, would show the girls how to use make-up at their next event. She would also take pictures of the girls' faces to add to the memory book each girl would receive which chronicled every event they participated in during the year-long activity.

However, on the day of the cotillion, Cheryl was planning to take the girls to the spa she used for the works—massage, hair salon, mani-pedi, full body scrub and make-up as her gift to the girls for their improvements in school over the summer. The cotillion was to be held just before the new school year started.

The girls sold all of the tickets each had for the final event. They were excited about getting dressed up and having their families and friends attend the festivities. A number of the school faculty members would attend as well as the school board members. Cheryl arranged for her pal, Tina Justice to film the event and do an exposé on the success of the school's program. Peter's twelve boys would also attend and next spring they would participate in a cotillion.

Cheryl was elated because it had been six weeks since Kendal Cassia was born. Adhering to her doctor's advice, she and Peter abstained from having intercourse during that time. That didn't stop them from making mad, passionate love to each other. Still, she was itching to get her hands on him and feel him inside her again. The grands were staying in the hotel with Kendal Cassia for the night to give Peter and Cheryl some quality time alone together. Cheryl was primed to take full advantage of the opportunity. After the cotillion, she and Peter were going to their beach home for an extended weekend to work on baby number two.

Cheryl steered the van into the underground hotel parking lot into an available spot. The girls were excited and chatting about the upcoming event mere hours away. They were early for their lunch reservations at the hotel. Cheryl planned to tell them about their surprise spa appointments after lunch. When all of the girls were out of the van, Cheryl locked it and noticed the girls had gone uncharacteristically quiet. She looked up and saw the three African men, one holding a gun.

Fear galvanized in the pit of her stomach as she sized up the situation. The men had rope they obviously intended to use to tie them up. Then instinctively she said, *"Spread!"* Her girls began to move around causing the men to be surrounded. They were not going to make it easy for the men to capture them. When the one with the gun moved toward her, Cheryl went into defensive mode momentarily surprising her would-be attacker. That was all the time she needed to say *"Defend!"*

The lights were lowered, signaling the beginning of the Lawrence Twelve Crew Cotillion. Quiet fell in the room as the music rose and a spotlight focused on the center of a rose-colored curtain.

"Good evening, ladies and gentlemen," came the disembodied voice of a nationally well-known DJ, Francis Baylor, Franky B, "we present the Lawrence Ladies and their escorts for the evening.

The curtain parted and in alphabetical order, each girl came out one at a time and was escorted to the edge of the runway platform where she curtsied low, her snow-white gown billowing out around her while the audience stood cheering. When all twelve girls and their escorts had been introduced, they stood quietly arranged across the stage, looking more beautiful and confident than any Miss America contestant.

The lights lowered again and the room fell silent in anticipation.

"Ladies and gentlemen, I present the sponsors of this event," the master of ceremony continued.

Each of the twelve women who participated in preparing the young girls for this event was presented along with their escorts. Finally, the curtain parted again and Cheryl stepped through on the arm of Darrin Johnson. After returning from the runway amid rousing, energetic applause, Darrin and Cheryl led off the waltz.

No one would suspect the harrowing experience Cheryl and her twelve girls endured hours earlier. No one except the men and women who arrested the terrorists after Cheryl and the Lawrence Twelve gave them the beat-down they never expected. Those three men needed serious medical attention on their black ops flight to an undisclosed location.

"Are you sure you're all right?" asked Peter concerned.

"I am, yes," said Cheryl. She was tucked securely into Peter's right side as they rested on a chaise on the deck at their waterfront home. The light was fading and the tide was rolling in gently onto the sandy shore. "I admit, I was afraid that if we didn't protect ourselves, we could have been kidnapped and shipped out of the country without anyone knowing what happened to us."

"Disappeared the way Jillian Harris has?" Peter questioned.

"Exactly. However, the girls performed admirably and took down those three terrorists just as they had been taught.

"Still," Cheryl continued. "I'll forever be grateful that Stacy Alexander and her team were there in the garage when the attack started."

"Why do you believe it was Stacy Alexander?" Peter asked. "You said the people who came to your rescue wore black clothes, like Ninja warriors."

"It was something about the leader's eyes. I could see through the mesh screens over their faces. Stacy has light, crystal-brown eyes and one Chi-town girl knows another one. Although I will never tell anyone else, I'm sure the one leading our rescuers was Stacy Greene Alexander."

Peter was sure it was his wife's crystal clear persuasion that won him over to her point of view.

He, too, would be forever grateful. "Regardless, she saved the first woman I've ever truly been in love with," said Peter.

"You're the last man I'll ever be in love with. Let's go inside and make another baby."

As the light completely faded, Peter stood up and brought Cheryl to her feet. He didn't have to be asked twice.